Never Ask Why
By: Barbara Phipps
ISBN: 978-1-927220-55-9

G000081294

Bluewood Publishing Ltd
Christchurch, 8441, New Zealand
www.bluewoodpublishing.com

Special Note: This book contains UK Spellings.

Other titles by Barbara Phipps:

The Threlfalls!

Coming Soon:

Dancing Upstairs
Turn the Stones

For news of, or to purchase this or other
books, please visit:

www.bluewoodpublishing.com

Never Ask Why

by

Barbara Phipps

To Mavis,

with best wishes,

Barbara Phipps .

Dedication

To my mother, a very well read lady.

CHAPTER ONE

Over the past two years, Helen had travelled the whole gamut of grief without realising what was happening. Shock was followed by anger, followed by sadness, then more anger mixed with loneliness. Today was going to be an angry day. She just knew it.

Compared to other women of her age, and with a bit of effort, Helen McGuire reckoned she could still look good. Her battle with hormones, gravity, and the passage of time had begun some time before, but her skin was still relatively free of wrinkles, her brown hair relatively free of grey. The cheval mirror confirmed her figure was wider in the middle than it had been ten years before, but what the hell? And fifty was just a number.

She looked out of her bedroom window onto a frosty March morning. The old V-Dub camper van at the top of the drive looked forlorn, despite the dazzling efforts of the sunlight twinkling on the frozen windscreen. She was still angry with Phil. They had been planning a round-the-world trip to celebrate thirty years of marriage when he had dropped dead of a heart attack. She had been hoping he would buy her some pearls in Tahiti.

That had been nearly two years before and, because he hadn't planned to die at the age of forty-nine, there had been a lot of paper work to sort out. She had plenty of money, thanks to Phil and all his insurance policies. Their lovely house, number fourteen Jumbles Lane, was paid for, and she liked living in Chester.

When their first son, Robert, was born, she and Phil happily made the decision that she would be a stay-at-home-mum, and consequently she had had no career. Castle Lane Juniors PTA had been quite fun and she had made lots of friends. They all still had husbands as far as she knew. Her involvement with the school had taken Helen into the classrooms to help the children with their reading. Maybe she could do that again. Maybe not. Her 'boys', Robert and James, were twenty-eight and twenty-six now. Her stay-at-home-sons had given no hint that they wanted to fly the nest.

She went downstairs and into the kitchen. Everything about the house shouted 'Phil and Helen live here'.

She wagged her finger at Phil's smiling photograph on the window ledge. *You had no bloody business leaving me like this, Phil McGuire.* Helen remembered taking the picture on their last holiday, the last photograph she had of him, sitting in the driver's seat of the camper van, smiling his huge, happy smile. He had passed her the camera, she could hear him now.

"Take one of me and Valerie. She won't last forever, you know."

Phil always called the camper Valerie, or Valerie Drobshaw to give her full name. Helen hoped it was just a play on the initials of the old V-Dub, rather than the name of an ex-girlfriend. *Too late to ask him now.* Not that she would really want to, just in case she didn't like the answer. They had enjoyed many a holiday in Valerie when the boys had been little—and quite a few after they had grown up, when she and Phil had had her to themselves.

She picked up the picture and looked out the window at the old van, and then back at the photograph. It struck her that Valerie Drobshaw hadn't turned a wheel since Phil had parked her there. She sighed and put Phil and his smiling face back on the window ledge.

"Fair enough, Phil, now it's all sorted out I do have enough money, I'll grant you that, but will you please tell me what I'm supposed to do with the rest of my life?" He smiled at her. "Oh, piss off. You're no bloody help at all," she shouted.

The trouble was she was so bloody bored. So bloody bored she had taken to swearing a lot. She never swore out loud in front of Robert or James. The 'out louds' were reserved for when she was on her own, which was quite a lot. Sudden acute pain, such as stumping a toe on an innocent piece of furniture, would evoke a 'bastard' or a 'bugger', or if it didn't hurt too much it would be a 'bollocks'. It somehow released the tension, and kept her tears under control at the same time. Phil had never heard her swear, and he wouldn't, not now. Not unless he was floating around somewhere, marvelling at the speed and tenacity with which she had grasped the new vocabulary. With a few notable exceptions, she concluded that swear words began with the letter 'b' or 's'.

She pulled on her fleece jacket and woolly hat, kicked her slippers off and stamped into her boots. Once outside, she breathed in deeply, the icy air making her cough. Her neighbour's kitchen window was directly opposite Helen's door, distanced by the parallel driveways. Susan Townsend. It seemed to Helen that whenever she went out, or came home, Susan was at the window, waving.

Waving back, she stomped off up the drive. For no reason at all, she began to scrape the frost from Valerie Drobshaw's windscreen with her fingernails. She worked slowly at first, and then furiously, until her fingertips were numb and her nails broken.

"Shit!" She bit off the ragged edge of her thumb nail before sucking her fingers to warm them. Peering through the scraped patch of windscreen, she saw Phil's sunglasses on the driver's seat. Her shoulders sagged and her arms dropped to her sides. She dragged her feet back to the house and sat on the doorstep, taking a packet of cigarettes from her pocket, and hoping Susan wouldn't come out for a chat. She could see her out of the corner of her eye, bobbing around at the sink. The mixture of cold air and smoke made her cough again. She threw the cigarette on the drive, resolving to quit the habit, as she twisted her booted foot to put it out. Another day stretched out before her.

Back inside, she pulled off her boots and threw her hat and coat on the floor. She made a cup of hot chocolate and toasted a crumpet. Butter dripped through the holes and onto her plate. Helen licked the fingers of her left hand and ran them under the waistband of her trousers. When Phil died, she could barely eat a thing, and had lost over a stone. At some indefinable moment she had turned to comfort eating. She wasn't so blind as to fail to recognise the toasted crumpet and hot chocolate for what it was. She had regained all the weight and a bit more…and counting. Still, if she sat up straight she felt a bit thinner. She took a pen and paper to write a shopping list.

Salad
Skimmed milk
Fish.

Her thoughts turned to her sons. They wouldn't thank her for a low fat diet. Robert and James had good jobs, and had been towers of strength when their dad died.

There had been a variety of girlfriends in the past but, as far as she knew, there were none around at the moment. They were far too dependent on her, and that was the trouble. Not financially, of course. They paid their board without being asked. No, it wasn't that, the problem was they were too comfortable. Shirts were ironed by Mum, socks paired up by Mum, favourite food cooked by Mum. It was her doing, of course. Perhaps it was selfish. Perhaps she made them so comfortable because she couldn't bear to be on her own. Such thoughts made her uneasy, so she pushed them away. They were good sons. Robert was the more staid one, working steadily at Carleton's Bank since he had gained his degree in economics. He played golf every Saturday afternoon. During the summer, he sometimes played weekday evenings as well. If Robert wasn't going to walk through the door at 6.15 p.m. precisely, he would send her a text message. His job suited him. He once told Helen that, when possible, he liked to schedule his day into twenty-minute time slots. It sounded rather too orderly. Helen feared this obsession with punctuality had spilled into his private life.

James was the complete opposite of his brother in every way she could think of. He was fair haired and tall, whereas Robert was much shorter, and dark. At twenty-eight, Robert was showing the first signs of baldness at his temples, whereas James's hair was an uncontrollable riot. James never knew what time he would finish work. His job with the police meant his hours were anything but regular. He kept his sports and swimming gear in his car, and would call at the gym whenever time permitted. Sometimes Helen heard his mobile ring late at night, or in the early hours of the morning. Minutes later, he would quietly close the front door. His work took him abroad sometimes, mostly to Europe, but he had been to the States a few times last year. She worried about him when he was away. His work was bound to be dangerous at times.

Helen wiped her fingers on a paper serviette. The solution popped into her head quite unexpectedly. *She* would fly the nest and leave them to it. They wouldn't like it, they wouldn't like a low fat diet either; they would try to discourage her on both counts.

She pushed away the buttery plate and opened her laptop. She could splash out on a round-the-world ticket, visiting the places she and Phil had planned to visit together; but after half an hour of googling, the idea was fading. The organised packages seemed to be designed for gap year students, singles looking for love, or oldies. She rocked on the back legs of her chair in a way that would have infuriated Phil. She heard his voice, loud and clear.

"You'll break the chair doing that. You're as bad as the boys."

She looked out of the window and Valerie Drobshaw looked back. As she stood up, the chair fell over, clattering across the kitchen floor.

"That's it, Phil. We'll go in Valerie. We can go wherever we want. What about Scarborough? You said you wanted to go there one day." She picked up her mobile and rang Freddie Dixon's garage. With Valerie Drobshaw booked in for an MOT the following morning, Helen spent the rest of the day cleaning Valerie's interior, the housework and diet forgotten.

The bodywork will have to wait. Robert and James might notice and ask me what I'm up to. I'll tell them when the plan is firmed up a bit.

Her own deviousness amazed her; she revelled in her thoughts all day as she cleaned and polished Valerie Drobshaw.

Phil always used to take their cars to Freddie Dixon.

"He's the best mechanic for miles around. Freddie won't give you any bullshit."

* * * *

Next morning, when Helen bump-started Valerie down the drive, and a pall of black smoke billowed from the exhaust, she was in high spirits. Partly because, having slept on it, the idea still felt good, and partly because she had managed to keep her plans a secret from Robert and James. Valerie stuttered and coughed up the short incline that took her to the top of Jumbles Lane, and then her engine cut out. No amount of clutch work from Helen would bring a spark of life to the engine, and so she and Valerie free-wheeled down to Freddie's garage and rolled into the forecourt, coming to a halt in front of the MOT sign.

"G'mornin', Mrs McGuire." Freddie emerged from

underneath an old Volvo, rubbing his hands on an oily rag. "You made it, then?" He had a habit of nodding whenever he finished a sentence as if answering his own question. He was short and wiry, with years of oil ingrained in his hands. He squinted as if unaccustomed to daylight.

"Only just, Freddie. The engine cut out at the top of the hill." Helen jumped out of the driver's seat and slammed the door shut. "The good news is the brakes work." Freddie walked to the back of the old van and opened the engine compartment. He wafted away the smoke, and rubbed his chin.

"Told your 'ubby, I did, last time 'e brought 'er 'ere." Freddie nodded, as he pursed his lips. "I said MOT is no problem, Mr McGuire, just a bit o' welding 'ere and there, but 'er engine's wor' out. It is, Mrs McGuire, it's wor' out." He tugged on the fan belt and twiddled various wires before closing the engine cover. "Were you thinking o' goin' far? She needs a new engine, by rights. Wouldn't want you goin' off on yer own in 'er, Mrs M."

Helen smiled as she thought of Phil's words. *No bullshit from Freddie Dixon.*

"What's your advice, Freddie? Phil always trusted your opinion."

"My advice, Mrs M, seeing as you're askin', is to sell 'er. Fetch a good price, they do, even non runners like this old lady." He nodded enthusiastically. "You take a look on that ebay, you'll be nicely surprised."

"I know you'll say I'm silly, Freddie, but I had this idea that if I went away for a while in Valerie, it'd be like Phil was still with me." Her voice trailed off. How could she possibly expect Freddie Dixon to understand? Even as she spoke, she knew it sounded stupid. Freddie stared at her with his mouth open. He had stopped nodding. Helen continued. "Can I think about it, Freddie? Can I leave her here and let you know?" He started nodding again, happy to have a question he could answer.

"O' 'course you can, give us a ring when you've decided. No rush."

Helen walked back up the hill, deep in thought. It hadn't crossed her mind that Valerie might not be up to it, though come to think of it, Phil had said she wouldn't last forever.

* * * *

Robert was home first. "Where's the camper, Mum? What have you done with it?" The question came before his briefcase hit the floor. Helen had hoped Freddie Dixon would work his magic and Valerie would be back in the drive, complete with MOT certificate before either of the boys came home. The idea of keeping her plans secret hadn't made it past the first hurdle. She didn't want to tell any lies, though. Not unless she really had to.

"She's with Freddie Dixon. I thought you might have seen her in the forecourt."

Robert took off his gloves, carefully folding them and placing one in each pocket. He took off his coat, and pulled his scarf through one of the sleeves before hanging it up. "How on earth did it get there?" His incredulous tone irritated her.

"I drove her there, of course. I had to bump-start her—the battery was flat—but we made it just fine." She saw no reason to tell Robert about free-wheeling down the hill to Freddie's. The 'just fine' bit was only a little fib.

"But why? You're not thinking of going anywhere, are you?"

"I might. Why not?"

Before he could answer, James came crashing through the door.

"What's the camper doing at Freddie Dixon's, Mum?"

Helen wasn't surprised that James had seen Valerie; it was part of his job with the police to be observant.

"I took her for an MOT. Thought I might go away for a few days at Easter."

"Did Freddie pick it up or did you drive it down there?" James ran his fingers through his hair, pushing it from his eyes.

"I took her, of course. Do you both think I'm incapable of driving old Valerie for half a mile?" The irritation in their mother's voice bordered on anger.

Robert and James exchanged a puzzled glance.

"Not at all, Mum." James said. "It's just that if you were caught driving without insurance, you'd get six points on your licence."

Helen didn't reply.

The brief silence gave James his answer. "I take it, then, that you don't have insurance."

"I only drove half a mile." She sounded defensive.

"Yeah, well, no harm done, I suppose. Just be glad you're saying that to me and not to a magistrate." James kicked off his trainers and went into the lounge and slumped into an armchair, TV remote in his hand. He put on the news.

Robert followed him. "Is that right, James, Mum could've been in court?"

"Forget it, Robert. It didn't happen."

"Don't you see? She's thinking of going off on her own in that old van and she can't even get half a mile away without breaking the law." Robert hadn't realised Helen was standing in the doorway.

"That old van," she shouted, "is Valerie Drobshaw. Your dad and I loved her, and I still do, and I want to go away in her so I can be with your dad again." Tears flowed down her cheeks. Anger, frustration, sadness and loneliness all mingled together. For the first time since Phil's funeral, she cried in front of her sons. "Have you two no idea how I feel?"

Helen turned from the room, walking quickly to the kitchen, annoyed with herself for losing control and unable to look at their shocked faces. That was definitely *not* part of her plan. She pressed her hands down hard, fingers outstretched on the edge of the stainless steel sink.

She was staring at her white knuckles and bright red fingers when Robert touched her shoulder. "Come on, Mum. Let's have dinner. Smells good."

She turned to look at his bewildered face as James set the table.

"Sorry, boys. I shouldn't've shouted at you." Helen sniffed, and then blew her nose.

James put his arm around her shoulder. "It's okay, Mum, we understand."

She managed a thin smile. Maybe James understood a little, but Robert would struggle to cope with her tears. He controlled his emotions too much. She opened the oven door, and a wall of steam was thrown into the kitchen. The lasagne looked a bit crisp around the edges. She served it up with garlic bread. Both boys said it was delicious, and all three of them cleared their plates. The air was filled with unspoken words. No one made eye contact. Apple crumble and custard followed, accompanied by more silence.

"We'll wash up. We will, won't we, James? You go and put your feet up, Mum." Robert was doing his best to comfort her, she knew that.

"I'm sorry boys…I…"

"Please, Mum," James said, "don't apologise. You have nothing to apologise for."

Helen looked down at her feet. Robert had bought her slippers for Christmas, and she had dropped custard on them. She sniffed away her tears before they got out of control again.

"If you don't mind, I'll go up to my bedroom. Watch a bit of telly, you know, bit of rubbish. Have an early night."

"Would you like a cup of tea?" Robert asked.

"No, thanks."

"Coffee?"

"No, thanks, Robert, but thanks for asking." Helen was aware they were watching as she left the kitchen and dragged her weary feet up the stairs. She shut the bedroom door and undressed slowly before wandering into her bathroom. The hot water of the shower helped dissolve the tension in her shoulders. She turned to let the water run directly onto her face, massaging her swollen eyes with its gentle force.

* * * *

James looked at Robert, who shrugged his shoulders, saying, "I'll wash if you dry."

"Fuck the washing up, Robert, stick them in the dishwasher. We need to talk about Mum."

"You mean about the van insurance?"

"No, Robert, I don't mean the van insurance. I mean *Mum.*"

"What about her? She'll be okay in the morning."

James felt himself getting angry. He knew Robert wasn't being churlish or rude, he just simply didn't get it. They loaded the dishwasher. He made two cups of coffee and they sat down opposite each other at the kitchen table.

Robert wrapped his hands around the hot mug, staring at its contents. He was clearly out of his comfort zone. "You think this is all about Dad, then."

"I do. She said it herself, if you remember."

"Said what?"

"She said she wanted to go away in the van, so she could be with Dad."

"You don't think she's going to do something silly, do you?"

"If you mean do I think she is going to commit fucking suicide, no, I don't."

Robert flinched at his brother's words. "Dad always

11

used to say you were as subtle as a brick. I suppose that's useful in your line of work." The brothers made eye contact across the table. "So what's this all about then?"

"I reckon she's still grieving. We thought she was okay, yeah?"

Robert nodded in agreement. "We thought she was just fine, that she had got over Dad and was happy." He nodded again, the truth dawning on him. "We were wrong?"

"Yes, Robert. We were wrong."

"What about her friends? Do you think they know she's still upset?"

"Dunno."

"What about this idea she has about going on holiday?"

"I think it's a great idea." James saw the horrified look on his brother's face. "But going away in Valerie Drobshaw so she can be with Dad? Not such a good idea."

"I could go to the travel agent tomorrow and get a load of brochures," Robert said, looking relieved to have come up with something positive. "I'd be a lot happier if she went on a package holiday somewhere."

"Me too, if I get any free time, I'll go online and see what I can find. I'd be happier still if she went away with one of her friends, but I get the feeling she wants to be on her own."

They drank their coffee, deep in thought.

* * * *

Upstairs, Helen lay on her bed, wrapped in the comforting folds of her soft towelling dressing gown. With her elbow on the pillow, she supported her head with her left hand while leafing through a magazine. A soap opera played on the television, and with the volume turned down low, the characters shouted at each other quietly. She switched it off with the remote. When she heard the front door close, she assumed James had gone back to work, so tiptoed downstairs, thinking Robert was in the sitting room. Quietly picking up her laptop, she crept back to her bedroom and arranged her pillows so she could sit up in bed comfortably, and googled for campsites in North Wales.

CHAPTER TWO

Robert and James walked along the footpath to The Lock-Keepers pub. They had never walked to the pub together before. They had explored the paths as young boys on bikes, under the busy dual carriageway of the A41, and along the canal towpath. The calm, black water mirrored the bright pub lights. The white paintwork on the top of the lock marked where the top of the gates doubled as a footbridge.

Once inside, Robert bought two pints of bitter, and they took a table next to the folding glass doors. In summer, the doors were opened and tables set out at the canal side. In winter, the Lock-Keepers was a traditional cosy pub.

The quiz was just starting.

"All for charity, lads, that's a quid each." They took the piece of paper from the landlady; James handed her two pound coins. Robert began to fumble in his jacket pockets for a pen.

"We don't have to do it, you know, just 'cos I gave her the money."

"No, I suppose not." They each took a long drink of the hand-pumped bitter before setting their glasses down on the cardboard beer mats. The quiz and the enthusiastic quizmaster provided plenty of background noise, but thankfully their table was far enough from the microphone for them to have a conversation.

"What exactly is it you do at the bank then, Robert?"

"Investments."

"You're not behind the counter, then? A teller? That's what they're called, aren't they?"

"Good God, no. I mean yes, that's what they're called...tellers, but that's not what I do. I had to do a stint of that when I first started on the graduate scheme.

Hated it. Didn't stay in retail banking a minute longer than I had to. I thought you knew that."

"Yeah, I think I remember something about you saying you wanted to be in a department. Can't say I understood it, or even took much notice, to be honest."

"Thanks." They sat in silence for a while. "What about you? What exactly do you do?"

"Drugs. I look at the information we get from…well…anywhere. You know, informants, anonymous tips from the public, the internet. We're after the suppliers."

"So when you sneak off in the night, what's that all about?"

"Anything that won't wait 'til morning. Usually when we think there's a major deal on the move. Or it could be the execution of a warrant. Best time to do that is when people are in bed, asleep. Take them by surprise."

"Execution?"

"Execution of a warrant, Robert. It's when we batter doors down. Nobody gets their heads chopped off."

"Right. I see," Robert said, although he didn't, not really. It all sounded far too dangerous to him.

Another silence hung between them, each considering how little they knew of each other's lives. The quiz continuing in the background, James took their empty glasses to the bar and bought a second round.

"The thing is, now," James said, "I have the chance of working for the N.C.A., used to be SOCA."

Robert frowned, he hated acronyms in his own work, and *he* understood them. "What's the N.C.A? What's SOCA?"

"National Crime Agency. It has replaced the Serious Organised Crime Agency. Supposed to be joined-up thinking with the Border Agency and a few others."

"Is that another police department, then?"

"No." James paused, turning his pint around on the beer mat with this thumb and forefinger, watching the condensation run down the side of the glass. "It would mean I'd be based in London."

"Oh…right…well…I wasn't going to say anything just yet, because it's not confirmed, but Carleton's may want me to move to London later this year."

"Oh, Christ. What about Mum? We can't leave her on her own. It never occurred to me that you'd be on the move."

"You mean boring old Robert in his boring old bank?"

"No, 'course not," James replied.

"Just because my job involves regular hours and wearing a suit doesn't mean it's boring, you know. Well, not to me, anyway. It might be to you. I happen to prefer working within a framework."

"Sorry. I didn't mean…"

"No, 'course not," Robert said.

James took a long drink from his glass before continuing, his tone conciliatory. "I think it's best if we don't tell Mum we might be leaving home, not until it's definite. No point worrying her about something that may not happen."

"Agreed. When will you know?"

"Quite soon, but it will be at least three months after that before I actually go anywhere. And you? When will you know?"

"Couple of weeks, max."

* * * *

Helen surfed through the links from campsites to campervans. Inevitably, the links took her to ebay. Freddie Dixon was right, Valerie was quite valuable. She was worth a lot more than her car and that was only four years old. Helen read the descriptions of several similar V-Dubs and learned that she had all the bits that made her more desirable. Apparently, a curved windscreen was called a bay window. Valerie had a split windscreen, which was rarer and consequently more valuable. She had a pop-up roof and a Westfalia interior, all of which evidently put her at the top of the V-Dub desirability tree. Valerie, it seemed, was worth a small fortune, and if her plans were to succeed, Helen knew she would have to sell her and buy something more reliable. There were certainly plenty to choose from.

She put on her dressing gown and went downstairs to make a cup of tea. As she waited for the kettle to boil, she went into the lounge to ask Robert if he wanted anything. Finding the room empty, she was about to go upstairs to see if he was in his room when he and James came in together.

"Oh, I didn't know you'd gone out as well, Robert. I thought..."

"We went for a pint," Robert said. He looked almost sheepish. "Sorry, Mum, we should have left a note."

Helen knew she must have looked surprised. "Good, yes...that's nice."

She saw James stifle a giggle. "We are old enough, you know," he said.

"I am your mother, James. If nothing else, that means I *do* know how old you are. I wish the pair of you would go out more often. Together or not together."

They smiled at each other.

She re-tied her dressing gown cord more tightly and turned towards the kitchen. "Cup of tea, anyone? I'm taking mine up to my bedroom."

James and Robert looked at each other and suppressed their smiles. For some unknown reason, they felt like naughty schoolboys. Their differences forgotten by the prickly way their mother had spoken to them.

Once back in her room, Helen gave her pillows a good thumping before settling back with her laptop. More determined than ever to get away, she fired off an email to a V-Dub enthusiasts' club. She described Valerie

Drobshaw and asked if they knew anyone who might be interested in buying her, then squandered a couple of hours looking at modern motorhomes. Comparing them to Valerie was like comparing a Rolls Royce to a pushbike, albeit a very collectable pushbike. She closed her laptop and turned out the light long after Robert and James had gone to bed.

* * * *

Things started to happen quite quickly over the following few days. The very next morning, Helen had an email from Leonard Bulmer, President of the Hyton and Seafield Volkswagen Club. She arranged to meet him that afternoon at Freddie Dixon's garage.

She and Freddie were chatting about old times when Leonard Bulmer drove into the forecourt in a Land Rover with a large trailer.

"Well, that's a good sign," Freddie said. "He hasn't come just for a nosey, Mrs M. He means business."

Leonard Bulmer turned out to be a gentlemanly sort. Helen was happy with the price he offered, and happy that Valerie was going to a good home where she would be appreciated. When he drove away with Valerie carefully strapped down on the trailer, Helen had a huge grin on her face, and twenty thousand pounds in her copious handbag. She jumped in her car and, with a wave to Freddie, drove straight to Billington's Motorhome Sales on the other side of Chester.

A man in his fifties came out of the showroom as she locked her car. He turned back inside and spoke to someone out of Helen's view, then got into a Jag and drove off. There was only one other car in the car park. Helen wanted to have a good look around without any sales patter being drilled into her ears. If Phil had been with her, it would have been different. They would have looked like serious contenders for a sale, and either the Jag man or his colleague would have been at their side by now. Such thoughts didn't insult Helen, they amused her. She had long since deduced that a lone woman is seldom taken seriously by the male of the species when it comes to a major purchase. There is an assumption she will have to consult her other half before a deal is done. She knew how to work chauvinistic attitudes to her advantage. Even the nice Leonard Bulmer had spoken the body language of disbelief at her selling Valerie without consulting a male. He was mollified to a degree by Freddie's presence. Helen reckoned her 'poor widow' status had done her no harm and may even have added a bit to the price.

Grinning, she moved between the motorhomes. The second-hand, or 'pre-loved', models, as the notices in the windscreens described them, were neatly parked in a vast car park. Row upon row of them, and all slightly different. Not one was more than five years old, judging by the registration plates. Helen tried the door of one, but it was locked. She hadn't really expected it to be open. Mr Billington wouldn't let the public go poking about in the vans unattended. A precaution against wheelkickers. She had learned the term whilst browsing on ebay. Some of the ebay sellers had written in their description 'no wheelkickers', and it hadn't taken her long to realise what it meant. Her ebay browsing had also taught Helen the difference between a campervan and a motorhome. She hadn't thought about it before, but you could *live* in a motorhome. A campervan was more...well...for civilised camping. They were what they said they were. What it said on the tin, so to speak. She stood on her tiptoes to peer through a window.

"Hello, Mrs McGuire." Helen was so startled she almost fell as she turned, jolted from her reverie. The young salesman knew her name. She, on the other hand, was entirely lost for words, due partly to the young man's hairstyle and the incongruous suit and tie that stood directly beneath it. Surely, he hadn't paid someone to make his hair look like that. One side was all shaved off, the hair on top standing to rigid attention in various shades of red—scarlet to orange to pink. The other side was shiny rat tails of various lengths and at various angles to his head. She wanted to ask him to turn around so she could see the back.

"I'm Bobby, Mrs McGuire. Bobby Billington." A huge smile spread over his face. "My Dad owns the business here." Helen was still incapable of speech. She blinked stupidly, trying to recognise that smile. She had definitely not seen anything else she might recognise. "You taught me to read, Mrs McGuire. At Castle Lane Juniors. Don't you remember me? We played sausages and cabbages."

"Of course I remember you, Bobby, sorry. You took me by surprise and…well…you've changed a bit." Helen remembered very well the Bobby Billington from school. During her stint on the PTA, she had helped out with the slow learners. Bobby hadn't had the slightest interest in learning to read until she had asked him if he knew how to play sausages and cabbages.

"Do you remember it, when we came to a word that began with 's' we said 'sausages', and if a word began with 'c' we said 'cabbages'?

"I remember, Bobby."

"I liked that story 'The Elves and the Shoemaker' best 'cos we made it 'The Elves and the Sausagemaker' and, instead of making shoes on a counter, they made sausages on a cabbage." Bobby dissolved into fits of laughter. It was infectious. Helen smiled. Her smile grew until she was laughing with him. Then, as quickly as he started, he stopped. "What you doing here, Mrs McGuire?"

Helen took a tissue from her bag and wiped the tears of laughter from her eyes. "Well, Bobby, funnily enough, I've come to buy a motorhome."

Bobby's face dropped. He looked quite disappointed. "My dad's not here, you just missed him. It's quiet at this time of year."

"I'd like to look inside this one, Bobby. Do you have any keys?"

"Oh, yes. Sorry. They're in the showroom. I'll get them. Do you want to come with me? It's cold enough to freeze the b…" He clearly thought better of finishing the phrase.

Helen closed her eyes and nodded.

Inside the showroom, on the larger of two desks, a photo of Bobby as a small boy with a rather large lady, presumably Mrs Billington, was almost lost amongst a pile of papers and brochures. Helen vaguely recognised her from school, when they had waited for the bell to ring, and for the children to come tumbling out into the playground. Bobby was a couple of years younger than James, and had been one of the last children Helen had helped with their reading.

A printer stood on a small table to the side of a smaller desk with a computer, a peg board with bunches of keys hung on the wall, each with a number over it. A hot drinks machine gurgled in the corner in a self-satisfied, smug sort of way. Billington's Motorhomes had the air of organised chaos, with the emphasis on the chaos. But what really caught Helen's eye was the brand new motorhome on display, with a picnic table and barbecue set out on a green carpet. A wind out awning added some sophistication to the idyllic scene.

Bobby went to the peg board. "Number forty-seven, wasn't it? The one you wanted to look inside."

Helen stepped inside the display model.

Bobby walked over and stood on the step. "Dad says I'm a bloody useless salesman."

Opening and closing cupboards, touching the smooth shiny surfaces, the fridge, oven, hob, sink, she made no reply. The table was set with shiny cutlery and sparkling glasses. She was like a child in a toyshop. "I never sold a motorhome, not one. He only keeps me on 'cos I can use the computer and he can't. He says it's to keep me out of trouble, and so he knows where I am, but I know he needs me really." Helen still didn't reply. "Dad says if anyone wants this beauty, they can have fifteen grand off the price. He'll even throw in all the knives and forks and stuff. There's even a special bit for the telly." Bobby leaned inside, pressed a button, and a bracket lowered from a wall cupboard. "It's last year's model, see, and they're sending the next one in two weeks, so we've got to get rid of this."

She sat in the driver's seat that doubled as an armchair when facing the interior, and swivelled around in it. Bobby stepped inside and opened a door towards the rear of the van. "In here is the shower and loo, see. There's a washbasin. It's all a bit poky, but that's motorhomes for you." She stood up and took the couple of paces towards it as he opened another door. "In here is the bedroom. Some people don't like having to make up a bed every night. This one has a proper little bedroom. Very little...see."

Helen saw. To her it was the height of luxury; but then Bobby hadn't seen Valerie Drobshaw.

"'Cos it's a display model, it's got all the bells and whistles. There's even a space at the back for a bike. They call it a garage, in the brochure. How weird is that?"

"It's lovely, Bobby. Even the little shower room. But I don't think I'll be riding a bike anytime in the near future."

"What about your hubby, Mrs McGuire? Won't he want to come and look before you decide? Dad says—"

Helen didn't particularly want to know what Bobby's father had to say about women on their own, so she cut him off.

"No, Bobby. Mr McGuire died some time ago, so it would be difficult for him." A silence followed as she looked in all the cupboards, inspecting the handles and the devices to hold the doors and drawers closed when the van was on the road.

"I call this the Goldilocks van." He laughed nervously, as if anxious to put his gaffe behind him.

"Goldilocks? I'm not getting the joke, Bobby." Helen continued to inspect the van, or pretended to. Bobby hadn't meant any harm, and she'd even tried to make light of his innocent remark.

"You know," he continued. "The kids' story. Everything is just right. Not too big, not too small. Even that bed, for one person, I mean. Not too soft and not too hard either."

"You're absolutely right." She turned to him, her smile restored.

"I thought you wanted a second-hand one, Mrs McGuire. Shall we go and look at number forty-seven?"

Mr Billington was right, his son was not a salesman.

"No, I don't think I do, Bobby. I think I'd like to buy Goldilocks here."

It was his turn to sit down. He looked down at his uncomfortable-looking shiny shoes. "You mean from me, Mrs McGuire?"

Helen looked out of the window, and then stepped towards the door, looking to her left and right. "Well, there doesn't seem to be anyone else here, Bobby."

"You know, what I think about getting a new one is this…"

Helen waited, expecting to be persuaded she had made a good decision.

"You pay an awful lot more for a brand spanker." Bobby spoke as if he were trying to get something off his chest, as if no one had asked for his opinion before, let alone listened to him. He spoke with conviction. "Even this one, and this is a bargain all right. Think about it, Mrs McGuire, are you sure you want to pay thousands of pounds more just so your arse is the first arse to sit on an undersized loo?"

Helen couldn't help it. Her smile burst into gales of laughter. Bobby caught the infection from her, though she wasn't quite sure he knew what she was laughing at. She wiped her eyes in an effort to regain control. She tried to speak but just burst out laughing again. She signalled to Bobby that she was going to the desk and stepped out of the van.

Bobby followed her. "Coffee, Mrs McGuire? Dad says always give punters a coffee if they look like they might be good for a sale."

Helen nodded as she sat in the chair opposite his desk, still incapable of speech.

"I'm right, aren't I? Some customers say they don't want to sleep in a second-hand bed but think nothing of it when they go to a hotel. If they're that picky, they could buy a new mattress, or cushions, yeah?"

She nodded again.

"Milk and sugar?"

"No, thanks, Bobby, plain black for me."

As he operated the hot drinks machine, Helen took the opportunity to study the back of his hairstyle while attempting to regain her composure.

He handed her the polystyrene cup. She took a sip and winced. The coffee was awful. It succeeded in wiping the smile off her face, where the rear view of his hairstyle could not. There was no denying his logic, but she still wanted, as Bobby called it, 'the brand spanker'. She put the cup on his desk, definitely not thirsty enough to drink it. If Mr Billington gave that to prospective customers, she dreaded to think what he did to wheelkickers.

"Tell me about your hair, Bobby." Even as he spoke, she was acutely aware she had broken her own rule: *Never ask a question unless you are sure you want the answer.*

He grinned. "You like it, Mrs McGuire?"

"Let's say it's very interesting."

"Dad hates it. I knew he would. Cost a bit, I can tell

you." There was a brief silence before he continued. "Mum and Dad had a proper go at me when I had it done, but it's their own fault."

Helen was intrigued. She asked another question. Another two, in fact. How could she not? "How do you make that out, Bobby? How is it your parents' fault?"

"I'm twenty-four, Mrs McGuire." He sounded defensive. A seriousness crossed his face. "I got pissed once and hated it. I don't do drugs, nothing like that. Mum and Dad said I wasn't allowed to get a tattoo or have anything pierced. Said they would chuck me out if I did. Pronto. They didn't say anything about hair."

Helen nodded. She again approved of his logic, if not the hairstyle. She tried to imagine Robert or James with such a style, but couldn't.

"Can I tell you a secret, Mrs McGuire?"

"Of course you can, Bobby."

"I got a dragon tattooed on me bum."

"Bobby!" She couldn't say anything else, she was in fits of laughter again. Reaching in her handbag for a tissue, she buried her face in it.

"You all right, Mrs McGuire? Do you want some more coffee? You're not crying in there, are you? You won't tell me dad about the dragon, will you?"

Helen emerged red-faced from the tissue. "No, Bobby. I won't tell a soul." She wiped her eyes. "Did it hurt?" Before he replied, she knew she really had asked one question too many.

"Yeah. It did. Especially when—"

"It's okay, please don't tell me. I shouldn't've asked. Now, on to business. I can leave a deposit today."

"You mean for number forty-seven? You haven't even been inside it, and it's getting a bit dark now. I hate going round them in the dark. It's dead spooky."

"No. Not number forty-seven. I mean Goldilocks."

"Right. Wow. Dad will be surprised. I'll get right on it." He turned to his computer screen and started to type, explaining in great and professional details the legal ins and outs of the sale. Helen noted his dexterity with the keyboard. Where he lacked in salesmanship, he excelled in computer skills. She produced the cash from the sale of Valerie, and the figures were entered into the computer. In no time at all, the printer spewed out a 'Contract of Sale'.

"There you go, Mrs McGuire, your Cabbage of Sausages!"

CHAPTER THREE

Helen ached with laughter as she drove home. She hadn't laughed so much since before Phil had d...the thought took the smile from her face, but not for long. The image of Bobby Billington in his suit and tie and mad hairstyle soon had her smiling again.

Her phone rang from the depths of her handbag. She was tempted to rummage about with her left hand to stop the compelling noise. James would be furious if she were caught. Anyway, it would only be Robert asking where she was, and she would be home in ten minutes. She lit a cigarette, resolving to quit when she set off in Goldilocks. It would be a new start, a new smokeless Helen McGuire. She wasn't going to tell the boys about her purchase. Not yet. Bobby had said he would tell his dad not to phone, and she was to ring the next day to arrange things in more detail. In return, she wasn't going to tell Mr Billington that she knew Bobby at school. That had been Helen's idea, and she had convinced Bobby his dad would be more impressed that way.

"Your first sale to a total stranger is more impressive than to an old friend, Bobby."

Bobby agreed, mostly because he liked the idea of Mrs McGuire being an old friend.

* * * *

"Where on earth have you been, Mum? I've been trying to ring you." Robert looked frantic.

Helen glanced at the kitchen clock. It was six-thirty.

"Why didn't you answer?"

"Sorry, Robert. I've been out. I lost track of time." She hung up her coat. "I daren't answer while I was driving. What would your brother have said?"

Robert ignored the question. "Where's the campervan? It's not at Freddie's. I thought you'd gone off in it somewhere."

"No, of course not. I wouldn't go off without telling you, and I'm not going anywhere in 'that old van' as you called it last night, because I've sold it."

"You've sold Valerie Drobshaw?"

"Yes, Robert. Sold it. For cash. Today. Okay?"

He gaped at her, open-mouthed.

"You can close your mouth now, Robert, unless you have something intelligent to say." She put on an apron and started to peel potatoes with more vigour than was necessary. "Egg and chips tonight? I haven't had time to do any cooking today."

"Does James know?"

"That it's egg and chips for tea? No, he doesn't."

"No, Mother. That's not what I mean, as you are well aware. Does James know you've sold the camper?"

"No. How could he?"

Robert ran his fingers through his thinning hair, drew a deep breath and sighed as he opened his briefcase. "I picked these up today at the travel agents." He pulled out some holiday brochures and put them on the table.

Helen turned from her vigorous potato peeling. She saw his face and her irritation dissolved. "Thanks, Robert. I'll have a look after tea." She returned to the peeling at a more leisurely pace.

Robert pulled out a chair and watched her put two potatoes in a basin and push it to the back of the worktop for James. The hiss of the frying chips and the hum of the extractor fan exaggerated the lack of conversation. He set the table for three, tomato ketchup and brown sauce, with pepper and salt in the centre.

Helen served the food. It was she who eventually broke the silence. "Had a good day then, Robert?"

"Yes, thanks, Mum. And you?"

"You're happy at Carleton's, aren't you?"

"Very, thanks."

"You got a girlfriend, Robert?"

He dropped his knife with a clatter on the plate.

Helen had no idea why she asked. "Is that a 'yes,' then?"

"No. Yes. Maybe…how did you know?"

"Mums know these things, Robert," she lied.

"How?" Robert seemed astonished. Helen thought it made him look vulnerable. She couldn't answer his question, so she asked one. "What is a 'no, yes, maybe' girlfriend, Robert? What does she look like? Where did you meet her?"

"I haven't. Not yet."

There was a pause while she worked it out. It took about five seconds. "Internet?"

Robert nodded. Another five seconds of silence.

"Good for you." She tried to sound positive. She could have said, 'Oh, dear' or 'Be careful', or she could have spoken her mind and said, 'Christ Almighty, Robert, what the hell are you thinking of?'

He smiled at her, so she had said the right thing. It struck her that if Robert had been a Roberta, her response would definitely have been of the 'Christ Almighty' type.

"Keep me posted," was all she said as she started to clear the table. Questions and worries scrambled about in her head.

"She lives in London. Works at Carleton's London headquarters," Robert said.

"That's a coincidence."

"Not really. You can tailor searches quite specifically. I requested someone in banking, thought it would make sure we had at least one thing in common."

"Does she have a name?"

"Jayne."

Helen put her hand on his shoulder and stood on

tiptoe to kiss his cheek, before picking up the travel brochures and disappearing into the lounge. She called back to the kitchen, "You finish the washing up, will you? I'm not in the mood, and the practise might come in useful one day."

He followed her as far as the doorway. "Don't tell James, will you, Mum?"

"'Course not, not if you don't want me to."

"He'd laugh at me." Robert returned to the kitchen and the washing up.

Helen switched on the television, and idly flicked through the travel brochures. They were of no interest to her, but Robert didn't know that and she didn't want to hurt his feelings. She conceded Jersey looked nice and made a mental note to research the ferries on the internet.

* * * *

A quick glance at the alarm clock told Helen that Robert would have left for work. She pulled her dressing gown on and slid her feet into the custard-stained slippers, and went downstairs. A pair of trainers with their laces still tied told her James was home. He must have come in very late. There was no evidence of his having eaten anything. The potatoes were still in the bowl where she had left them, along with her note about egg and chips. There was a note in his handwriting and a printed sheet of A4 paper with website addresses.

Thought you might like to check these travel sites out. There's hundreds out there but these looked good. Everything from Bognor to Bali.

Helen sighed and put the kettle on. As she sat down at the table with a mug of coffee, the phone rang. It was George Billington

"Oh, good morning, Mr Billington…yes, that's right…the display model…oh, I see. Well, yes, I can, I suppose…two o'clock? Okay. We can sort everything out then. And might I say, Mr Billington, you should be very proud of Bobby. He's a fine young man. Very polite and professional. You really didn't need to phone me."

George Billington didn't reply. Helen was enjoying herself.

"I'll see you at two o'clock, then. Bye for now." She replaced the receiver and went back into the kitchen, grinning widely, envisaging George Billington's stupefied face. Sipping her coffee, daydreaming about Goldilocks, driving the open country roads, like a snail, or a tortoise with her home on her back, but a bit quicker, of course. She imagined herself parking on a cliff top overlooking the open sea, listening to the waves breaking on a pebble beach.

Her reverie was broken by James thundering downstairs and into the kitchen. It was impossible to tell whether he was dressed for work or not, for he always wore casual clothes. He looked scruffy, no other word for it. She knew she shouldn't compare them, but couldn't help it. They were so different in every way. James was tall and blond; Robert was shorter and dark, and always neat and tidy. They didn't even look like brothers. James had explained some time ago that he had to 'blend in' with the public. But to Helen, he was scruffy.

"What was all that about then?" he asked.

"What was all what about?"

"You. On the phone. Who's Mr Billington? And where's the old camper? It's not at Freddie's."

Helen felt herself bristling. She had thought James was fast asleep.

"It's none of your business—"

"Oh, I get it," he interrupted, and then paused. "You're not selling the camper to George Billington, are you? He'll rip you off as soon as he looks at you. Old V-Dubs are worth a bit, you know. I'm not saying he's a criminal, but he sails pretty close." James made himself a coffee and sat down opposite his mother.

"Oh, shut up, James. I have *not* sold the campervan to George Billington. I know exactly what they're worth, and I have sold it for a good price. Okay? Stop treating me like a child," she snapped.

"Who to? What did you get for it?"

"None of your business."

James leaned back in his chair, rocking on the back legs.

"Don't do that, you'll break the chair." Helen remembered doing the same thing herself. *Was that really only two days ago?*

"So why is George Billington phoning you at nine o'clock in the morning, Mum?"

She sighed deeply. Not ready to talk about her long-term plans, she didn't want to say anything until it was all settled.

"I'm thinking of buying another camper, maybe something a bit bigger."

"I could come with you if you like." He sounded concerned, as if he wanted to protect her.

"That's very kind of you, James, but no. I might buy something, but there again I might not..." As the words left her lips, Helen realised she had told a lie. She stopped speaking abruptly, and then continued, "I'd just rather go on my own, that's all."

"Okay. Have it your own way. I'm off to work."

"What about some breakfast?"

"No, thanks, no time. I'll grab something in the canteen when I get there. It's manic just now, but I'm hoping to have some time off next week. We'll catch up then." He pushed his feet into his trainers.

"Thanks for the website addresses, James. I'll have a look through them this morning." It was another lie. She'd be far too busy making lists.

James nodded as he grabbed his keys and left for work. As he closed the door, Helen took a notebook and pen from her handbag.

What to take, and what not to take? There was no point taking stuff she wouldn't need. On the other hand, she didn't want to end up buying things she already had, but forgot to pack. Shopping trips would replenish the fridge and larder. There was just so much to consider. Packets of soup weighed light and were easy to store. The first aid kit took some thinking about.

Plasters, yes. Paracetamol, yes. Antiseptic cream, yes. Sling, no. If I'm stupid enough to do something that needs a sling, I won't be driving anywhere.

She made another coffee, and her thoughts drifted to the conversation with George Billington. She wished he hadn't phoned. The cat was creeping stealthily out of the bag. What with her having to say she had sold the camper, and James overhearing her side of the phone call, it was proving very difficult to keep anything a secret. George Billington was obviously having difficulty believing Bobby had made a sale. He had phoned to confirm she intended to complete the purchase of Goldilocks. *I left a cash deposit, for goodness sake. Did he think Bobby had printed the money?* He had asked if she could complete within two weeks, as he needed the space in the showroom for the new model. He had assured her he would be happy to hold it for longer, but it would have to be outside, and fully paid for. It was plain as day that the reason for the phone call was to confirm Bobby's amazing success. She didn't like the word, but George Billington was, indeed, gobsmacked.

The practicalities of going away for a year had to be worked out, and these went much further than making the decision of whether or not to pack a sling. The household finances would have to be attended to. Robert would be the obvious choice. He and James could sort out the household bills between them, or she could ask them to pay their board into a bank account and manage everything online, herself, from wherever she was. The joys of the internet. Option number one seemed more attractive, at first, but when she scratched the surface she began to favour option two. That way she would be sure everything was being dealt with properly. More to the point, how could she start telling them about gas and electricity accounts if she were to continue the fallacy that she was only going away for two weeks?

"This is so bloody complicated!" She threw her pen down, and it scuttled across the table, falling to the floor and under the washing machine. "Sod it." She didn't try to retrieve the pen, instead got another out of a drawer and sat down again. Phil was still grinning at her from his photo on the kitchen windowsill. She wasn't cross with him anymore. It felt as if she and Phil had made a joint decision about selling old Valerie. Perhaps it was the knowledge that Phil and Freddie Dixon had discussed her possible departure from the McGuire family that made it feel so right.

* * * *

Helen didn't expect to like George Billington, and he didn't disappoint her. She thought him a simply dreadful man who thought he was God's gift to women. He stood too close to her and thought he was sexy and amusing. He wasn't, he was overweight and sweated profusely. Mercifully, he wore a decent aftershave. His suit was of good quality, but he must have put on a few pounds since the last visit to his tailor, and consequently the seams were doing stalwart work squeezing him together. The tie was firmly in the 'too loud' department. Worst of all, was the futile attempt to disguise his baldness with a few strands of long hair carefully crafted from a parting just above his left ear. The showroom lights mocked his efforts as they reflected his shiny scalp through the long thin strands of hair.

Bobby's cheap suit, on the other hand, looked as if his dad had bought it in the hope that Bobby would grow a bit more. His colourful, outrageous hairstyle was growing on her; anything was better than a comb-over. Helen was quite sure she would never have bought anything from Billington's Motorhomes had Mr George Billington been around the day before. She found herself avoiding eye contact with Bobby for fear of bursting into giggles.

George Billington put his hand under her left elbow.

"Come, Mrs McGuire, let me show you inside your motorhome. I'm sure Bobby didn't explain everything to you."

Helen stiffened at the unwelcome touch.

Bobby stepped forward.

"You stay there, Bobby," his father commanded. Helen took George Billington's hand from her elbow with her right hand, and lifted it away.

She looked directly into his piggy eyes, and with her best school-marmish voice said, "Mr Billington—"

"Mrs McGuire—Helen, if I may? Please call me George."

"Mr George, I believe Bobby is my point of contact. If you think he may not have explained everything to me, and you would like him to learn, then I suggest he comes with us." She smiled her most benevolent smile. From the corner of her eye, she could see Bobby grinning. As his father turned to him, Bobby put his hand to his mouth to stifle a giggle. He pretended to yawn.

"Pay attention, Bobby. You heard what Mrs McGuire said. Get in the motorhome," George Billington snapped. He seemed annoyed that he wasn't going to have Helen to himself.

Maybe he fancies me, she thought, frowning.

Mr Billington made Bobby stand in the shower room while he converted the dining table into a double bed. Mercifully for Helen, the shower room door opened inwards so there was no opportunity to shut the poor boy inside. Sitting on the edge of the cushions, he ran his fingers over the fabric. His arms folded, Bobby looked at the ceiling of the shower room, humming the tune to 'Daddy Cool'. Helen still dared not look at him for fear she would laugh.

"Why don't you sit down next to me, Mrs McGuire? You need to appreciate just how very comfortable this bed is."

"I'll take your word for it, Mr Billington. I shall use the little bedroom at the back when I'm on my travels."

"Will you be travelling alone, dear?"

"Mr Billington, I am not your 'dear'. I am your customer, or more correctly, I believe I am Bobby's customer. As to whether or not I am to travel alone is for me to know, and for you to ponder about." She stepped out of the motorhome, struggling to keep a straight face, as she walked towards their desks. She half turned and called back to him over her shoulder. "Paperwork, Mr Billington. We need to complete the paperwork. I believe you need Bobby's help with that."

Twenty minutes later, with all the necessary forms completed and signed, she shook hands with Bobby, and then with his father.

"A word of advice, Mr Billington," Helen said as she pulled on her gloves.

"Yes, Mrs McGuire?" He sounded apprehensive.

"Let Bobby wear something more casual for work. He looks perfectly ridiculous in that cheap suit."

This time Bobby laughed out loud. His father was speechless.

"I'll see you in three weeks when I collect my motorhome." She smiled and turned to the door.

Bobby darted round and opened it for her. "Thank you, Mrs McGuire." His cheeky smile spoke volumes. She gave a little wink as she nodded in acknowledgement and left.

* * * *

On the drive back to Jumbles Lane, her thoughts turned to the question of her departure. More specifically, how she was going to work it with Robert and James. Some ideas were already shaping up in her mind. Helen knew exactly what she wanted to do, but feared her sons would try to talk her out of it. If she said she was going on a package holiday, they would insist one of them took her to the airport, so although that idea had the advantage of telling them nothing about her true plans, she dismissed it almost as soon as she thought of it. There was really no alternative but to tell them about Goldilocks. Anything else would be impossible to sustain. She contemplated setting off on her travels straight from Billington's Motorhomes, but had to dismiss that idea too. She needed to drive it home and pack properly. There was nothing else for it, she would tell them at the first opportunity, and get it out of the way, just as soon as they were both home at the same time—hopefully that night. She finally came to the conclusion that the simplest way was to tell them she intended to take several short trips, starting with a week or two in North Wales over Easter. She would have her phone and laptop with her, so they could contact her whenever they wanted, and she could contact them. Keep it simple. That would be the key to keeping her long-term plans to herself.

* * * *

As luck would have it, James was home that evening, but Helen lost her courage and didn't say anything. As a result, she was in a foul mood by bedtime. She didn't understand what was holding her back. Was it her imagination, or were Robert and James tiptoeing around her, metaphorically speaking? What was wrong with them? What was wrong with her?

She tossed and turned in bed, drifting in and out of

sleep; sleep filled with bizarre dreams in which Phil stood on the drive, waving to her as she flew down Jumbles Lane in an aeroplane. In another dream, all the cupboards in her van were filled with sausages and cabbages, and she had to eat them all before Robert and James would allow her to go.

Helen didn't want to tell them separately. Something inside her insisted it would be better if they were together when she broke the news. She resolved to tell them next time they were together, definitely.

Her next opportunity came four days later, on Saturday.

"Sit down at the table, boys, I'll make a pot of coffee. I have something to tell you." She saw the anxious glance pass from Robert to James, and James's almost imperceptible shrug. She made their coffees the way they liked them. James: black, two sugars, Robert: white, no sugar, and her own: plain black. She sat opposite her sons and took a deep breath, speaking slowly as she told them about the beautiful motorhome she had bought, while all the time dreading their criticism.

"So my first stop will be North Wales, maybe Anglesey."

They stood up and put their arms around her. She didn't know what she had expected, but not that. They were delighted for her. The shock of their reaction caused tears of joy to run down Helen's cheeks as they hugged her. All her prevarications had been fear of their reaction. What a silly fool she had been. James took three glasses out of a cupboard and a bottle of sparkling wine from the fridge.

"I think we should crack this open, don't you, Robert?"

"It's a bit early, but why not? Good for you, Mum."

Helen smiled, relief written all over her face. She had said 'good for you' to Robert when he had told her about

Jayne. She could only hope he meant the words more sincerely than she had.

James filled the glasses and they chinked them together.

"What's the toast to be, Mum?" Robert asked.

Helen thought about it for a moment and raised her glass. "The future."

"To the future," they repeated in chorus.

CHAPTER FOUR

Helen's days became dominated by lists. Everything needed organising, and she was keen to put her plans into action. The list of 'things to do inside', such as changing dead light bulbs and cleaning the insides of all the windows, was as long as the list of 'things to do outside', such as sweeping leaves and washing window ledges. Finding a dusty bottle of champagne in the garage, she wiped it before wrapping it in two tea towels. She'd pop the cork on that when the boys told her they were leaving home.

The non-food list comprised of everything from washing powder to toothpaste to fly spray. Helen sang happy little tunes as she went about her self-imposed tasks, sometimes aloud, sometimes in her head. There were reminder lists to change the bed linen two days before she left so there was time to launder everything, and leave a clean set for each of them. All the boys' clothes had to be ironed—Robert having a wardrobe full of shirts for work—and her conscience wouldn't let her go without filling up the freezer with ready meals and loaves of bread.

Her lists seemed endless, but her personal packing became the biggest challenge of all. After several attempts to decide what to take and what not to, she came up with a systematic approach. She emptied everything out of her wardrobe and drawers, and put back only the things she wanted to keep, but leave behind. The rest went into two piles: one 'to take' and the other 'to charity shop'. The day before she was to collect Goldilocks, the 'to take' pile was stacked in the hall. It was somehow both cathartic and shocking to see her clothes and shoes all neatly piled up.

A box of non-perishable supplies contained such

things as washing up liquid, kitchen roll, cling film, shampoo, shower gel, deodorant, toothbrush and toothpaste.

"That's another advantage of a motorhome," she mumbled. "No need for suitcases."

Items were ticked off with great satisfaction as her carefully laid plans fell into place, while all the time a question constantly niggled in the back of her mind. Her worrying was out of proportion, but then, she told herself, all worries were like that. They never solved anything, but that didn't stop them either. This particular question needed a simple 'yes' or 'no' answer.

Should I take Phil's photo?

Helen took it from the windowsill and put it on top of some towels in the hall. He looked back at her. She picked it up and put it back on the windowsill.

"Well, do you want to come, or not?" She waited for a reply. "Oh, all right, then, you cheeky old sod, come on." She put him face down on the towels. "I think I knew all along you'd have to come with me."

* * * *

Two days later, on a bright sunny morning, Helen set off for North Wales. Her planning had paid off and everything had dovetailed together perfectly. She delayed telling her neighbour until the day before, that way it was a *'fait accompli'*, and Susan didn't have the opportunity to grill her too much. They had a coffee together, and Helen gave Susan her mobile number, 'just in case…' Helen had the feeling Susan thought she was nuts.

Robert and James were even more positive when they saw Goldilocks. They seemed genuinely happy for her. Robert said he felt quite jealous and wished he were coming along. He fixed her television to the bracket while James fiddled with all the gadgets. He was particularly impressed with the electric doorstep which folded in and out at the touch of a button.

The automatic gears and power steering made it an easy drive. Rod Stewart sang to her from a CD as she cruised happily along the coast road, shunning the busy dual carriageway of the A55, towards Llandudno. She would stay there for a week or two before moving on to Anglesey. There was no hurry, and the traffic was light. She should reach the campsite before lunchtime, and use the rest of the day to familiarise herself with the place and cook the first meal in her new home. She asked herself if Robert and James would have been so pleased had they known her long-term plan. The answer came bouncing back with a resounding *definitely not!*

Driving over the brow of a hill, the landmarks of the Little Orme and Great Orme peninsulas identified the town before her, as they stuck their heads into the Atlantic Ocean. The vast expanse of water epitomised her freedom. The first day of the rest of her life. A blank page. Helen sang at the top of her voice, along with Rod Stewart, at full volume.

Littletrees Caravan Park was easy to find. The receptionist handed her a leaflet that gave details of the showers and laundry block, how to hook up to the mains electricity, where to fill up with fresh water, and the location of the recycling bins. A plan of 'Littletrees', with plot sixteen circled, indicated her allotted site.

"The shop sells groceries and newspapers, and is open from seven 'til six. Have a nice day. If there's anything else you need, please ask."

Helen thanked her. So far, so good. Everything on the immaculately clean site had a freshly painted, cheerful look about it as the season had only just begun.

She reversed into plot sixteen—the nearside front neatly lined up to the electrical hook up point—and switched off the engine.

"First things first, Helen McGuire," she said as she swivelled her seat around. "Put that kettle on." She opened the door and set out the step, using the remote control and, taking the cable from its neat little hatch, she plugged into the mains electricity. Battery power would be useful on the road when she stopped for a cuppa, but there was no point using it on site. Bobby had given her a demonstration, and if all else failed, there was always the instruction manual to fall back on. The plots to either side of her were vacant, but it was early in the day. She was certain there would be neighbours before too long.

The kettle boiled and Helen savoured her first cup of tea sitting at the dining table. From there she could watch her fellow campers as they went about their day. There were a few young families about, but most of the population of 'Littletrees' appeared to be older people.

"Come on, Helen, things to do. You can't sit here on your backside all day." She went into her little bedroom and made up the bed. The double bed sheets were too big, but single ones would have been too small. Her quilt piled up against the wall on one side and hung to the floor on the other.

"I'll be as snug as a bug in a rug," she said as she put Phil's photograph on the little table. "I must remember to put you under the pillow when we're on the road, Phil. Don't want you getting smashed." She smiled at him. "I mean broken, not smashed as in drunk, silly arse."

From the bedroom she went to the shower room and organised her toiletries, and from there she pressed the button, as Bobby had demonstrated, to reveal the television. She attached the aerial and waited for it to pick up a signal. Helen had never watched much daytime television, but conceded it might have its uses on a rainy day, especially now her housework was drastically reduced, and there would be no shirts to iron.

She took her laptop from a cupboard and opened it at the table. There were emails from Robert and James wishing her a happy holiday. Robert told her to take care, James told her to have fun and not to talk to strange men.

She replied, telling Robert she was fine and he was not to worry, and James that she would only talk to strange women. She loved them both dearly.

"If only you knew I was doing all this for you."

She stared blankly at the laptop screen until her attention was diverted by the sound of a woman shouting and, looking out of the window, she saw an elderly couple parking a small caravan in the plot opposite. The man was at the wheel of the car, his wife shouting directions from behind the caravan.

"Left hand down, John." She waved her arms. Helen thought he probably couldn't see her. "No! Not that way, the other way...stop!" she yelled. He took no notice, and proceeded to park the caravan perfectly. Helen decided John was either stone deaf or pretended to be. He got out of the car and began to unhitch the caravan.

"Thank you, dear," he said. "Couldn't have done it without you."

"I'll sort out inside while you faff about getting the legs down," she replied.

"No jigging about in there, Betty, not until I've got her stable."

The caravan, like the car, was far from new.

If Phil had lived, that would have been us in a few years' time, in old Valerie. But then, maybe not. Valerie was past her best, and Phil would have had to spend a lot of time and money on her.

She felt no nostalgia for Valerie. Goldilocks was home, and Helen revelled in the sheer, unadulterated luxury, well aware the novelty might wear off. Time would tell on that one, but for now she was content to watch John and Betty setting up their caravan.

They worked without further conversation in what looked like a well-honed routine. Outside, John wound down the legs and checked everything was level before winding out the awning. A slight breeze ruffled the striped canvas and, after looking skyward, observing the scurrying clouds, he shook his head and wound it back in again. He reached inside the caravan with one hand and, without any exchange of words, Betty passed him a small doormat that he carefully laid out in front of the step. Their dining area and window faced Helen. Betty looked across and waved as she placed a vase of plastic flowers on the table. Helen smiled and waved back before returning her attention to her laptop. Next time she looked across, they were reading newspapers. Betty had spread hers on the table; John held his paper up in front of him. They couldn't see each other, and if Helen's observations were correct, John was in a silent world.

A teenage girl, hands deep in her pockets, walked along the narrow road between the caravans and motorhomes. This area of 'Littletrees' was reserved for tourers, separated by a hawthorn hedge from the large static vans available to hire by the week. The girl wore black denim jeans and a black tracksuit top with its hood up, hiding her face almost completely. Wisps of long blonde hair escaped and blew in the breeze. A wire from her hood to her pocket verified she was listening to music, as deaf to the world around her as John was to the real world. She walked towards reception and into the shop.

Helen leaned back and shut her eyes. The image of the teenage girl dressed in black imprinted on the inside of her eyelids. Even her trainers were black. That was an odd thing about girls. Not that she claimed to know anything much about girls, not having been blessed with a daughter. They seemed to be all pink and pretty and then everything goes black, as if the pink fairy flies out of the bedroom window one night to be replaced with a Goth.

Boys were much simpler. Robert had always been particular about his appearance and would save his pocket money to buy a certain T-shirt, whereas James didn't really care what he looked like, just that his clothes were dry and comfortable.

A revving engine took Helen from her daydream. A

large motorhome pulled into her neighbouring plot. As soon as the engine stopped, hoards of children appeared, all laughing and running around. The mum and dad shouted instructions as four of them set off towards the beach with buckets and spades.

"Keep Ellie in your sight all the time, Daniel...and don't forget to watch the tide."

Helen reckoned mum and dad were in their mid-thirties, the children ranging from about six to twelve. The eldest, evidently called Daniel, waved his acknowledgement without turning round as they all ran off. Mum lifted out a baby buggy, and Dad started to unfasten bikes from the rear of the motorhome.

Helen stepped outside. "Can I help at all? You seem to have your hands full."

"That's very kind of you. I'm Jeffrey, please call me Jeff. This lovely lady is my wife Miranda, or Mindy as she prefers to be called, mother of our unruly brood."

"Helen, Helen McGuire." She proffered her hand and Jeff shook it firmly, then Mindy shook her hand with a lighter touch. "Do you come here often?" The three of them laughed at her words. The worn phrase sounded silly. "I mean, the children seem to know their way around."

"We do, yes. Every holiday," Mindy said. "We've taken the older ones out of school one day early so we could get here before the Bank Holiday rush. We shouldn't really, I know."

"A lot of the people here are regulars," Jeff said. "It's a nice site. The kids love the freedom." He pointed to the little caravan opposite. "John and Betty over there, they come every Easter. Lovely old couple. He's as deaf as a post."

"I gathered that," Helen said with a smile. Just then a cry came from inside their motorhome, and Mindy stepped inside, coming out moments later with a little girl in her arms.

"This is our youngest, Poppy," Mindy said as she put her in the buggy. "She's just eight months. We decided she was the last one, but there's another on the way." Mindy smiled as she patted her stomach. "Due September."

"I'll make a pot of tea," Jeff said. "Would you and your other half care to join us, Helen? I'll get the table out."

"That would be lovely, but I'll make the tea. You must have plenty to do." Without waiting for a reply, Helen went inside and filled the kettle. With a deep sigh, she lifted three mugs from the cupboard and put them on a tray with a little jug of milk, a sugar bowl and two teaspoons. For all her lists and careful planning, Helen hadn't considered the possibility of entertaining. She didn't have a teapot. By the time she stepped outside again, Jeff had set out a table with four folding chairs.

"Your hubby not joining us, Helen?" Mindy asked.

"No. There's just me. No other half." Helen saw Mindy's eyes dart to her left hand as she held the tray. Helen still wore her rings. "My Phil died a couple of years ago." An empty silence hung between them. Helen felt obliged to say something, to fill the gap in conversation. "Please don't feel badly about it. It's okay." She busied herself setting out the tea.

"Sorry...I..."

"It's okay, Jeff, really it is. You weren't to know."

The three of them sat down. The teenage girl in black walked by with a large plastic bottle of milk.

"I see the Davidsons are here, Mindy." He turned to Helen. "They're regulars too. They have a caravan. Come every year from Scarborough. That's the daughter, Tashy. Her mum and dad are divorced. She comes here with her dad and his new wife."

"They'll have the baby now," Mindy said. "Don't you remember, Jeff? Fiona told us at the end of last summer the baby was due in February."

"You're right. I'd forgotten that."

Helen was content to sit and listen to the relaxed conversation between them. 'Littletrees' was apparently a second home to a lot of people, but she didn't feel like an outsider. They all seemed friendly enough, and it said something about the site if they had so many regulars.

"Well, must get on," Mindy said, "The children will be back before we know it and starving hungry. I'll get something for Poppy first. Will you put the windbreaks up, Jeff?" Turning to Helen, she said, "It's so much easier if we can eat outside. Keeps the crumbs out of the motorhome."

"I'll leave you to it, then." Helen put the empty mugs back on the tray. "I fancy a walk along the beach."

"It'll be breezy," Mindy said. "Hang on to your hat."

"I will." Helen smiled as she took the tray back inside. Washing the mugs, she could hear Jeff hammering the windbreak poles into the ground.

* * * *

Natasha Jayne Davidson, aged fifteen, found the deepest sand dune she could and sat down with her back resting on the steep sides. She was pretty much sheltered from the bloody wind down here, and could listen to her music in peace. Her life was shit. Being fifteen was shit for a start. Too old for kids' stuff and too young to be allowed to do anything she wanted to. 'Go get some milk, Tashy. Put the kettle on, Tashy.' She was treated like shit. She'd insisted on being called 'Tashy' by refusing to answer to 'Natasha'. Her parents were too busy getting on with their own lives to think about her. It was all very well for them. Mum with her gorgeous Roger, and Dad with his gorgeous Fiona. Now there was a baby brother to put up with as well. If Dad and Fiona thought she was going to be a resident babysitter, they could think again.

They made it quite obvious they didn't really want

her around. Mum had gone and suggested to Dad she went on holiday with him and Fiona. No one asked her if she wanted to go; she was simply told what a good idea it was. Worse still, she knew Dad and Fiona felt they had to take her, once the suggestion had been made. She had thought the one good thing to come out of Mum and Dad splitting up was that she wouldn't have to come to bloody Llandudno any more. She'd tried to tell Mum she would rather stay with her. That wasn't quite true, of course. What she really wanted was to stay at home, so she could hang around with her friends.

She put her hand in her tracksuit jacket pocket, pulled out a small tin, opened it carefully and took out a hand-rolled cigarette, holding it lightly between her lips. Cupping her hands against any gusts of wind that might find their way into the dune, she lit up, drew deeply on the spliff, and rested her head back, eyes closed. Her whole body relaxed. She smiled and revelled in the deliciously blissful sensation. Her dad had accused her of smoking, which she had denied, of course. Then she had admitted it in a non-committal shrug when he had said he could smell it on her clothes. Mum smoked, so Dad blamed Mum for setting a bad example and all that crap. They had no idea. The thought made her smile again, this time at their stupidity. Anyway, they were only little spliffs. She bought them ready rolled for two reasons. Firstly, because she was rubbish at rolling her own, and secondly because she didn't want Mum or Dad finding any dope in her stuff. If they were ever annoying enough to go looking, they would only find roll-ups.

After two more long drags, she pushed the tiny stub into the sand.

CHAPTER FIVE

With her warm fleece zipped up and her hat firmly pulled down, Helen set off for the beach. A high spring tide with huge, thunderous waves filled the air with roaring and a misty spray, forcing Helen to walk in the dunes. The soft sand made for hard going as she climbed up and down the little hills. Tussocks of coarse marram grass waved in the wind, their tough roots clinging to the curved shapes sculpted by the breeze. She grabbed at the grass to pull herself up the steep slopes, sliding slowly into deep hollows.

It hadn't occurred to her that there might be anyone else in the dunes. The first indication she wasn't alone was a faint, sweet smell. The momentary distraction caused her to miss her footing, and she fell into one of the hollows. "Bugger it."

"Are you okay?"

Helen turned round quickly to see the girl in black pushing a cigarette stub into the sand as she jumped to her feet.

"Oh! Yes. Sorry about the language. I didn't know anyone was here." Helen dusted the sand from her fleece.

Tashy stifled a giggle. "Perhaps you should sit down for a bit."

"It's Tashy, isn't it?" Helen asked.

Tashy stepped back, crossing her arms defensively. "How d'you know my name?"

"I'm staying at 'Littletrees'." Helen sat down, rubbing her right ankle. "The family next to me told me your name. I'm Helen."

"Oh, right." Tashy sighed deeply. "That's one of the things I hate about that place."

"Sorry. Didn't mean to offend, I'm sure."

"It's the same every bloody Easter. They all park in exactly the same plot every year. They're like fucking homing pigeons. All they talk about is who's died and who's had a baby."

Helen took her sock off, and immediately regretted it. Her ankle was swelling rapidly.

"I suppose it's my turn to apologise for the bad language."

Helen shrugged. She didn't care whether Tashy apologised or not. It didn't sound as though she meant it. Right now, she would like to use some bad language herself because her ankle hurt like mad. In fact, it was fucking agony. She tried to get her sock back on.

"So whose plot am I in then? I'm parked opposite John and Betty, next to Jeff and Mindy."

"Oh, them. I suppose they've had another baby."

"Yes, Poppy, and another on the way."

"They're like bloody rabbits, those two. You must be in Mr and Mrs Beaumont's plot. No one ever knew their first names. Proper old fashioned. Their caravan was ancient. One of them must've snuffed it. They were dead old." Tashy's face burst into a huge grin at her unintended pun. "Dead old...get it?"

Helen faked a smile. "I get it."

"Your ankle looks gross."

"Thanks. I think I might have a problem getting back."

"I could go and get my dad, if you like."

"I'll manage, thanks." Helen didn't want any fuss. She tried to get to her feet but fell back with a cry of pain. She pointed to a piece of driftwood. "Pass that over, would you, Tashy? It might serve as a crutch."

Tashy did as she was asked. "I'm having a smoke before I go back." She put her hand in her pocket, pulled out her tin, and opened it carefully to reveal three hand-rolled cigarettes. Helen saw they were small and neat, with tips. "Fancy one?" She held out the tin.

Helen hesitated for a moment, and then took one, her resolve to quit crushed by the pain.

"I need another before I go back to play happy families." Tashy lit up, and then handed the lighter to Helen.

She looked at the cigarette for a while before putting it to her lips. The strength of the little roll-up made her cough. She watched Tashy draw deeply with her eyes closed, burning away a third of her cigarette. The pain in Helen's ankle was getting worse. Then her head began to swim and she lay back on the sand, eyes closed. The pain floated away and she began to giggle.

* * * *

Doctor Haines at Llandudno A&E was impressed with Helen's stoicism. The x-ray confirmed she hadn't broken any bones, but how she had walked for almost a mile across soft sand, with no more than a make-shift crutch, he had no idea. He'd qualified as a doctor the previous summer and was three months into his stint at A&E. His disenchantment with his own generation had developed in equal proportion to his respect for the oldies. The under-forties seemed to think doctors were magicians, but the over-forties listened to him with respect, accepting his diagnosis. The over-seventies thought he was God, even when God was likely to be their next visitor. It was all a huge generalisation, of course, but generally true.

Mrs McGuire had waited calmly, more concerned with wasting the precious holiday time of the people who accompanied her, than by her own injury. "Really, Doctor, I can manage perfectly well, once I'm back in my motorhome. It's very convenient. I have all I need. Mr Davidson and Tashy here have been very kind, but now I've wasted enough of everybody's time."

"I'll get some painkillers sent up from the pharmacy

for you." The doctor started to write a prescription.

"No, thanks. It'll take hours, and I'm not sitting here for a few pills that I won't need. You've been very kind, and I'm sure you're spot on with the bad sprain diagnosis. I'm very grateful, but I'll be off now." Helen struggled to her feet, taking her weight on her right foot, and touching the floor lightly with her left to gain balance. She winced. "Come on, Tashy, give me your arm."

Doctor Haines shook his head as he turned to his next patient.

* * * *

Alan Davidson stepped in front of his daughter. He knew Tashy wouldn't want to help. He'd been surprised she had wanted to come to A&E with them at all. In fact, there was a lot he didn't understand about the last two hours. Apparently, Tashy had met Mrs McGuire on the beach. They had been walking in the dunes chatting about 'Littletrees'. That in itself was incredible. Tashy barely spoke to anyone. He'd had to insist on taking Mrs McGuire to the hospital, and she had only agreed when Tashy had said she'd thought it was a good idea. As they had waited to see the doctor, Helen—as she had asked to be called—had told him how she had lost her footing, and how Tashy had helped her back to the campsite. He was speechless. Here was this stranger telling him what a lovely daughter he had, and that he must be very proud of her. As he put out his arm to assist Helen, Tashy darted forward.

"Come on, Helen. I'll help you to the car." Tashy put her arm under Helen's elbow.

Alan followed his daughter and a hopping Helen on their slow progression to the car park. He watched Tashy check the front passenger seat was as far back as it would go to make it easier for Helen to get in. She placed a cushion under her injured ankle before climbing into the back of the car. During the short drive back to 'Littletrees', Helen thanked Tashy for her thoughtfulness, and told him again how proud he must be of his daughter. The words were music to his ears, a strange but wonderful music he hadn't heard before. They were driving through the entrance to 'Littletrees' when Tashy asked to be dropped off with Helen at the Beaumont's old plot. Alan Davidson nodded slowly, speaking for the first time since leaving the hospital.

"Okay, but you come back to the caravan if Helen needs a rest." Tashy didn't reply. As he pulled up at plot sixteen, she leapt out of the car. He didn't try to help. He'd got the message: Tashy didn't want him interfering, and he wasn't going to rock the boat. Once Helen was on her feet, or rather on one foot, Tashy slammed the door, and he drove off.

Alan Davidson was baffled. Happy, pleased and proud…and completely baffled.

* * * *

"Thanks, Helen."

Helen and Tashy were inside with the door shut.

"For what?" Helen was genuinely puzzled. "It is I who must thank you, but I expect you're fed up hearing that by now." She lowered herself slowly, sitting sideways to the table with her injured foot raised on the seat.

There was a knock on the door. Tashy opened it.

It was Jeff. "How are you, Helen? What happened? Fiona said you had gone to hospital."

Helen opened her mouth to speak, but Tashy answered for her. "She's okay. Needs to rest her ankle, that's all."

"Tashy's right. Just a silly sprain, Jeff. Thanks for asking."

"If there's anything we can do to help—"

"I'll do it," Tashy said.

"Very kind of you to offer." Helen winced as she spoke. She hadn't attempted to get up, but her ankle hurt like hell, and she was struggling to hide it in her voice. "You have plenty to do, with your children. Tashy here will help me."

"John and Betty have been asking what happened." Mindy was standing behind him now, Poppy on her hip.

They were all very kind, but Helen found herself wishing they would sod off. "Tell them I'm fine, just need to rest. See you tomorrow."

"You're sure we can't help?" He looked quizzically at Tashy.

"She's sure," Tashy said, as she smiled and closed the door. "Right set of nosey parkers. They'll all have been trying to work out how it was my fault, I suppose."

"Who's Fiona?" Helen asked. "Jeff said Fiona had told him."

Making no reply, Tashy turned to the sink and filled the kettle.

Helen let the question go. "Plain black for me. The coffee and mugs are in the cupboard over the sink."

Two steaming mugs of coffee were on the table before Tashy answered, sitting opposite her new friend, her hands gripped around the hot mug.

"She's Dad's new wife." A dark look crossed Tashy's face.

A short silence hung between them.

"Just before Jeff knocked on the door, you said 'thank you'."

"Mmmm. I meant, thanks for not telling anyone about the spliff."

"Ah. Yes. Well, I was worried, you see. Worried about going to the hospital and someone smelling it on me or something." Another silence followed. Helen thought she could have felt very cross with Tashy, tricking her like that. She had no idea why she had accepted the cigarette, even when she'd thought it was just a roll-up. "I've been trying to give up smoking, and that was definitely my last cigarette. Maybe you did me a favour, Tashy."

They sipped their coffee, putting their cups down on the table simultaneously. Their eyes met and they smiled, then laughed, the ridiculousness of the situation dawning on the new, unlikely friends.

Tashy looked around the motorhome. "Nice. Very nice."

"Thanks. It's going to suit me just fine. I like the separate bedroom. It means I won't have to make the bed up each night. That's going to be a real bonus, especially now I've done this." Helen pointed to her ankle, which had swollen so much her ankle bone had disappeared into a balloon of flesh. "I hope the mattress is comfortable."

"Haven't you slept in it before, then? Is it brand new?"

"Tonight will be my first night. I expect this bloody ankle will keep me awake though. Would you look in there for me, Tashy?" Helen pointed to a cupboard above the hob. "For some paracetamol."

"Bet you wish you'd waited for the stronger ones now," Tashy said as she passed the packet of tablets to Helen. "Can I get you something to eat?"

With Helen giving directions, Tashy had a ham salad tea for two ready in a matter of minutes. She told Tashy she should send a text to her dad telling him she was staying for tea.

"Look at it from Fiona's point of view. She'll be making a meal for someone who doesn't turn up. I know how that feels."

Tashy sighed heavily. It took her no more than ten seconds to send the message.

"There," Helen said, "that wasn't too difficult, was it? I expect you text your friends all the time."

Tashy's phone buzzed. She looked at it briefly, and then put it back in her pocket.

Helen didn't ask what the message was. She was sure it was her dad saying 'okay' or 'thanks'. She was equally sure he would be surprised to receive the message. They ate in silence for a while.

Tashy looked out of the window. "I hate this fucking place."

Helen didn't reply. She had the feeling Tashy wanted to talk; to be listened to.

"We come here every Easter. It used to be with Mum and Dad, now it's with Dad and Fiona and their baby. Next year I'll be sixteen and old enough to tell them to stick their bloody caravan up their stupid arses. I can do that, you know, legally. Mum's gone away with her boyfriend, and I told them I wanted to stay at my friend's house, but oh, no. All I get is the 'you'll like it when you get there' speech."

The image of a caravan legally stuck up Alan Davidson's arse flickered through Helen's mind. She stifled a smile.

"I can leave home and get my own place, and I'll tell you it won't be in sodding Llandudno, or bloody Scarborough. It will be as far away as I can get from any of them." Tashy continued to gaze out of the window. Helen saw the tears welling up, and knew Tashy was waiting for her to speak. To criticise. To argue. The tear-filled eyes looked at her. "We live in Scarborough and come here for holidays. Can you imagine anything so boring? Where is the imagination in that? We come from a boring East coast town to a boring West coast town."

Helen rummaged in her handbag and passed her a tissue.

"I bet you're going to lots of interesting places. You won't stay in this dump for long." She took the tissue from Helen and wiped her eyes. "You can go where you want, and do what you want. I hate being me." Tashy stood up and started to clear the table.

Helen didn't know what to say, so she changed the

subject. "The cling film's in the cupboard to the left of the sink."

Tashy cleared the table and washed up without another word. When she'd finished, she wrote her mobile number on a piece of paper and handed it to Helen. "You can text or email me if you need anything." She looked around the spotless camper. "Looks like you have all you need."

"Thanks, Tashy. Will I see you in the morning?"

"If you like. Dunno why, with you being old and all that, but I can talk to you." Tashy smiled and left.

* * * *

Helen sighed deeply, happy to be on her own at last. She reflected on Tashy's parting words. It puzzled her that this girl could talk to her when her own sons couldn't. The 'old' tag had been unpleasant, but fair enough from a teenager. If she'd had her way, there wouldn't have been any trip to hospital, with or without the fear that the doctor would somehow diagnose her as a pot-smoking junkie. She'd been scared half to death when she'd realised the cigarette was a spliff. Why had she accepted it in the first place when she was supposed to be quitting? So much for her resolve. Madness. Sheer unadulterated madness. It could only be put down to some mid-life thing, trying to connect with the younger generation. Stupid cow.

Her thoughts drifted to Robert and James. Shuffling sideways on the seat, she leaned over to lift her laptop out of the cupboard, deleted their emails, and smiled. She'd been gone for about twelve hours and, so far, had been taken to hospital and had smoked her first joint. James would be horrified. Robert would insist she went straight back home like a naughty child.

She googled 'marijuana' and, for the next hour, visited websites to learn as much as she could about the drug. Opinions varied from 'it's okay because it's natural' to convincing arguments regarding the powerful effects on the mind, short term and long term. Articles about artificially-modified skunk, and its powerful smell, proved that views and fears about genetic modification weren't limited to supermarket shelves. She was fascinated. Cannabis. Hash. Grass. Weed. She learned that in the UK it was downgraded to a class 'C' drug, only to be re-classed back up to 'B'. She learned of the popular misconception that to possess the drug for personal use wasn't illegal. It was. As a medicine, it was legal in Holland, Canada, Germany, Austria, Portugal, Spain, Italy, Israel and Finland. North America gave a confused message, making cannabis totally illegal by federal law, but legal for medicinal use in some of the fifty-two states. There was debate regarding its painkilling qualities. Helen had a firm opinion on that one. *It worked a bloody sight better than paracetamol.* She closed the laptop and, with difficulty, got undressed and went to bed, sinking gratefully into Goldilocks' mattress. *Not too soft, not too hard, just right.*

Phil smiled at her from his picture on the little table.

"Stop smirking, Phil McGuire." Helen put the picture flat. "Sod off." She turned out the light. As her eyes grew accustomed to the dark, the vent in the roof provided sufficient light for her to look around her little bedroom. A 'what on earth do you think you're doing?' moment crept into her mind, but it didn't last long. She couldn't afford to let it, not now she'd got so far. If self doubt was to have had a chance, it should've taken it before she sold Valerie and bought Goldilocks.

The events of the day and the people she'd met whirled around in her head. Tashy was definitely the most interesting. Were all teenage girls so full of angst? She couldn't remember feeling like that when she was that age. As her eyes closed, she concluded that her plans hadn't changed that much. She'd stay in Llandudno for a while, self sufficient in her new home. Tashy would do any bits of shopping for her. By the time the Davidson's left the following week, she'd be able to hobble to the 'Littletrees' shop by herself. There wouldn't be any climbing of the famous Llandudno 'Great Orme', or long walks on the beach, but what the hell. Looking on the bright side, she'd sprained her left ankle, and as Goldilocks was automatic, her injury wouldn't stop her driving.

* * * *

When Tashy came back the next morning, Helen was already up, showered and dressed. The skin on her ankle was shiny and tight, with swelling starting at the base of her toes and continuing up her leg. Shades of red and purple mingled in a painful array. The table set for two, she put her foot up on the seat. Four sausages and four rashers of bacon sizzled slowly in a frying pan.

"Come in."

Tashy stood in the doorway.

"I was hoping you'd be here soon, breakfast's almost ready. You haven't eaten already, have you?"

"I don't eat breakfast. I only came to see you were okay. How's your ankle?" Tashy's eyes left the offending contents of the frying pan, widening as they focussed on Helen's foot. "Oh…my…God."

"It's painful, I admit, but not too bad." Helen had no idea why she was being so stoical. It hurt like mad, and she'd done lots of swearing as she'd struggled to get dressed and make breakfast. It had been a challenge, and she'd been terrified of bumping into something in the confined space.

"You should've waited for me. I'd have made your breakfast."

"Well, it's made now. Just need some toast. Sure you won't have any?"

Tashy shook her head and put all the sausages and

bacon on one plate, setting it down in front of Helen.

"I can't eat all this, Tashy. You'll have to have something. Pass that other plate. You're not anorexic, are you?" Helen immediately regretted asking the question.

Tashy's reply came a bit too quickly. "'Course not."

As if to prove her point, the girl passed the plate, pushed the lever down on the toaster, and made two coffees before sitting down opposite Helen. They shared the food equally. Tashy pushed her food around before putting it in her mouth, chewing and chewing before swallowing. Helen said nothing because she didn't know what to say. She had read somewhere that people could be bulimic as well as anorexic. Tashy couldn't very well throw up in Goldilocks' bathroom without her knowing, motorhomes not being renowned for their soundproofing. She started to think of excuses to keep Tashy with her, maybe ask her to wash up, and then they could watch television together, or play cards.

"Would you like to put the television on? I don't know if there's anything that might interest you."

"The Jeremy Kyle show's on, I like watching that." Helen felt her body stiffen, and hoped Tashy hadn't noticed the slight movement, or the sharp intake of breath. She found the programme cringingly unwatchable.

"Me too," she lied. "If you press that button there the television comes down from behind the cupboard."

Tashy pressed the button. "Neat. Very neat."

CHAPTER SIX

Robert tipped the packet of *Stir Fry Vegetables for One* into the wok with some chicken goujons. As usual, there was no way of knowing what time James would be home, and he wasn't going to start cooking meals just to throw them in the bin like Mum used to. He jabbed at the sizzling food with a wooden spatula. James's whole attitude annoyed him. When at home, he forever whistled or hummed about the house as if he were really happy. Everything had been fine until a few weeks before. Mum had seemed happy enough. She hadn't gone out much, but she had given no indication she wanted to travel, or do anything other than stay at home.

He was pleased she was having a holiday, but buying a motorhome clearly meant she intended to go away a lot. That part of his grumpiness was caused by a guilty conscience, which made him grumpy about being grumpy. He was happy for her, of course he was, but at the same time he was annoyed that his well-ordered life had been interrupted. It was all so unexpected, starting with her taking the old camper to the garage, and then that evening kicking off about missing Dad.

Deep inside he wanted to jump in his car and go find her, to talk to her, but he would have to wait another week until she came home. She'd been gone for seven nights, and he really missed her. The house was horribly empty. No cooking smells to greet him as he came through the door. No fresh coffee wafting upstairs as he showered each morning.

He tipped the food from the wok onto a cold plate. If Mum had cooked it, the plate would've been warmed.

James came whistling through the door. "Smells good, Robert. Any for me?"

"No. Cook your own bloody food."

"Who's bitten your arse, then?"

"Just sod off, James." Robert stabbed a piece of chicken.

James took his phone from his pocket and ordered a pizza. "Yeah, Jumbles Lane, number fourteen. Twenty minutes? Okay." He put his phone back in his pocket. "What's the grief, Robert? You've been sulking about all week. Missing your mummy, are you?"

"Yes, I am," he shouted. "But not in the way you're implying. I'm worried about her."

"Why?" James seemed genuinely surprised. "What's there to worry about? It's not as if she's gone off in the old camper."

"There's everything to worry about." Robert stood up and threw his plate in the sink. It smashed.

"Temper, temper."

Robert knew James was teasing him and was determined not to rise to the bait. He picked out the pieces of broken plate and threw them in the pedal bin, taking a deep breath before speaking again. His voice was calm.

"I've been emailing her all week. She says she's fine and not to worry."

"So why are you worrying?"

"Because I don't know where she is, and I get the feeling she might not be coming back."

"Has she said she's not coming back?"

"No. It's just that I don't see her buying that expensive motorhome for a one-off trip. She could be anywhere."

"Well, it's my guess she intends to do lots of short trips. That's the impression I got, anyway. Right now she's in Llandudno. She didn't even get as far as Anglesey."

"How do you know that?"

"I put a tracking device under the wheel arch."

"What?"

"You heard. A tracking device—G.P.S—bought it on the internet and fitted it while the motorhome was still at Billingtons. Wait here, I'll show you." James left the kitchen and ran upstairs two at a time, returning seconds later with his laptop. He showed Robert a map of Llandudno with a red spot flashing near the beach.

"There she is," James said, with a note of triumph in his voice. "Littletrees Caravan Site. The motorhome hasn't turned a wheel since she arrived last Thursday."

"You bought it on the internet?"

"Yep."

"You didn't nick it from work, then?"

"No, Robert. I didn't nick it from work. I'll show you the invoice if you like."

"No need. So we know where she is. I still don't like all this, though. Something's not right."

"Well, now you know where she is, you can go and see her."

Robert thought about it for a few moments. "No. If I do that, she'll want to know how I found her."

"Good. Now you're thinking. Stop worrying. You're like an old woman."

"So can you explain why she stacked the freezer with ready meals before she left?"

"Did she?" James raised his eyebrows.

"Yes, she did. The big freezer in the garage. There's enough food in there to last us for months."

"If I'd known that, I wouldn't have ordered a pizza."

Robert didn't reply. He went into the sitting room and sat on the sofa, turned on the television and watched the local news programme, staring unfocused at the screen. Jayne Manners wanted him to go to London at the weekend. He wanted to go, all right, but Mum was due home. His intuition said she wasn't coming, but he could be wrong; intuition had never been his strong point, so why should he be right this time? It had all happened far too quickly.

The door bell interrupted his train of thought. James's pizza had arrived.

* * * *

Bobby Billington sat back in his chair, comfortably dressed in an open-neck checked shirt and black trousers. Not exactly his choice of clothes, but a bloody sight better than that stupid suit. Dad never let him wear his proper clothes for work and, he conceded, in his own way, Dad was right. His low slung jeans and black T-shirts weren't really suitable for Billington's Motorhomes. Dad had said his jeans suited him, and for a brief moment Bobby had thought his dad liked them. Then he had said 'slack arsed', and Bobby had known it wasn't a compliment, after all.

He stared at his screensaver, the recently uploaded photo of Billington's Motorhomes. Dad had been impressed with that. He'd even said he'd use it on the following year's brochure. Dad liked the logo he'd designed, too. They were getting white shirts with his design embroidered on them. He reckoned he'd earned enough merit points to last him quite a while. Easter weekend had been really busy, and he'd clinched three sales: one new, and two pre-loved. Dad had only sold one, but it was a six berth brand spanker. His three sales didn't add up to the price of that one, but Bobby worked it out on the computer that his three had actually pulled in more profit. He felt he was beginning to get the hang of this business lark.

Now things had quietened down, he had time to think about Mrs McGuire, and the bloke who had fixed the tracking device on her motorhome. He had had sleepless nights over it. Dad said he was a copper, and Dad was usually right about things like that. Bobby remembered every word of the conversation. It went around and around in his head. He had been in the showroom, the day before Mrs McGuire had been due to collect her Goldilocks. As soon as the bloke had got out of his car, Dad had said he was a copper. He had walked straight up to Dad and said, "George Billington?"

Bobby had wanted to laugh, seeing Dad shitting himself. He'd gone bright red, shifting his weight from one foot to the other.

"Who wants to know?" Dad's voice had gone all squeaky. Bobby had turned away and gone to the coffee machine to hide his grin.

"James McGuire. My mother is supposed to be collecting a new motorhome tomorrow." At that point, Bobby had dropped the stack of polystyrene cups he'd been trying to load into the machine. They'd bounced and scattered all over the place. He'd said "bollocks" without thinking, and Dad and the copper had turned around to stare at him. He had been convinced the sale was off, that the James bloke had talked her out of buying it or something. Dad had coughed and said, "Is there a problem?" his voice a bit more normal.

James, or whoever he was, had given him a funny look and then said, "I'd like a look at it. The motorhome. Can we talk in private?"

The more he thought about it, the more he thought his Dad was right. It was the way this bloke said 'George Billington' like it was a question. Only a copper would do that. Dad had told him to get on with the paperwork, but he hadn't. He'd watched them walk round Mrs McGuire's motorhome a couple of times. They'd stayed round the far side for a couple of minutes, and then the bloke had left.

"What was all that about, then?" Bobby had asked when his dad came back inside.

"Dunno. But I reckon your Helen McGuire isn't quite what she seems."

"What d'yer mean?"

"Tell me this, Bobby." Dad had sat down heavily at his desk. "Why would a copper put a tracking device on her motorhome?"

That had been nearly two weeks before.

Bobby sat up straight and flexed his fingers backwards to make his joints crack. Dad hated it when he did that, but Dad wasn't there. He went to his hotmail account and clicked on 'new', and typed in Helen McGuire's email address.

* * * *

Helen sighed as she watched the Davidson's caravan go by. Tashy sat in the back of the car next to her baby brother in his baby seat. Tashy nodded in acknowledgement as Helen waved. She had been a huge help, and Helen was sorry to see her go, but at least she wouldn't have to watch any more Jeremy Kyle. John and Betty had left the day before, as had Jeff and Miranda with their happy, noisy tribe. 'Littletrees' still had a few visitors, but the holiday atmosphere of Easter had passed.

Helen inspected her foot. The swelling had reduced considerably, and she was able to put on her slipper, though the bruising was still pretty spectacular. She made herself a coffee. Sure she'd put on weight with all the enforced idleness, she hesitated before taking the biscuits from the cupboard.

A scrap of paper, carefully folded, was in the top of the tin. Neatly written, it simply said 'tashyd@hotmail.com'. She smiled. Typical Tashy. She'd made no mention of keeping in touch, and Helen hadn't pushed it. Delighted, before she sat down with her coffee and comfort food, she took her laptop from the cupboard, accessed her email, saved Tashy's address, and then wrote 'Look forward to hearing from you. You have my mobile number, from Helen.' She clicked 'send'. The ball was in Tashy's court if she wanted to keep in touch.

Two new messages flagged up in her inbox, one from Robert and one from Bobby Billington. She opened Robert's first.

Hi Mum, I hope you are enjoying your holiday and that everything is okay with the motorhome. Everything is good here. I don't see much of James as he's working a lot. I was wondering when you would be home, as I'm thinking of going to London on Friday and wouldn't want to miss your arrival back home. You left plenty of food for us in the freezer and I found the washing machine instructions, so there's no need for you to come back if you are enjoying yourself. Have you made many friends at the campsite? I miss you a lot.

Love from Robert.

Helen read it twice, and then leaned back with a sigh, not quite knowing what to make of it. Through his words, she sensed his unease. It was unusual, unheard of even, for him to go to London for a weekend. She would have to tell him she wasn't going home that weekend; but his references to the food in the freezer, and the instructions for the washing machine, hinted that he had worked it out for himself. Her reply would be carefully worded. She needed time to think it through, and so decided to open Bobby's email. No doubt that would cheer her up.

Hi Mrs McGuire, Bobby here. I hope you're having a nice time in your Goldilocks. There's something I have to tell you. I've been dead worried. The day before you collected your Goldilocks, this bloke came into the showroom. Dad said straightaway he was a copper. He came over to Dad and said you were his mum. I suppose you could be his mum and he could be a copper as well. You said you had two boys, but you never said nothing about one of them being a copper, so I don't know. He talked to Dad for a bit, I couldn't hear what they said, but after he'd gone, Dad showed me where he'd put a tracking device under the front nearside wheel arch of your motorhome. Dad said not to tell you under any circumstances, but you said you were my friend, and I don't believe you've ever done anything wrong. From your friend,

Bobby Billington.

Helen felt her jaw tighten as she drew a long breath, not knowing whether to laugh or cry. She shuffled to the edge of the seat and stood up, taking most of her weight on her right foot and a little on her left to balance. She opened the door and hopped outside. Holding the side of the van, she crouched down by the wheel arch. Bobby was right. Her instinct was to rip the device off, but she decided to leave it, to think about it, and limped back inside.

"You cheeky little shit, James McGuire!" she shouted. "How dare you? How fucking dare you?" She sat down with a bump, jarring her ankle. "Shit…fucking shit!" The words did nothing to calm her down. Tears welled up in her eyes and began to flow down her cheeks. Uncontrollable, hot, silent, irrational tears. Reaching for a tissue, she dabbed her eyes, but the tears kept flowing. She stared at her wedding ring, the image of her hand blurred by tears. Leaning forward with her forehead resting on the palms of her hands, tears flowed onto the table. She didn't know who she was any more, and it was all Phil's fault. He'd died and thrown her to the wind. Her sons were like bloody limpets, and she wanted to get as far away as she could from everybody and everything she had ever known. The sanguine Helen McGuire who sold Valerie Drobshaw and bought Goldilocks didn't exist any more.

She limped to the bathroom and buried her face in a towel, pressing the soft absorbent fabric as hard as she could against her skin, rubbing away the futile tears. As she looked up, the little mirror above the wash basin reflected the face of the most stupid, incompetent, weak person to ever have existed. All rationality was blinded by the impotence of anger. Her sons were hopelessly dependent on her, sticking like shit to a blanket. Angry tears mingled with tears of self pity. She stared at the reflection of an angry stranger.

Slowly, her fury subsided, her facial muscles relaxed,

allowing the seed of an idea to filter through. In her volatile state, it made perfect sense. The thought of the device attached to her Goldilocks was abhorrent to her; a violation, an unwelcome guest who had followed her, uninvited. Well, she'd make it go away. She'd turn the tables, and that would show Mr Clever-arse James.

Her first email was to both James and Robert. She clicked their individual addresses and began to type.

Hi James and Robert,

I've decided to stay away a little longer. It's lovely here in Llandudno, the campsite is very well run, and I'm enjoying the peace and quiet, long walks on the beach, and so on. I always take my phone with me so you mustn't worry at all. You can phone me if there's an emergency, and I can always summon help if necessary. You know I prefer the email. I hope you have a nice weekend in London, Robert. I might move on to Anglesey next week, I haven't decided yet.

Love to you both, Mum. X

The next one was to Bobby, but before she started to type, she read his message again. The wording was so typically Bobby, she could hear his voice as she read. She chuckled to herself as she read the last sentence, recalling her first conversation with him. *'I don't do drugs, nothing like that.'* It was she, the respectable Helen McGuire—who had helped Bobby Billington learn to read—who 'did' drugs. Maybe she should get a tattoo on her bum. She laughed out loud; a high pitched, nervous laugh that didn't sound like her at all. It didn't matter. Bobby had cheered her up, all right.

Hi Bobby, Thanks for the email. There's nothing to worry about. It will have been my son who came to see your dad. James is a policeman, and I expect he was just worried about me going off on my own. Everything is fine with Goldilocks and me.

Your friend,

Helen.

She clicked 'send' and closed down her laptop. She had lied and lied to her sons, and to Bobby. A bubble of excitement whirled around inside her. The lying to Bobby was harmless enough. She had done it to allay his fears. James and Robert were playing head games with her. Well, they were going to lose, or her name wasn't Helen McGuire.

She stormed outside with as much stamping as her ankle would allow. It hurt like fuck, but the pain had become cathartic. Kneeling at the side of the wheel arch, she removed the tracking device with a carefulness that belied her emotions. She struggled to her feet, lifted the flap of the electrical hook up box, and unplugged Goldilocks. The offending tracker inside, she pulled down the flap with a satisfying thud.

Back inside, she stowed away the television, kettle and toaster. All the cupboards were tightly closed and their contents safe for the journey ahead. Helen drove to the reception area and checked out, answering politely the obvious and courteous questions about her stay at 'Littletrees', casually mentioning Anglesey as a possible destination.

A quiet motivation to break free from everything that had gone before brewed inside her. A rekindling of her idea to travel, but not just physically, this really was about moving on. The grey sky started to drizzle, but nothing could stop her now, certainly not the North Wales rain. She turned on the C.D. player and Rod Stewart accompanied her out through the gates of 'Littletrees Caravan Park' as he had accompanied her in.

Helen set off in the gloriously liberating knowledge that she hadn't a clue where she was going. Only that she was not going to Anglesey.

CHAPTER SEVEN

Nathan Sadler, also known as Naz, sat in the driving seat of his brand new black Range Rover, inhaling the smell of leather. He considered the personal number plate—B16 NAZ—a fitting symbol of his position. Like all successful businessmen, he kept his finger on the button. There was no room for error if he was going to keep the competition out. He drummed his fingers on the steering wheel and waited for Jorge. Neither he nor Jorge smoked or drank. They never had, so didn't miss it. He forbade Jorge to touch alcohol or cigarettes, and Jorge did as he was told. Since the recent expansion, Naz had delegated some of the distribution work to him. It was a calculated risk, as he wasn't the sharpest knife in the drawer, but he was honest. He lacked the intelligence to be anything else.

There simply wasn't time for Naz to do everything himself. He had to concentrate on the imports. What his wholesalers and retailers did was up to them. Their stupidity worked in his favour, as it kept them dependant on him to maintain the supplies. Most of them had started as his customers, back in the days when he had walked the streets at night to sell the drugs himself. He'd been arrested once. The pigs had found a few E's on him, so few that he got away with saying they were for his own personal use. It meant he had a record, though, and his photo was on file. Still, it was all years ago, he had just been a stupid kid then, so no big deal.

These days he preferred to think of his dealers as wholesalers. The retailers came lower down the chain. Customers were scum, so stupid they didn't realise they had paid for his new car. Some of them had even admired it. He demanded their respect and took pleasure in their fear.

He had detailed strategies for all eventualities. He was nobody's fool. The red velvet bag in the locked glove compartment held his guarantee that he would never be caught. The passports all bore his photograph and the names of dead men. No one would ever catch Naz Sadler. He smiled as he took the little books from their hiding place, running his fingers over the embossed covers. They were his protection, his security. One credit card even showed one of the names. That really was a stroke of genius. Everything else he needed was in his head, being adept at figures. The details of his foreign bank accounts were in the safest place of all, and cash was never going to be a problem.

There was one ambition left, an obsession, a weakness in his armour, his Achilles heel. Sometimes he recognised it, but for most of the time Carrie Halstead made him lose all rationality. He could have as many women as he wanted, but he didn't want them, he wanted Carrie. She would respect him and do as he said, in time. The little bitch didn't know it, but he had marked her out; and the one obstacle in his way had been removed.

* * * *

Bright sunlight streamed through the thin curtains, lifting Carrie from a deep sleep into semi-consciousness. A rhythmic thumping in her head awoke her, as it did every morning. Her awareness increased, and she heard another noise, another banging, someone shouting. She lifted her head from the pillow and waited for the pain to kick in, taking her weight on her elbow, and tried to sit up.

"Police. Open up, Carrie." She fell back on the pillow and reached out to push Jono from the bed.

"Come on, Carrie. It's Pete Levens. Open up."

She opened her eyes. Jono wasn't there. Her dull

tangled hair fell across her face. Naturally dark in colour, it reached to her shoulders before turning to a lifeless, bleached blonde.

The banging and shouting continued. She tried to shout back, but her voice was little more than a whisper. "Okay, okay, I'm coming." There was no need to get dressed. She still had her clothes on from the day before. The bare wooden stairs were rough on the soles of her feet.

Pig's eyes peered through the letterbox. "Come on, Carrie." His voice had a kindness to it that didn't fool her. It was odd though, he usually shouted for Jono. Carrie put one hand to the back of the door for support as she crouched down to the letterbox. Pete Levens wasn't as bad as most of the pigs, but she still didn't want to let him in.

"He's not here."

"I know that, Carrie. It's you I need to talk to."

Trying to remember if there was any heroin left, she put her hand to her forehead. She didn't want Pete Levens stealing it. The events of the night before began to filter through her mind. She and Jono had chased the dragon, and he'd gone out to get more.

"What time is it? Jono should be back by now."

"Just open the door, Carrie."

She turned the lock just a fraction and the policeman pushed his way in. He was alone.

"Just me, Carrie. I'm not searching, no warrant. You need to come with me."

"You arresting me? I've done nothing."

"No. I'm not arresting you."

"Then I'm not coming. Where is he? Where's Jono?"

P.C. Levens took a deep breath before speaking. "He's at the hospital."

Carrie's eyes widened. Turning, she ran upstairs, pulled on some trainers, grabbed a denim jacket and ran down again, tying her uncombed hair back in an elastic band as she slammed the door behind her. The pain was starting in her legs and shoulders. She tried to ignore it. For Pete Levens to come to the house and pick her up, it must be bad. She climbed into the passenger seat of the patrol car. He turned to face her. "What?" Carrie accused.

"It's Jono, Carrie."

"I know its Jono. You said it was. That's why I'm here. I did as you said, and now you take me to see him. Right?"

"I'm taking you to identify him, Carrie. Jono's dead."

Seconds elapsed. Her pale face grew paler, her jaw dropped in shock. Then she started screaming, and beating her fists on the dashboard.

"No! No, he isn't. He can't be. Not my Jono." She hit out at the policeman, her fists landing wherever they could. Gradually, as the rage of disbelief buckled into reality, she began to sob. "You lied to me. You said he was at the hospital." Her face swollen with angry tears, her body shook.

"He is at the hospital, Carrie. He's in the morgue." He spoke softly.

"Can you wait here a minute? There's something I need."

"Okay. Don't be long."

Carrie ran from the car back into the house. She knew Pete would know what she was doing. He wasn't stupid.

She opened the cupboard above the washbasin and grabbed a small bottle, swallowing the contents in one gulp. It was only methadone. Right now, she needed the real thing like she'd never needed it before, but this stuff would take the edge off until Jono got back. An immediate and overwhelming panic shot through her. She gripped the edge of the sink and threw up. Jono was dead, and she had just chucked up the last drop of methadone.

Carrie walked slowly down the stairs, deliberately

delaying what she knew she had to do, as she struggled to accept the undeniable truth of Pete Levens' words. She closed the car door and fastened her seat belt. Pete started the engine and set off for the hospital, Carrie sitting in silence beside him, wringing her hands continuously, her head down.

* * * *

Pete drove the patrol car out of Eastgate and towards the hospital. The picture postcard appearance of Pennington-on-Sea, a seaside resort on the beautiful south Devon coast, belied the town he knew. Pete Levens had seen the recent statistics, and the seaside town had an average problem. The drugs engendered shoplifters and burglars with the need to steal on a daily basis. Selling whatever they could get their hands on for the price of a wrap. Families were broken, lives wasted, and for Jono, death had won. He had no idea where Jono had come from. He had turned up in Pennington-on-Sea two summers before, and stayed. Carrie and Jono had been together for a year or more, and she was the only one he knew who could identify him. She would know his surname and maybe even his hometown. He must have family somewhere.

For all their addictions, neither Jono nor Carrie had ever been caught stealing anything. They did steal. Of course they did. How else could they find the money to feed their habit? He'd known Carrie Halstead for a long time; watched her change from a pretty, intelligent girl called Caroline into the heroin-soaked wreck beside him. She came from a decent middle class family. Her father was a councillor in Pennington-on-Sea. Carrie had nine G.C.S.E.'s, all good grades. Her family blamed Jono, but there was more to it than that. If it hadn't been Jono, it would've been someone else. Her father put too much pressure on her, and she rebelled, big time. He had seen the signs the first time he'd taken her home, too drunk to stand up. Councillor Halstead had tried to give him fifty quid to keep quiet about it, more worried about his position in society than his beautiful, vulnerable daughter.

Pete parked in a small secluded car park within the hospital grounds. The morgue was discreetly sited away from the main entrance. Large shrubs surrounded the parking area and shaded the doorway. He ushered Carrie in, her frightened face an ashen grey, her eyes red. He spoke quietly to the mortuary technician, and then turned to her. "You okay with this, Carrie?"

She nodded and followed the two men into a small room. The body on the table was shrouded in a green cloth. The technician slowly turned it back to reveal Jono's grey face. Carrie made no sound as the tears flowed down her cheeks. She nodded and stepped forward to kiss his forehead. Shock darted across her face.

"He's cold...so cold!"

The technician and the policeman exchanged glances.

"Come on, Carrie." Pete Levens' manner reflected his feelings towards her. His eldest daughter was only a few months younger than her. Times like this reminded him how lucky he and his wife were with their family. "Come with me. I'll buy you a cuppa." He knew she wouldn't want it, that her mind would already be focussing on her next fix. She was in shock, and this might be his best opportunity to get her to speak to him.

He bought two cups of tea and a bag of crisps in the hospital canteen. "I need to ask you a few things, Carrie." He sat beside her. Experience had taught him that sitting side by side was less confrontational, better than sitting opposite someone in an interview room, across a bare table. Carrie was far more likely to answer his questions if she didn't feel threatened.

She opened the crisps and offered the bag to him.

He declined with a wave of his hand as he sipped his tea. "Do you know his second name?"

"Lister." Carrie concentrated on her tea and crisps. "He's from Leicester. I could always remember it 'cos it's easy. Lister from Leicester. Jonathan George Lister. Didn't have much family, his parents are dead. He once said he had a brother. That's all I know." She put the tea cup down and turned to face him. Her pallor was not unlike that of Jono, lying on the mortuary slab. Her face had a yellow tinge to the grey; and yet her blue eyes still had an innocence and beauty, despite the heroin.

"Do you know his date of birth?"

"No. He was twenty-six, though, if that helps. His birthday was in December, before Christmas, but I don't remember the actual date."

They finished their tea. Pete hoped she would say more, but she didn't. He offered to drop her off at her parents' house. She declined, as he knew she would. For all he knew, they didn't want her back and, anyway, he wasn't a social worker. If she wanted to go home, Carrie would go of her own free will, and in her own good time.

"I'll get back to the station then, Carrie. You know where to find me if you want me. I may need to talk to you again, depending on what the post mortem comes up with."

* * * *

Naz and Jorge let her have two wraps on account. Naz hadn't heard about Jono. He said he was real sorry and put his arm around her. Carrie wanted to think he was being kind, but there was something about the way he touched her that didn't feel right. The boys looked alike with their dark hair and dark eyes, but Jorge was always scruffy. Naz wore expensive clothes and was neat looking. Jono had once told her he thought they were half brothers, but Naz called Jorge his associate. Carrie suspected Jorge didn't know what it meant, but it sounded important and seemed to please him.

She promised to pay the following day, and told herself she'd give up the stuff, that these two wraps would be the last.

To prove to herself she was going clean, Carrie resolved to wait until she went home before injecting. Pete Levens had told her Jono had had no drugs on him when his body was found in an alleyway. In her confused logic it explained why Naz and Jorge didn't know; it was because Jono died before buying. The post mortem results would take a few days. She didn't care what they said, or what anyone said. Jono had looked after her, and now he was dead and she was all alone.

Carrie decided to get fixed up, then go to the supermarket and lift enough to settle the deal with Jorge. From there, she'd go to the doctor to pick up her methadone. This was a long term plan; it took her to the next day.

Back in the bedroom, she snapped the tourniquet on her arm, raising a vein in the scarred skin of her left forearm. The needle slid in, and within seconds the physical pain dissolved. With the relief came the positive, unshakable belief that she could do anything she wanted. In that moment, Carrie knew for a fact she'd quit doing this stuff. Jono would want her to. He wouldn't want her to go lifting. He'd always looked after that side of things.

Slowly at first, and then more quickly, the high which used to last much longer fell from its sky-scraping peak and Carrie was cocooned in the envelope of oblivion. She was on a beach of white sand. Crystal clear water lapped over her suntanned body. She would lie here until the sun went in and the cold light of day threw her back on the rocks. After that short, blissful dream ebbed away, all the heroin could do was make her feel normal.

* * * *

Every time she woke, Carrie relived the morning Pete Levens had taken her to see Jono's cold body. Pete was okay for a pig, he'd even asked if she wanted to go home to her family. It was an obvious question coming from him, but Carrie knew that as far as her father was concerned she had crossed an invisible line. There was no going back, not in any sense. Her mother would never stand up to him. Pete Levens meant well, but he was wrong. Without her twice-a-day fix she was a wreck, unable to function at any level. With it she could walk in a straight line without shaking or sweating.

Naz and Jorge were being really good; they let her have more wraps on account. She liked everything about Naz. He drove a big black four wheel drive with smoky black windows. He had given her some tips on lifting and had been a real friend. She didn't love Naz, she could only ever love Jono, but she respected him.

Carrie carefully lined her bag with foil the way he'd shown her. She'd found almost a full roll in the cupboard, from the times when she and Jono had chased the dragon together. Chasing the dragon was something she had only ever done with Jono. No Jono, no dragon-chasing. It wouldn't feel right. She hadn't believed Naz about the foil at first, and then reasoned he wouldn't lie to her, not about that, anyway. Something deep inside told her Naz and Jorge knew something about Jono's death, but she didn't dare to ask them. Jorge seemed really nervous recently, he was all jumpy and looked over his shoulder all the time.

"Line it carefully, Carrie," Naz had said to her. "I'll give you a list of DVD's to lift. Put them in the bag and the security alarm won't go off at the door. The security people in the High Street don't know you, so it'll be easy. Just relax."

Naz always sold good stuff and he really wanted to help her out. It'd pay off her debt. He had tried to kiss her on the lips, but she'd turned her head so he could only peck her on the cheek.

She waited for the bus, her bag slung over her shoulder. The foil made a crinkling noise whenever she moved. Two old ladies before her in the queue were deeply engrossed in conversation, and a girl about her age joined the queue. Carrie stared straight ahead, avoiding eye contact with anyone. No one took any notice of her. She was happy to be ignored; her invisibility helped her detach from what she was doing. Naz had told her to go to Max's Music shop on the High Street in Pennington-on-Sea, but Carrie was on her way to Camford Retail Park. Jono always went out of town. She didn't know where he went, but he'd told her he never lifted close to home. He'd said you shouldn't shit on your own doorstep. Pennington was a small town, too small. Naz and Jorge didn't know who her father was, but there were plenty of people who might remember her as Councillor Halstead's daughter.

The journey to the retail park on the outskirts of Camford took about twenty minutes. Carrie headed straight for 'Music and More'. She needed to get this over with as quickly as possible and get back to Pennington and Naz.

Her hands shook as she entered the store. There was no need to check Naz's list, she hadn't even brought it with her. She had memorised the titles he'd ordered. She browsed around for a while, taking mental note of her targets before slipping her bag from her shoulder. Sweat trickled down her back. Her hand stretched out and touched a DVD. Her eyes focussed on the pale skin covering her bony fingers. As she touched the plastic cover, a security guard in a brown uniform appeared at her side. Her instinct was to put the DVD straight back on the shelf, but she didn't. She pretended to be interested in it, pretended to read the back cover. Her feet wanted to run and run and never stop running, but they didn't. She wouldn't let them.

The security guard's attention was diverted to three teenage boys who had entered the store and immediately split up. Carrie took her chance, taking the DVD and quickly putting it in her bag. Within a minute, she had another seven and her list was complete. She was out of the store. No alarms rang. Brilliant. She'd done it, and was only a short bus ride away from the pain-relieving fix her body craved. Naz was right about the foil. He'd be impressed. Her first lifting, and she'd completed the list, got every single thing he'd asked for.

The sweating was getting real bad now, her body tingled all over, her limbs taking most of the pain. She needed to get back to Naz before the shaking took over.

They had arranged to meet in one of the shelters on the sea front. He was waiting for her, his car parked at the roadside. She sat beside him on the wooden bench and handed her bag to him.

"Where the fuck did you get these?" He held them close to her face, scaring her. Carrie took her weight on her thin wrists as she backed away from him, sliding along the chipped paintwork of the seat. "I said," he shouted, "where the fuck did you get this crap, you stupid bitch?"

"Camford Retail Park," she whispered, barely able to hear her own voice above the crashing of the waves and the rattle of the pebbles as they were dragged away from the shore. Naz opened the DVD packs one at a time and laid the empty plastic covers between them on the bench. Dummy packs. Display stuff.

"Can I have a wrap, Naz? I need it real bad. I'll go back and—"

"No, you fucking can't, you stupid bitch." The empty cases shattered as he threw them onto the concrete floor of the shelter.

"But, Naz, you're my friend and I…" Her hands shook so much she could barely wipe the tears from her cheeks.

"But Naz nothing." He folded his arms and leaned back, his legs out straight in front of him. "No more Mr Nice Guy, Carrie. You owe me."

"But you're my friend, Naz, and I promise—"

He stood up and grabbed her by the shoulders, pulling her off her feet. He kissed her violently, his hands now inside her clothing, trying to rip them from her. Carrie struggled to free herself, but was no match for him.

Jorge leapt from the car, ran across the grass and pulled Naz away from her, throwing him against the side of the shelter, breaking the glass in one of the panes.

"Get off her, you fucking twat," Jorge yelled.

Naz stood up slowly, blood dripping from a gash on his cheek. He stared at Jorge as if in disbelief. Jorge walked away, taking the first few steps backwards across the grass before turning and running off as fast as he could.

Naz turned to Carrie. "I'm your dealer, Carrie." He pointed a jabbing finger into her breasts. "You're one more pathetic junkie who owes me. That's all." She watched him get in his beautiful black car and drive off, tyres squealing. The blood drained from her face and the salty breeze chilled her to the bone. She dragged her feet as she walked back to the house in Eastgate, took one of Jono's sweatshirts from a drawer and buried her face in it. Clutching it to her thin body, she crawled under the duvet, hoping sleep would take her away forever.

For Carrie, there was no reason to wake up.

* * * *

Next morning, Carrie lay with her eyes closed, delaying the start of another day for as long as she could. The dreamy moments between asleep and awake, when she thought Jono was lying beside her, had shrunk to a split second. Every morning, she reached out to touch him, forgetting for that brief moment that he wasn't there, that he would never be there. Her mind heard Pete Levens banging on the door, her closed eyes saw Jono's grey face, her lips felt the cold skin of his forehead.

He'd been dead for two weeks now. His brother had taken him back to Leicester, and she hadn't been able to go to the funeral to say a proper 'good-bye'. They probably wouldn't have wanted her there, anyway. She would have liked to go. It was hard to believe he wouldn't be coming back. If she had been at the funeral, maybe it would have sunk in. People called it closure. She didn't even know if he'd been buried or cremated. Probably cremated, that's what usually happens these days. If she had his ashes, she'd take him to their favourite place at the far end of Pennington beach. They even had a favourite rock they liked to sit on together and watch the waves.

She stretched out her thin legs to the bottom of the bed, flexing her ankles in an attempt to ease the pain. The events of the day before came crashing in, as unwelcome as the morning that took her from her dreams.

* * * *

Just when she thought things couldn't get any worse, the landlord had called. Carrie hadn't given a thought to the rent or any bills. Jono had seen to everything like that. She had asked him to call back the following week. Since Jono's death, her need for heroin had dominated every waking moment. Sleep was the only respite. The methadone came nowhere near. She had walked the streets, trying to find Naz. Eventually, she'd found Jorge, down by the sea front, though actually, Jorge had found her. She'd been sitting in the shelter where she and Naz had met up after her attempt at lifting. Jorge had told her that Naz wanted to see her, that he had a proposition for her, if she was interested.

Turning over in the bed, she opened her eyes slowly, reluctantly letting another day begin, staring at her tear-stained pillow, recalling Jorge's every word and picturing his face.

"What proposition?" she'd asked.

"Dunno exactly, a way to pay your debts."

"How?"

"Carrie, listen to me." She'd thought he'd looked a bit odd. He hadn't looked her in the face when he'd spoken to her, and that wasn't like Jorge at all. She'd frowned. It was also unusual to see him on his own, without Naz. "He puts other girls into houses."

"What you talking about, Jorge?"

"Houses. Brothels. In the bigger towns. He's got three." Jorge spoke quickly.

Carrie's eyes widened in disbelief. "You mean he wants me to be a prostitute?"

"No, not you. He wants you for himself. That's what this has all been about, Carrie."

"All what, Jorge?"

"I gotta go, Carrie. You're not like the others. I'll tell him you're interested, and will be here at eight tonight. Okay? If I'm not back soon, he'll want to know what took so long." Jorge had run off without waiting for her reply.

Carrie had gone back to the shelter at half past seven and waited until half past nine. Chilled to the bone, she'd dragged herself home and cried herself to sleep. She'd drifted in and out of consciousness, images of Naz and Jorge plaguing her. In one dream she was running, in another she was locked in a tiny room, tied to a filthy bed. All the time she was crying and Naz was laughing.

* * * *

Pete crouched down to peer through the letterbox as

he banged on the door with his fist. He saw Carrie coming downstairs, and stood up.

"Get dressed, Carrie. I need you to come to the station."

"What for?" She opened the door and stared at him. "I've done nothing. You can search if you want. There's nothing here."

"I need a statement."

"What about?

"Jono. Looks like it was murder, Carrie. We've made an arrest. You were the last one to see him alive, apart from his killer, of course."

Carrie's eyes grew wider, then slowly closed, and her knees buckled as she fell forward in a faint.

Pete Levens stumbled backwards down the steps in an attempt to break her fall. His colleague, Dan Greenway, was out of the patrol car and rushing towards them, already requesting an ambulance from his radio. Pete lifted her back inside and laid her down on the bare floorboards of the hallway. He grabbed a couple of old telephone directories and a coat from a shelf and raised her feet onto the makeshift pillow.

The ambulance arrived as Carrie stirred and began to come round. Her eyes suddenly wide open, she stared at Pete, panic written all over her face.

"Don't tell anyone. Please. Not *anyone*." She tried to sit up.

Pete nodded and gently pushed her back down. "Okay, Carrie, okay."

She made no protest about going to hospital. She looked small and fragile as the paramedics covered her in a blanket. Tears seeped from beneath her closed eyes. Pete and Dan followed the ambulance in their patrol car, blue lights flashing and sirens wailing, to Pennington General Hospital.

"What was all that about then?" Dan shouted above

the noise of the sirens. "All that don't tell anyone stuff."

"That, Dan, was about her father."

"Her father?"

"She doesn't want me to tell her father, the respectable Councillor Keith Halstead."

Dan pursed his lips as he exhaled with a long toneless whistle. Any relationship between Councillor Halstead and the pale, waif-like girl was difficult to believe.

Carrie's arrival at A&E as a stretcher case, escorted by two policemen, ensured she was seen immediately.

Pennington General Hospital was due for closure. Tired-looking posters, giving information about sexually transmitted diseases, vaccinations, e-coli, and contraception adorned the walls. Many locals had fought to keep it open, but in the days of spending cuts, a small town like Pennington-on-Sea was lucky to have kept its own hospital for as long as it had. Chipped paintwork, old furniture and equipment added to an air of neglect.

Parents struggled to amuse their children, discussing details of their injuries with complete strangers; their need to see a doctor creating transient, unlikely friendships. Three of the waiting children were the results of playing on back garden trampolines, a workman had a nail stuck in his hand—presumably from a nail gun—and a rather large lady supported her wrist in a make-shift sling. Resigned looks of total boredom were temporarily relieved by speculation on the reasons for the police presence.

A nurse approached the two officers. "Follow me, please. Doctor Lloyd will see you now." She led the way through the swinging double doors. Patterned curtains sectioned off the six cubicles, providing privacy but not soundproofing for the patients. Moans and groans and cries mingled with instructions and encouragement from the medical staff. Pete and Dan were led to a desk where a doctor was entering notes into a computer. Carrie sat at his side.

"Miss Halstead is anxious to leave. There is no reason to keep her here."

"Thank you, Doctor," Pete said. "Is there anything we need to know?"

Doctor Lloyd shrugged. "It's up to Miss Halstead to tell you. She has to make the decisions. Patient confidentiality, you understand. I'll be sending a letter to her G.P." He picked up some papers from the desk. "I have patients to see, Officers. Please excuse me. I believe you know the way out." He beckoned to a nurse, and they disappeared behind the curtains of another cubicle.

Carrie's beautiful blue eyes were framed by deep, dark shadows, her skin grey and dull, her lips paled into the same deathly colour. Her collar bones protruded through the worn fabric of her T-shirt: a pathetic sight, broken mentally and physically by heroin.

"I'll come with you and make a statement." Even her voice was thin, epitomising her weakness. She was powerless against the all-consuming strength of her addiction.

Carrie shuffled to the edge of the seat. With one hand on the doctor's desk, she slowly took her weight on shaking legs.

All eyes in the waiting area followed Carrie, Pete and Dan as they left, causing a brief silence in the busy room.

Pete decided to leave any questions until they were in the calmer surroundings of an interview room.

CHAPTER EIGHT

Keith Halstead commanded respect; he had been the youngest councillor ever to be elected in the community of Pennington-on-Sea. His wife, Gillian, was intelligent enough to know her place was by his side. She attended any function where her presence was required, and dressed appropriately in the clothes he bought for her. He approved of her voluntary work at the hospital with the 'Women's Royal Voluntary Service', taking her trolley of sweets, magazines and newspapers around the wards three times a week. She tended the garden of their detached house in Oakdene Avenue where they had lived for twenty years.

It was a shame about Caroline, his only daughter. If only he could have had a daughter he could be proud of. If he were a more honest man, he would have known he could never forget her, that he couldn't dismiss her from his mind as he would a voter who opposed him. He was deluding himself by thinking he could. His fists clenched automatically whenever he thought of her because he was angry. He hadn't been able to make her conform to his will, and deep down, he still loved her.

It had always been an ambition of his to buy a brand new house, and his position had opened doors he never thought existed. The builder had offered him one of the best plots on the new and exclusive Oakdene Estate at a knock-down price, no strings attached. Even back then, he'd had no desire to live anywhere near the majority of his voters, 'The Great Unwashed' as he thought of them—a reference never voiced.

Gillian's voluntary work at the hospital had been his suggestion, and a jolly good one at that. It meant she was able to tell him what was going on up at Pennington

General. Inside information on public opinion, and that of the staff, had helped him to know how to represent his voters. He was able to allay the gossip that Gillian relayed to him before it became a rumour. Predictably, a 'NO TO THE CLOSURE' campaign had sprung up with the mandatory petition attached. His joining the protestations to the plan was somehow further validated by Gillian's voluntary work. Of course, the hospital would close. It was pie in the sky to think anything else, but it wasn't his place to be brutally honest to the public about it. There would be heart-rending stories in the Pennington-on-Sea Gazette about vulnerable patients having to travel all the way to Camford. There would be platitudes about job transfers and better facilities, but for the time being, Councillor Keith Halstead would fight the losing battle, because that was what his voters wanted.

They would never know about his business arrangements with the building trade. More specifically, they would never know about his association with the contractor who was buying the land around the hospital. Keith would ease the passage of the necessary planning permissions when the time was right. There would be a fee, of course. After a while, when the hospital became a derelict eyesore, his builder friend would buy the hospital and grounds for a song, thereby ensuring Pennington-on-Sea remained the attractive seaside town they all knew and loved. His working relationship with the builder had always benefited both of them, right from the day they had done the deal on his house.

As far as he could see, it was a 'win-win' set up. What 'The Great Unwashed' didn't know about, they didn't worry about.

* * * *

Gillian Halstead pulled the purple tabard over her head and tied the tapes at each side. She smoothed her hair with her hands to neaten any stray curls, pulled herself up to her full five feet and two inches, and pinned her 'Gillian Volunteer' badge to her ample bosom. The first badge they had given her had had her surname on it, but after a week she'd asked for another. She said it looked friendlier though, in truth, she was fed up with people asking if she was related to Councillor Halstead.

Keith was popular, there was no denying it, but then the voters didn't know him like she did. The fact was he didn't have the principles for which he was so applauded. Her secret nickname for him was the 'Vicar of Bray' from the old English song. Like the fabled churchman changing his faith with the political wind, Keith took the opinion of the majority of the population of Pennington-on-Sea every time. That was his secret. That was how he retained his position where others failed. He told her this was his duty, that it was what was expected of him. He had to represent the people. It was a strong argument, but with Keith there was always more to it. Gillian was certain some of his colleagues saw through this thin veil of self preservation, but nothing ever stuck to Keith. He had a non-stick coating.

The thing she hated about him most was his refusal to talk about Caroline. They had rowed about it when she had first left home and taken up with that druggie, Jono. The row had ended with him telling her she must never mention Caroline's name again. If anyone asked, she was to say Caroline had gone travelling. Gillian tried to point out that Pennington-on-Sea was too small a town to get away with lies like that, but he had been adamant, and after a while no one asked or even mentioned her. Gillian had thought it strange at first, but in the end had concluded that everyone knew the facts, but did not know what to say, or how to broach the subject.

To the outside world, it was as if her only child had never existed, but she was never far from her thoughts. The twisting knife in her stomach was a constant reminder of her loss, like bereavement without a death. When someone died, there was a structure to it. A funeral, a mourning, an eventual acceptance of the finality of death. Caroline wasn't dead, she lived right there in Pennington-on-Sea, in that awful house in Eastgate. Gillian had followed her boyfriend there one day. She didn't know why. The knowledge that her daughter was living in the poor end of town gave her no comfort, just the opposite, in fact.

She collected her loaded trolley and set off with a sigh. The headline on the Pennington-on-Sea Gazette caught her eye: 'DRUG DEATH WAS MURDER: VICTIM NAMED'. Murder in Pennington-on-Sea was unheard of. When she saw the address, she was spellbound, standing motionless as she read and reread the article. Caroline's boyfriend, Jonathan George Lister, was dead.

A smile flashed briefly across her face, to be replaced by a frown. This could mean anything. Maybe Caroline would want to come home. Maybe she had been hurt. She put the newspaper back and started to push the trolley along the corridor in the direction of the wards. What if Caroline had killed him? She dismissed the notion. Her Caroline would never do anything like that.

Gillian carried out her round of duty like an automaton. An hour later, she put on her coat and walked out of the hospital, head down, looking at her shoes, down to the sea front. She needed time to think, to decide whether or not to tell Keith.

After a while, she sat in one of the shelters, protected from the worst of the sea breeze. The shelter needed a coat of paint, one of the panes was broken, and shards of glass were scattered all over the pavement. She would have to tell Keith. They were a disgrace to the town. Empty plastic DVD cases, beer cans, cigarette ends, empty crisp packets, along with other sundry litter, were scattered all over the place.

After a while, she concluded that Keith probably knew about Caroline's boyfriend being dead. He probably knew where Caroline lived. Keith liked to make everything his business. He said it was important for his position as councillor to have his finger on the pulse. Gillian translated this as having his fingers in the pie.

She walked away from the sea front and out of the chilling breeze, her pace slackening as she walked along Oakdene Avenue. The fresh air had been uplifting, and she didn't really want to go home.

The front door opened at a touch, before she turned the key. Fear rose in her chest. Keith was never home at this time of day. She tentatively stepped inside, fearing an intruder, and then her heart rose momentarily, hoping against hope that Caroline was home.

"That you, Gillian?" Keith called from the dining room.

Her shoulders sagged. "Yes, dear," she called in the convincingly cheerful voice she had perfected over the last twenty years.

"Where have you been? I thought you finished at twelve."

She took her time to hang up her coat before entering the spotless dining room, where framed photographs of Keith at various civic functions were propped up on the sideboard. A copy of 'The Pennington-on-Sea Gazette' was spread out on the mahogany table. It confirmed her theory that Keith had been secretly keeping track of their daughter.

"I went for a walk down on the front. Where's your car? Those shelters are a mess, you ought to—"

"Shut up, Gillian. I put the car in the garage. I don't want any nosey-parker neighbours asking why I'm home at this time of day." He tapped the newspaper with his forefinger. "Read this." As she read, she decided to play dumb, to pretend she didn't know of any possible connection between the headline and Caroline.

"Terrible, isn't it? I read it at the hospital. You don't expect murders here." She picked up the newspaper, shaking her head and making little tutting noises. Keith stared at her, a picture of impatience. If there was a possibility of Jono's death bringing Caroline home, she didn't want to say the wrong thing. Sometimes she was deliberately perverse, just to wind him up, but not now. Right now she was playing for time, trying to figure out his intentions. He was too arrogant to see it.

With a deep sigh, she put the paper back on the table. "Are you quite well? Would you like some lunch?"

"This Jonathan George Lister…"

"Terrible. Just terrible. Whenever I read anything like that, I think of the parents, you know. It must be awful to have a policeman knock on your door and tell you your child is dead. I can't imagine—"

"Just shut up, woman. Listen to me for a change."

"But I always—"

"Jonathan George Lister was Jono," Keith shouted at her. "He was our daughter's boyfriend."

Gillian pulled out one of the dining chairs from under the table and sat down quickly with feigned shock. She held her head in her hands, focussing on the grain of the polished wooden table. "Are you sure?" She spoke without looking up.

"Of course I'm bloody sure. This mustn't get out, Gillian. Understand?"

"What do you mean, it mustn't get out? It's all over the front page of the paper."

"What I mean is there must be no connection made between me and this sordid matter. If it is known that my daughter was involved in any way, any connection whatsoever, it could ruin me and everything I've worked for."

"How?" Gillian's voice remained calm as Keith grew more and more agitated.

"The man was a drug addict. Caroline's a drug addict.

Do I have to spell it out for you?"

Gillian looked up. Keith's face confirmed what she heard in his voice. She had never seen him look so angry. His eyes bulged, and a vein in his right temple twitched. There was no chance of Jono's death bringing him to his senses. He had no compassion, no love for their daughter, his puffed-up ego was more important.

Gillian wasn't afraid of her husband. In the early days of their married life, he'd once threatened to hit her. She couldn't remember what it had been about, only that she'd told him that if he did, she would leave. 'You won't hit me twice, Keith Halstead.' She was certain that over the years there had been many times when he had wanted to hit her, but had never done so. She was also certain this was because he simply wouldn't be able to stand the humiliation if she left him. It was not because he loved her. Keith loved himself, he loved power and he loved money.

"You remember her name then?"

"What?"

"Caroline. Our daughter. You spoke her name."

He didn't reply, just stared at her as if he would burst with rage.

"Not like you to have nothing to say, Keith."

Still he didn't speak. He wheezed and coughed, sweat breaking out on his face and neck. He tried to call out to her, and Gillian instantly knew he was having a heart attack. She lip read as, holding the edge of the table, trying to walk to her, he wheezed, "Help me."

She stood up and stepped backwards as he tried to grab the back of a chair, clutching his chest then his left arm, vomiting as he fell to the floor. Gillian avoided the stinking mess on the carpet as pleading eyes stared up at her.

"I'm just going to put the kettle on, Keith." She smiled. "I fancy a cup of tea. When I come back, I expect you'll be dead. When they've taken you to the morgue, I'll go to see Caroline, my daughter. Good-bye, Keith. I can't say it's been a pleasure knowing you, because it hasn't."

She closed the door behind her, not wanting the smell of vomit to spread through the house.

* * * *

Carrie was as sure as she could be that Pete Levens wouldn't tell her parents. Dad could find her easily enough if he wanted to. There hadn't been much to put in the statement, just that Jono had gone out that night and she had gone to sleep, and that Pete Levens had woken her up.

It took longer for Pete to explain what she had to do, and for her to give him her details, than it did to say what had happened. Carrie didn't see how it would help, but Pete said the time line was important. She wasn't even sure she'd got that right. She remembered it was dark when he had gone out, and that he had been wearing his warm black coat, but that was about all. The rest was guessing and she told him so.

Pete told her to say what she remembered, no more and no less. Jono had gone out to buy heroin and not come back. End of story. End of Jono. Pete gave her a cup of tea and some biscuits.

After she left the police station, she walked down to the sea front. She didn't know why, there was nothing to do, and nowhere to go. Sitting in the shelter, she thought, maybe, she felt hungry, and maybe the pain wasn't as bad as it had been the previous week. Carrie stretched out her legs. Her trainers had been lovely—all pink and white when they had been new. Now they were just grey and dirty, the fabric frayed out at one side, not quite in a hole yet. Naz had those brilliant black and red trainers. She recalled how he'd stretched out his legs to look at them just before he'd tried it on with her.

Her eyes narrowed as she looked up at the bright,

reflective light of the sea. She still needed heroin, but maybe not quite as much. A solitary black cloud hung overhead in the otherwise clear blue sky.

Jorge rushed into the shelter and sat beside her. "I can't stay long, Carrie. Listen."

"Where's Naz?"

"Arrested. He's locked up. Listen, Carrie, don't talk. I grassed him up. After I saw you, I went to the police. When Naz finds out it was me, he'll have me killed. He killed Jono, Carrie." Jorge took her hand as she gasped, throwing her head back on the wooden headboard of the shelter. The impact made her feel dizzy, and her head flopped forward to her chest. "Carrie! Carrie!"

She lifted her head, eyes half closed, and turned to look at him.

"I gotta go away from here, right away. Understand?"

She nodded slowly as his words sank in.

"He killed Jono 'cos he wanted you. He let you have those wraps on account, so he would have a hold on you. Don't you see? I gotta go. The police want me to give evidence. Naz is locked up for now, but not forever. You understand what I'm saying?"

Her expression blank, she was bewildered, disorientated. This couldn't be happening.

"So why are you telling me all this, Jorge?"

"It works like this: he makes girls indebted to him and then gets them to work in his houses. With you it was different, he wanted you for himself. I told him you wouldn't go with him, not for anything. He said if he couldn't have you he would kill you, too. 'It's no big deal.' That's what he said, honest."

"You grassed him up...your own brother...for me?" Tears rolled down her pale cheeks.

"Half brother, yes, I did, and I'd do it again for you." Jorge put his hand in his pocket and pulled out a small brown bag. "There's two wraps in here, Carrie. It's up to you. No charge, not now or ever. Understand? Our set up is gone. Stay safe." He kissed her cheek and left.

Carrie stood up and watched him walk quickly towards the town square. She hoped he would get far, far away. She didn't want to believe what he had told her, while at the same time knowing it had to be true. If anyone else had told her she wouldn't have believed it, but what with Pete Levens wanting a statement, and saying they had made an arrest, everything Jorge had said fell into place. Carrie knew she was more alone than ever.

* * * *

Councillor Halstead's widow walked down the aisle behind her husband's coffin. She scanned the crowd of faces, acknowledging those she recognised with a nod, while all the time looking for Caroline, the only face she wanted to see.

The undertaker guided her to the front pew, her back as straight as a ram rod, her head held high.

As soon as Keith's body had been removed from the dining room, she had donned her coat and walked to Eastgate. She had knocked quietly at first, then more loudly, but no one had answered. She'd thought she'd seen a dirty curtain twitch, but couldn't be certain. She had written a note, asking her daughter to get in touch, telling her that her father had died, and had pushed it through the letterbox. She had also said that a house key would be left in their usual hiding place, and that she could come home whenever she wanted, that her room would be ready and waiting for her, with no questions asked. There had been no response.

Once the funeral had been arranged, Gillian had returned to the house in Eastgate, but still no one had answered. She'd left another note, giving details of the service.

Keith had left very specific instructions about his

funeral: classical music, with traditional hymns, and the best oak coffin money could buy, covered in white orchids. Gillian had struggled to keep her face straight as she'd walked into St Marks to the loud and unmistakable voice of Frank Sinatra singing 'My Way'. Keith lay in an eco-friendly wicker coffin with white daisies on top. The funeral director had seemed surprised at her request, but Gillian had assured him it was what Keith had wanted.

The vicar droned on about what a wonderful man he had been, how he'd served his community in a selfless and admirable manner. The collection was to be donated to a hostel for the homeless—a cause Gillian informed the vicar had been close to Keith's heart. The hymns were all very modern, so no one knew the words. She hadn't gone to the expense of the church choir.

All she could think of was whether Caroline was there or not. It was quite possible; the place was packed to standing room only. Maybe she was right at the back somewhere.

Carly Simon singing 'You're so vain' accompanied Keith out of church. He'd always had a particular hatred for the song.

Gillian shook hands with everyone at the church door. It took a while for them all to shuffle out.

The hearse bearing Keith's coffin left alone for the Crematorium in Ellwood Road. Gillian explained Keith had wanted this, and that she should go straight to the Town Hall—where everyone was invited for refreshments after the service—to greet the many mourners he had expected.

Hushed voices admired her grace and stoicism. Her dignity on such an occasion would have made Keith very proud.

Her friends from the hospital smiled kindly as they shook her hand, uttering their platitudes. They hoped to see her soon at the hospital, and told her she had to give herself time, and not to rush anything. Gillian tilted her head to one side in a nod, but said nothing. No way was she going back there. She wasn't going to do anything that had been Keith's idea. As soon as she got home, she was going to crack open a bottle of champagne and rip up every photo she had of the selfish sod. Some of the more observant mourners might have detected a tear in her eye. Gillian was desperately sad, but not because her husband had died. She was sad because her beloved daughter hadn't turned up.

* * * *

The funeral director took her home. She thanked him for the excellent arrangements and asked him to send his bill as soon as possible. She turned the key in the lock and stepped inside, kicked off her shoes, pulled her hat from her head and threw it on the stairs.

The door from the hallway to the kitchen was open. Her heart jumped. She must be there.

"Caroline!" Gillian ran the few paces to the kitchen, flinging the door open. The room looked exactly as she had left it, everything spotlessly clean and tidy. Her eyes were drawn to the note propped up against the kettle. Just five words, neatly written in Caroline's unmistakeable handwriting.

Sorry, Mum, with love, Carrie.

Tears blurred the words as she tried to read it again. What was she sorry for? It was she, her mother, who needed to apologise. She should've stood up to Keith and his precious reputation. Instead, she had taken the path of least resistance, and lost her daughter on the way. Gillian lifted the note to her lips and kissed the paper her daughter had held so recently. This was the closest she'd been to her for three years. She took off her jacket and carried it upstairs, picking up her hat on the way. Both Caroline's bedroom and her bedroom door were wide open. Somehow, she knew she wasn't there. She peeped in her daughter's room without crossing the threshold, and saw everything was in its place.

"Did you just want a look, my love, to see if it really was just as you left it?" She closed the door quietly and went to her own room, the one which until eight days before she had shared with Keith. In a split second, she saw the reason for her daughter's apology. Her open jewellery box was on the bed. The only thing left was a fake pearl necklace that Caroline had bought for her with her pocket money when she was a child.

Gillian sat on the bed and wept. Rivers of hot, angry lava burned her cheeks, falling onto her black skirt. Her love for Caroline was matched by her hatred for Keith, and an even greater hatred for her own weakness. Caroline had stolen her jewellery to buy drugs, and would be far away, high on heroin. The knowledge increased her anxiety.

Twisting off all her rings, including her wedding ring, she placed them carefully in the empty box. Keith had bought all the jewellery, everything except the little pearl necklace that meant so much to her.

She undressed and took a long, hot shower. As the bathroom filled with steam, the tiles and mirror ran with condensation. She then turned the control to 'cold' and stood under the freezing spray until her head hurt and her shoulders were numb. Shaking fingers turned the water off. Naked, but for a towel wrapped around her hair, Gillian walked back to the bedroom. Taking a handle in each hand, she opened Keith's double wardrobe. His suits hung neatly in bags from the dry cleaners. Crisp, starched shirts, beautifully ironed by a downtrodden wife hung in colour-coded order. His three best shirts selected, she took them to the landing, briefly holding them at arm's length before throwing them down the stairs. She grabbed more shirts, then suits, laughing hysterically as she threw them down to the hall below. Socks, vests, underpants, ties—anything and everything that had belonged to her husband thrown over the banister.

She then threw open her own wardrobe doors. Suits and dresses she'd worn to civic functions as the dutiful wife of Councillor Halstead were added to the growing pile on the stairs. Hats, shoes and handbags all received the same treatment. When she finally sat down on the edge of the bed, her wardrobe contained only the clothes she'd chosen herself, for herself. She dressed in her favourite white trousers and a yellow T-shirt.

The pile of discarded clothing stacked half way up the stairs. Gillian slid down onto it, pushing the hated garments with her feet. Her next task was to remove his photographs from the dining room. One by one, she systematically took them from their frames and ripped them up. The frames were added to the pile of clothes in the hall. Gillian was enjoying herself. For the rest of the day, she methodically searched every drawer and cupboard in the house, taking everything that had belonged to Keith, and adding it to the pile. It could all go to a charity shop.

At five o'clock, she put on some shoes and a jacket and drove to a Chinese take-away. Something Keith would never allow. Back home, she ate her Hung Ling Special from its polystyrene box and washed it down with a glass of Keith's best red wine. She threw the box in the kitchen bin with a smile, and forced the cork back in the wine bottle. Now she was ready to tackle the study: his den, his inner sanctum. She had only ever been allowed in there to clean, and had been strictly forbidden to touch anything, or open any drawers.

"So let's have a look at your secrets then, Keith."

Shelves filled with box files lined the walls. Gillian looked in a couple of them. They contained old housing plans. To anyone else, it would have seemed strange that there was no computer in the room, conspicuous by its absence, but not to Gillian. Keith was afraid of hackers, or so he said. Gillian knew it was more to do with the nature of his connections with the building trade. He didn't want his dealings to be traceable. She opened the third and lowest drawer of his desk. To her surprise, she found a brown A4 envelope with her name on it. Inside a white envelope bore the words: *'The Last Will and Testament of Keith Halstead.'*

"Ah, now we're getting somewhere." She ripped open the envelope and read it quickly. There wasn't much to read. He'd left everything to her. "Well, that's a relief, I suppose."

A broad smile filled her face. About to throw the envelope in the wastepaper basket, she felt something inside it. She tipped it up and a small key fell out. The tag read *Carleton's Bank, Camford High Street. 2569.'* Gillian sat on the studded leather chair, swivelling from side to side, as she twisted the key in her hand.

CHAPTER NINE

Detective Inspector James McGuire could trace the path of criminal activity like a bloodhound following a scent. He used 'The Proceeds of Crime Act' to track down the vast sums of money and the assets of criminals. He had impounded cars, boats and even an aeroplane as part of his dogged determination. Big boys' toys, as he liked to call the officially named 'white goods'.

A small, apparently legitimate business would be brought to his attention. Fast food outlets, second hand car sales, or a taxi firm were typical. They were a front for the real money maker: the drugs. James wasn't after the little shits on the streets, he was after the so-called barons. Main suppliers had a penchant for buying houses for their parents, mistresses and children. Property was easy to trace. One of his greatest joys was the predictable phone call from a solicitor along the lines of, *"You have frozen all my client's assets without any proof of a crime having been committed."*

"Yep."

"You can't do that. My client cannot run his business."

"I can, and I have. I suspect his assets are the proceeds of crime, and that's all I need."

He would then quote the Proceeds of Crime Act of 2002, put the phone down and punch the air with satisfaction. *"Yes! Yes! Yes!"*

James McGuire usually celebrated success with a long workout at the gym. He swam extra lengths and ran extra miles on such a high that he didn't count the lengths or watch the clock. He just went for it.

That day, the magistrate had signed the order to detain fifty grand in cash found at the office of 'Ivan's Ices'. James hadn't been directly involved in the case, but

Maddie had, so it was a good result for her. The information had come in via an anonymous phone message to Crimestoppers:

'It's not ice cream Ivan's sellin'. He's sellin' to th' kids, but it in't just ice cream, if yer know what ah mean. Yer need to get down th' far end o' th' Lanes Estate. Playing his bloody Nellie the Elephant tune at all fuckin' hours, 'e is.'

Ivan had been selling ecstasy, amphetamines and other class B drugs. The raid had been successful, with thousands of tablets removed from his office, along with fifty thousand, one hundred and four pounds. Ivan lived alone in the flat above the office, and parked his van in the yard at the back. Maddie's team had gone in just before dawn, smashing down the drain pipes to prevent any evidence being flushed into the sewers. Seconds later, the front and back doors had been forced open simultaneously. There was always the chance that nothing would be found, but Maddie had done her research. Ivan had taken a delivery the night before the warrant was executed. To find so much cash in the place was a bonus.

As James ran on the treadmill, his eyes on the television screen, his thoughts moved to Robert, and home…and Mum. He agreed with Robert about a lot of things, but Robert was just so bloody irritating, the way he kept going on about Mum not coming back. He was right about the house not feeling the same. It hadn't felt the same when Dad had died, and no doubt it would feel different again if Robert left home. Mum's email had told him about London. James assumed it was to do with the promotion Robert had talked about that night at the Lock-Keepers. He made a mental note that they should have another pint together the following week. Maybe they'd both know a bit more about London by then.

He had a lot to discuss with Maddie that night. She knew he was in line for promotion, that it would mean him moving away from Chester, but they hadn't talked about it. They hadn't spoken about the long term at all.

When he was with Maddie, he knew he wanted her to be a part of his life, but he couldn't imagine stifling in the North West of England for the rest of his career, either. If she wasn't willing to apply for a transfer to London, he would have a difficult decision to make. The following week he was going to Rotterdam for three days to work alongside the police there, to observe operational procedures. Then he was going straight to London for two days to debrief, and have another interview with the National Crime Agency. Hopefully, he would have a clearer idea of where things were going by then.

He switched off the treadmill and went for a shower. The cool water running through his thick blond hair helped to clarify his mind. He would discuss the future with Maddie when he got back from London. Then he would take Robert for a pint to find out what he was planning to do. Mum should be back home by then, but if not, he would email her. No point telling her until he knew the details himself. She kept saying she wanted to be left alone with her peace and quiet and, anyway, he was sure Robert was wrong. Mum would be back soon.

* * * *

Robert couldn't concentrate on his work. His computer held no interest, as his mind darted between being annoyed with his mum, and the beautiful photograph of Jayne Manners. Mum shouldn't have sent her email to both James and himself. He had written to her about a personal matter and expected a personal reply. He'd wanted to tell James about his trip to London in his own good time, and now James would be quizzing him about it. Quite apart from that, he had a particular hatred for shared emails, like the one-size-fits-all letters that sometimes came with Christmas cards, the ones that gave detailed accounts of the activities of ex-colleagues' children, whom he would never meet. He tried to be more laid back about such things, but somehow he couldn't. His own attitude annoyed him even more than the 'round robins', making him feel thoroughly miserable.

He changed the subject within his head. It wasn't difficult. The thought of meeting Jayne made him smile. She had her own apartment in London, but hadn't said whereabouts. The plan was that he would travel to London that evening and stay in the White Dolphin Hotel, where she would join him for breakfast on Saturday morning. They would have the whole day together.

She looked beautiful in her photograph, with big blue eyes and blonde hair falling about her shoulders. The thought of meeting her made him feel warm and happy inside. He looked away from his computer screen and saw one of his colleagues staring at him.

"Penny for 'em, Robert. What's the joke?"

Robert didn't reply, the smile wiped from his face by the intrusion. There was less than twenty-four hours to go before he would meet her. He had been terrified she'd be put off by his photo, but she hadn't. She'd even commented on his kind face, and now, with a bit of luck he wouldn't see James before he left. If it all went wrong, and Jayne didn't want to see him again, he wouldn't have any explaining to do, or any jibes to suffer. In a way, he could see that Mum had done him a favour by letting the cat out of the bag. He didn't have to tell James why he was going to London, but she still shouldn't have done it; it still irritated him.

He shuffled in his chair, wishing he'd taken his overnight bag to work. That way he could have taken an earlier train to London, and avoided all possibility of seeing his brother. It was packed and on his bed ready for him to pick up after work. The day dragged. Robert began to understand the term 'clock watcher'. It was something he'd never done before.

James ordered a pint of bitter and a glass of white wine with soda. He didn't need to ask Maddie what she would like to drink, and they rarely discussed where they would go. 'The Lock-Keepers' suited them well. Few police went there, so they wouldn't be dragged into talking shop, and it wasn't a known haunt of the criminal fraternity, either.

He put the drinks down on the table and thought how lovely she looked. Regulations demanded that her red hair be tied back at work, for safety reasons, and to see her with her hair falling about her slender shoulders was a delight. It transformed her into a different person. At five foot six, Maddie was slim, but not skinny. Her green eyes fascinated him.

He sat beside her and was about to say how good she looked, but Maddie spoke first.

"I've got some news."

"I heard you got a result with Ivan."

"We did, yes, good one, but that's not what I wanted to talk about."

"Oh? What then?" James was immediately wary. In the split second before she replied, a multitude of thoughts ran through his head. Had she heard he might be going to London? Should he have told her about that? He wanted to tell her in his own time, after Rotterdam and the interview, when he could be more sure of what was happening.

He turned towards her and looked at those green eyes. The tension there worried him. Was she going to ditch him, to pursue her career? Had she gone off him? Was she pregnant? He was terrified of losing her and knew then, if he hadn't fully acknowledged it before, that Maddie was the one for him, that he was in love with her, and was about to lose her.

"I've been offered a secondment. It would mean moving to London for two years."

Dumbstruck, his surprise at her news quickly changed to relief, spreading across his face like a flood tide. He smiled the broadest smile imaginable.

"What?" Maddie asked. A short silence lay between them. She waited for him to speak. "Say something, then." He still didn't say anything. He didn't know what to say. So much now depended on his getting the job at the National Crime Agency. "You pleased I'm going, then?"

"Yes...no..." He grabbed her hands. "Maddie..." The usually calm, controlled, articulate James had turned into a tongue-tied boy. He let go of one hand to take a long drink from his pint. Setting it down, he turned to her again, melting under the gaze of those enigmatic eyes. Slowly, and choosing his words carefully, he told her of his hopes for promotion, and how he had feared telling her. "I wasn't going to say anything until I knew for sure, Maddie."

"I could be cross about that, James McGuire." She poked him in the ribs and giggled as she spoke, "except that's exactly what I did. This promotion has been in the pipeline for a while, but I didn't see any point in telling you until it was nailed on. I start next month, based at Paddington Green."

They sat in silence for a while, holding hands and sipping their drinks. The fact that they were both likely to be in London changed everything. Each had thought they were to be separated by their careers, when in fact their careers were about to bring them closer together. On the proviso, of course, that he got his promotion.

"Have you eaten yet?"

Maddie shook her head in reply.

James stood up. "Come on, then, let's go to Chan's to celebrate. I'll get that job, I know I will."

Heads turned as they left, for they made an eye-catching couple with Maddie's red hair, and James's uncontrollable blond mop. Their happiness held a charisma as they smiled and chatted, arms linked, on their walk to Chan's Chinese Restaurant. James ordered champagne, and somehow, without any mention of 'commitment', Maddie and James had conveyed exactly that to each other.

Fate had played a big part in mapping their immediate future.

* * * *

Robert had never been so nervous in his life, not even when he had gone for his first interview at Carleton's. He'd known what he was talking about then, and had had a list of questions. He'd known the protocol and the rules. Right now he was worried his chinos and checked shirt were too casual. He was way out of his comfort zone as he waited in the dining room of the White Dolphin Hotel. Jayne had recommended it because of its location, close to Euston Station, and not too expensive by London standards. He had purposely chosen a table tucked away in a corner, partly hidden by a palm tree that appeared to grow straight out of the floor. It gave him a perfect view of the entrance. Twice he had been invited to the buffet by the immaculately dressed waiters, and twice he had said, "No, thanks, I'm waiting for someone." He was beginning to think they didn't believe him, and he was beginning to wonder if they were right, and Jayne wasn't coming at all. He had it all planned out. As soon as he saw Jayne enter the dining room he would wave to her casually and move to her side of the table, drawing a chair out politely.

He compared the scene before him to that of the night before when he had dined alone. This morning there was no music, and the buffet of everything imaginable for breakfast was laid out in the centre of the room. The lighting wasn't the same, but otherwise nothing had changed as far as he could see, and yet the atmosphere was completely different. This morning, his fellow diners appeared to be talking business, whereas last night there had been raucous laughter as the red wine of expenses relaxed the executive stress.

"Robert?" He was shocked out of his daydream by Jayne's magical appearance at the opposite side of the table. *Had he not been watching the entrance to the dining room? How had she got here without his noticing?* He jumped up, and his chair fell over, crashing into the palm tree. Several seconds of silence followed as conversations paused to locate the disruption. Embarrassed, Robert turned to retrieve the chair, but a waiter beat him to it. He muttered his thanks and turned back to see Jayne struggling to keep a straight face. He rushed round to assist her to her seat, but a wretched waiter again beat him to it. With as much dignity as he could muster, which wasn't very much at all, he returned to his seat. It took effort to look up, to look her in the face, and when he did so he was so struck by her loveliness that he was incapable of speech. He sat there looking like a bloody cod fish with his mouth gaping open and no words coming out.

"I'm Jayne Manners." She waited for him to reply, but he didn't. "And you're Robert McGuire?" He nodded. "Well, Robert, it's a good job we exchanged photos, or I might think I was at the wrong table. Shall we get something to eat?"

He followed her to the buffet. Jayne picked up a tray and chose orange juice, scrambled egg, two slices of brown bread toast, two portions of butter and a large black coffee. Robert chose exactly the same. Only when they were once again seated did he realise what he had done. Jayne looked at his plate, and then back at her own. He saw her straighten her shoulders in a way that said, 'I'm out of here as soon as possible.' He heard the sharp intake of breath as she picked up her knife and spread butter on her toast. Robert picked up his knife and spread butter on his toast. Jayne had a drink of orange juice.

Robert sipped his coffee. They put their respective drinks down and looked each other in the eye. Robert saw a twinkle there, and relaxed a little. He even managed a smile.

"See, I am capable of independent actions." The tension between them disappeared in a flash, and they laughed together at their inauspicious start to the day. By the time they finished eating, Jayne admitted to him that she had almost walked out when he'd copied her choice of food, and Robert admitted he'd almost run away when he realised what he had done.

They had finished eating before he noticed what she was wearing. The bright pink blouse and white linen jacket looked expensive. As they stepped out into the spring sunshine, the day stretched ahead with limitless anticipation.

"Well, Robert, we've both got the day off work, so we might as well make the most of it." Jayne slung her bag over her shoulder. "Where would you like to go?"

If he'd answered truthfully, he would've said he didn't care, as long as they were together, but even love-struck Robert realised how totally naff it would sound. The way she said it made it perfectly clear she considered they had the day together, and no more. What did he expect? A life-time commitment from a beautiful girl like Jayne, and after no more than a breakfast?

"Your choice, Jayne. I'm the northerner in the big city for a day."

"You must have some idea."

"Okay, I'll go for the obvious: London Eye, Buckingham Palace, and the Houses of Parliament."

"Right, we'll go for the Eye first, that way you'll see the whole city and gain your bearings. We could take an open top tour bus and do the total tourist day out if you like." She nodded briefly to the uniformed concierge of the White Dolphin Hotel. He raised his hand and a taxi drew up. The concierge opened the taxi door. Jayne thanked him as she stepped inside the shiny black car. Robert sat beside her and the door was closed. They were on their way to the London Eye, cocooned in the taxi with the driver weaving through the traffic with inches to spare on either side. Robert was filled with admiration for her. The sophisticated way she dressed, walked, talked, and was generally in control of herself and everything, and everybody, around her. Even the concierge, though to be fair that was his job, had taken notice of her. Other hotel guests were waiting for taxis, but Jayne, with an almost imperceptible nod, had attracted his attention. A taxi had magically appeared, just like the way Jayne had magically appeared in the dining room. Robert was awestruck, love-struck, and very nearly, for the second time that day, dumbstruck.

After the London Eye, they took an open top tour bus. Jayne bought two 'hop on, hop off' tickets, insisting on paying because Robert had bought breakfast. She had paid for the taxi, he had paid for the Eye, so, she reasoned, it was her turn.

"So far I'm getting a good deal, Robert."

He wanted to argue with her, but when he opened his mouth to protest, she put her finger across his lips with a "Shush...I insist." Robert could still feel her touch burning his lips as she checked their tickets and they waited for the bus.

They 'hopped on' and 'hopped off' for the rest of the morning. Robert eventually relaxed, and they chatted about London and all its wonderful sights. They saw the guards at Buckingham Palace. Jayne pointed out that there were four of them, and that the Royal Ensign was flying above the palace. She explained this meant the Queen was in residence. "When she isn't there, the Union flag flies, and there are just two guards."

"Don't you mean the Union Jack?"

"No. It's only a Union Jack if it's on a ship."

"Oh, right. I didn't know that."

"Not many people do."

Robert began to hum the tune of 'They're changing guard at Buckingham Palace, Christopher Robin went down with Alice'.

Jayne laughed, and he began to hope she liked him. They hopped off for a light lunch at Harvey Nics, and then went to the Saatchi Gallery. Robert was bemused by the exhibitions. He felt Jayne was watching for his reactions.

Once outside, she looked at him quizzically. "Well? What did you think of it?" she asked.

Robert had to decide whether to be non committal, pretend to have understood it, or be honest and say he thought it was...well...the sculptures were grotesque twists of metal, the paintings were disturbing. He thought it was quite mad. He looked in her blue eyes and saw that twinkle he'd first seen at breakfast. This time he had the confidence to laugh.

"Mmm. Me too," Jayne said. "What time is your train back?"

"They go every half hour, last one twenty-three thirty. I can go whenever."

"Good. We can go to a show if you like."

"Of course I'd love to, but..."

"But what?"

"I need to go back to the hotel and collect my bag, check out and..."

"Tell you what, Robert, I'll send someone to the hotel to pick up your bag and bring it to my apartment. I'll settle the bill and you can pay me back. That way we'll have a chance to freshen up before we go to the theatre." Before Robert could reply, she'd taken her I-Phone from her bag, and switched it on.

"Jayne, you can't do that, it's not—"

She waved away his protest as she dialled. She gave instructions to someone at the hotel and put her phone back in her bag. It buzzed incessantly as messages came in. She took it out again and switched it off. Robert's phone was in his inside pocket, switched on and fully charged, and hadn't made a sound all day. Jayne raised her hand and a taxi appeared.

She gave an address and, once again, she had worked her magic, and they were weaving through the traffic.

Her apartment was near the river. Not for the first time, Robert wondered what it was Jayne did at the bank. Clearly, it was much better paid than his job in Chester, or the salary he would receive if he moved to London. This place was not cheap. Nothing about it was cheap. The liveried doorman had Robert's sports bag in his hand.

"Good afternoon, Ma'am, shall I bring this up for you?" He held the lift door open for them.

"It's okay, Henry." Jayne held out her hand and took it from him. "I can take it."

"Let me take that." Robert moved forward, and Jayne passed the bag to him as they entered the lift.

The apartment was immaculately clean. Cream leather sofas and a black glass coffee table with a vase of fresh lilies furnished the lounge. The simple minimalist decor was complimented by an uninterrupted view of the River Thames.

Robert put his bag down and stepped towards the window. Jayne stood beside him.

"Nice view." He turned and looked around the room. "Nice apartment." Robert spoke quietly, as if he feared breaking a spell. He was in Jayne's personal space, and was flattered that she had brought him there. Away from the bustle of London, in what should have been the calming peace of the room, he felt awkward.

"The kitchen's through there." Jayne pointed to a glass door on the far side of the room. "There are some beers in the fridge, wine if you prefer it. I'll take a shower, and then you can, if you want to. Tramping round London always makes me feel dusty." She flicked on the television and handed him the remote. "Make yourself at home." She smiled broadly and disappeared through a door next to the kitchen.

Robert felt like a fish out of water, out of his league. For a brief and inexplicable moment, he wished he was back at his desk in Chester. He knew what he was doing there. He knew who he was and what to do. What on earth was this beautiful, independent, educated, rich young woman doing on an internet date with him?

He went to the kitchen. It was small, but expensively furnished. Granite worktops shone, the sink shone, the whole apartment shone. After taking a beer from the fridge, he went back into the lounge, twisted the top off and took a gulp of the cool, refreshing liquid. He'd had a lovely day, and it wasn't over yet, but he was sure she wouldn't want to see him again. Too polite to dump him, she'd done the tour guide of London thing.

By the time Robert finished his beer, he was convinced she would put him on his train straight after the show and shove him back up north where he belonged.

CHAPTER TEN

"Your turn for the shower." Jayne's voice came from behind him. She wore a white towelling dressing gown, with a white towel wrapped around her head in a turban. Before Robert could say anything, she disappeared into the bedroom.

He picked up his sports bag.

Like the kitchen, the bathroom was small, with expensive fittings. A stack of thick white towels lay neatly folded over a warm rail. Jayne's perfumes and shower gels—all upmarket brands—filled the glass shelves.

The refreshing water danced over his shoulders. The whole day had had a dream-like quality to it, a beautiful dream that would end when the day did. The thought of that made it difficult to enjoy. He let the water run through his hair, and rubbed his face with both hands to dispel the confusion. Stepping out, he chose one of the towels and wrapped himself in the comforting warmth of the soft fabric. He took a fresh shirt from his bag. It was a bit crumpled, but there was nothing he could do about that. He didn't want to ask for an iron, and then stand there like an old woman doing the chores.

Jayne switched off the television as he entered the room. Black olives with cocktail sticks and crisps sat in little glass dishes on the table. Jayne handed him a glass of lager. She had a glass of white wine in her hand.

"Here's to the rest of our day, Robert." She raised her glass.

"To our day." He managed to smile, and once again relaxed in her company. "What is it you do at the bank, Jayne?" He didn't know why, but he regretted asking as soon as the words left his lips. The question seemed to hang between them.

"Oh, please, Robert, let's not spoil the day by talking about work. This is our day off, right?" She picked up the olives and offered him the dish. He could only nod dumbly and pick up a little cocktail stick to eat the purple fruit, his mind diverted to the problem of the stone.

"I tried to book the theatre while you were in the shower, but being Saturday all the best shows are fully booked. All I managed to get was a couple of tickets for "The Armourer" at The Grande. It's only been running for a week, and I'm told it's not going to last, but I'm game to give it a try if you are." Jayne smiled her enigmatic smile and passed an empty dish for the disposal of the stone.

Robert felt hungry. They hadn't eaten since the salad at Harvey Nics. If all he ate was crisps and olives, and he drank any more beer, he would be half way to drunk before they reached the theatre. His empty stomach provided inspiration for his reply.

"Only if you let me buy you a meal first."

"Italian?"

"My favourite."

They ate in the noisy atmosphere of Bella Italia. After some excellent food and a glass of wine, Robert began to unwind and chat freely about their day. The Eye had been the best.

"Tell me about your family."

"Not much to tell, really," Robert said. "There's my younger brother, James, he's a sort of policeman, and there's our mother. I'm worried about her." Even as he spoke, Robert didn't know why he was saying it. It meant he had to tell Jayne all about his fear that she wouldn't come back.

Jayne listened intently as he told her about his mother buying a motorhome, and James's tracking device.

"So why don't you go to Llandudno and visit her?" Jayne said. "Just ask her what her plans are." It sounded so simple when she said it.

"I don't know. Something tells me she doesn't want that."

"Look at it this way, Robert, the worst thing that can happen is she'll tell you to go away." She looked straight at him, through the doubt in his eyes. "Tell you what, Robert, if your mum doesn't come home next week, I'll come up to Chester at the weekend, and we'll go together. How does that sound?"

He didn't answer for several seconds. The blood drained from his face and then flooded back in a blush. "You...you want to see me again?"

"Would you like that?"

"Yes, of course, I would love it. It's just that I thought you—"

"I've enjoyed today, Robert, and I'd like to see you again. I think we should leave it at that for now, don't you?"

Robert smiled widely as he nodded in agreement. He paid the bill and they left Bella Italia, holding hands for the short walk to the theatre.

* * * *

His train pulled out of Euston Station at twenty-three thirty hours. Jayne had kissed him on the cheek, and promised to email him. He had no idea what the show had been about or if it was any good. He'd sat through the whole performance in a trance. Jayne Manners had enjoyed his company and wanted to see him again. Robert McGuire was the happiest man alive.

* * * *

Robert didn't wake until almost eleven o'clock. His train had been delayed at Birmingham and hadn't arrived in Chester until three fifteen. There were voices coming from the kitchen. He pulled on his dressing gown and ran downstairs.

"Hi, Mum." Swinging around the newel post, he yelled, "Good to have you...ah...I don't think we've met."

"Good morning, you must be Robert. I'm Maddie Ridgeway." Maddie swapped her mug of coffee from her right hand to her left, proffering it forward to shake hands with Robert. "I work with James."

"So I see," he said. James's red dressing gown clashed with her red hair.

Maddie let the remark go.

"Coffee?" She turned and filled the kettle.

Robert blushed. James tried, unsuccessfully, to hide his amusement. "I thought you were in London for the weekend," he said. "I take it your early return means you didn't get the job."

"Wrong on both counts, smart arse." Maddie handed him a mug of coffee. "Thank-you, Maddie."

"You haven't been snooping on Mum, have you?"

"Wrong again."

"Well, what then?"

"None of your bloody business." The rising irritation in his voice was unmistakable.

"Boys, boys." Maddie stepped between them, holding up her hands. "What's the matter with you two? You sound like spoilt children. Can't you be civilised?"

The brothers looked at each other sheepishly.

James spoke first. "Mum said in her email that you were away for the weekend."

"I told Mum I was going to London on Friday, and she assumed that meant the whole weekend."

James took a packet of digestive biscuits from the cupboard and sat at the table. Robert sat opposite him, wanting to tell him about Jayne but not knowing where to start.

Maddie broke the silence. "Don't you two ever talk

to each other about what you're doing?"

Robert and James looked at each other but neither of them spoke.

"I'll take that as a 'no' then." She waited for one of them to speak. Several seconds passed. "Right, I'm going for a shower. I suggest you two do the same. There's more than one bathroom, yes?" James and Robert nodded. "When we're all freshened up, we'll go for Sunday lunch at the Lock-Keepers. It's my guess you two have a lot to talk about."

* * * *

Maddie took her time drying her hair and applying a bit of make-up. When she wasn't at work, she liked to be more feminine. It transformed her from the hard-nosed copper her career demanded into the real Maddie Ridgeway. At work, her hair was tightly tied back to keep it under control, and she never wore make-up on duty. She hoped James and Robert were being civilised towards each other. Her first meeting with Robert had been embarrassing by any standards. She'd get over it, probably more quickly than Robert.

As the three of them walked to the pub, it became clear to Maddie that a bristling resentment fanned between the brothers. She was no longer sure her Sunday lunch idea was going to work. Either they were going to constantly bicker or sit in stony silence. Maybe she would have to mediate. Today wasn't turning out the way she had hoped at all. She and James had planned a lazy day together. Perhaps that was part of the reason for James's mood. If he and Robert communicated better, or even at all, he would have known his brother was coming home the previous night.

The Lock-Keepers was busy. The folding doors were open, and all the tables, inside and outside, were occupied. Children ran around to the constant warnings from anxious parents about keeping away from the water's edge.

"If I had kids," James grumbled, "I wouldn't bring them here. Too dangerous."

"What you really mean is that you wish there weren't so many kids here so you could get a seat," Robert replied.

"No, it isn't." James gritted the words from clenched teeth.

"I'll get the first round," Robert said. "You two stay out here and grab a table when one comes empty."

"Lime and soda for me, please, Robert," Maddie said. "I'm driving later."

Robert turned to James.

"Pint of bitter."

Robert went inside. The bright sunshine made the interior of the pub seem very dark. He ordered the drinks and was told it would be at least an hour's wait for lunch.

"Is it usually this busy on Sundays?" Robert asked the barman.

He was clearly harassed, and didn't look up from pulling the beer. "It's Mothers' Day. Busiest Sunday lunch of the year."

"Oh, right." Robert paid for the round and carried the drinks outside on a small round tray. All the tables were still occupied.

"Did you know it was Mothers' Day, James?" He put the tray down on the grass.

"Shit."

"Me neither." He took a large gulp of lager.

"Since when did you drink that stuff?"

"It's lager, James, not stuff. I had some in London, if you must know. I like it."

Maddie sipped her drink. "Do you two squabble all the time?" She looked first at James and then at Robert.

"No, 'course not," they said simultaneously.

"Then do yourselves a favour and stop doing it now."

A silence followed. Robert was embarrassed by the whole thing, and James probably felt Maddie had made him look stupid.

"Are you both sulking now?"

"No, 'course not," they repeated, again simultaneously.

"I take it neither of you sent a card to your mum?" Another silence. "Text message? Email?" Neither of the brothers spoke. "Right. I have a suggestion. Your mum is on holiday in Llandudno. Yes?"

"That's right," James said.

"Maybe, maybe not."

"Don't start that again, Robert, Maddie knows all about the tracking device. We know exactly where she is."

"Okay, okay. Just listen, you two. I suggest we jump in my car and go see her. Llandudno is only an hour away."

James and Robert looked at each other, trying to make out what the other thought of Maddie's suggestion. "You can wish her 'Happy Mothers' Day' and discuss her future plans with her." Neither of the brothers spoke. "Just you two could go if you think it's better I don't join you."

"No," James said. "I mean yes, I want you to come."

"That means we're going, then." Maddie sighed. "What about you, Robert?"

"Count me in." He wasn't sure he wanted to go, but there was no way James was going without him. He would rather have been going with Jayne. It crossed his mind that both Maddie and Jayne had had the same idea. Strange that. He decided it must be one of these intuition things that women go on about.

They finished their drinks and walked back to Jumbles Lane. Before long, they were on the way to Llandudno, taking the direct route along the A55, with

Robert in the back of the car, and James in the passenger seat.

* * * *

They pulled into the car park at 'Littletrees' Caravan Park just after three o'clock.

"You two stay here," James said. "I'll find out exactly where she's parked." He went into the reception area. Maddie and Robert could see the receptionist shaking her head, and then point into the caravan park. It looked as though she was giving directions. Moments later, a pale-faced James was back in the car.

"What's wrong?" Maddie asked.

"She's gone. Left yesterday."

"But what about...?" Robert started to ask.

"Yes, yes. I know. What about the tracking device? I don't bloody know, but we'll soon find out. Drive down there, please, Maddie. Plot sixteen, that's where she was. I checked the tracker just this morning and it was there then."

"So what went wrong?" Robert asked as Maddie drove between the touring vans and motorhomes. "Where is she now?"

"I don't fucking know."

Maddie glared at him, but it made no difference. His face flushed with anger.

"What a stupid fucking question," James muttered.

They arrived at a vacant plot sixteen. The three of them got out of the car, and James paced up and down in disbelief.

"What exactly did the receptionist say?" Maddie asked.

"Just that she left yesterday...and that she seemed upset."

"Anything else?"

James paused at her question.

"She said she was walking much better, hardly limping at all."

"What?" Robert shouted. "What do you mean? I told you something was wrong but oh, no, mister smart-arse policeman knows everything."

"Apparently, she sprained her ankle walking on the dunes soon after she arrived." James frowned.

Maddie stood next to the hook-up box. She opened it and looked inside. "James, Robert, I think you should come and take a look at this." The brothers walked over and stared in disbelief at the tracking device. "Your mum's far too smart for you."

"What do you mean?" James asked.

"Work it out for yourselves."

They looked at each other. Robert shrugged in a 'haven't a clue' sort of way. "You're the policeman, James, what do we do now?" he asked.

James wandered around plot sixteen, his hands deep in his pockets, his head down. "It's obvious she found the tracker, fuck knows how, it was well hidden." He paused for a moment, scratching his head. "Must've been that little shit at Billington's. He must've told her."

"And instead of thinking you did it for her safety, Mum didn't like the idea of being tracked. She went off to Anglesey in a huff, emailing us to say she was staying here."

"Maybe," James said, clearly not wanting to admit his idea had backfired. "The receptionist said she was upset."

"Yeah, well, bloody furious can look like upset. Let's go home." They got back in the car.

Maddie started the engine. "I'll drive to Anglesey if you like. There's time to look round a few campsites, but it's my guess she's not gone there at all." She reversed the car. "Don't know about you two, but I'm starving. How does fish and chips sound?"

"Let's go home," James and Robert replied in unison.

"Hey! Maybe you two can communicate." Maddie laughed. James glowered at her. Robert smiled at his brother's discomfort.

"First thing tomorrow, I'm going to upgrade my phone to something with a better internet connection. I'll be able to email all the time. Will that please you?" James asked sarcastically.

"This isn't about me, James," Maddie replied, her smile gone. "This is about your relationship with your brother here, and your mother, wherever she is." She looked in the rear view mirror. Robert grinned. "Take that stupid smile off your face, Robert. I only met you today, and I don't want to fall out with you, but I could do quite easily."

It was Robert's turn to feel uncomfortable.

"Food sounds good to me," he said, "then home."

James nodded in agreement, so Maddie drove to the seafront. They ate their fish and chips from the paper, each deep in their own thoughts.

Their hunger satisfied, the mood lifted. James broke the silence. "When we get home, we need to email her. I'll send a text, just to tell her to check her inbox. Maddie's right, Robert, we need to communicate."

"Where do you think she is?" Robert asked.

"No idea. Did she take her passport?"

"No idea."

"Well, then, we need to start by looking for it," James said.

"What good would that do? It wouldn't prove anything, would it? If we can't find it, that doesn't mean she's abroad."

"No, Robert, it doesn't, but if we do find it, that means she's still in the U.K."

CHAPTER ELEVEN

Helen headed along the A5, through Llangollen, joining the M6 near Stoke-on-Trent. Tears of rage dried on her cheeks. Her eyes felt swollen, her skin taut. She subconsciously followed signposts to 'The South'. Slowly, her anger began to subside with the calming monotony of the motorway, only to be replaced by numbness, an empty detached feeling. The ache in her ankle was a constant reminder of Llandudno, and yet she felt she had no past and no future. There was nothing to look forward to. Her life was passing by as unnoticed as the scenery of Gloucestershire. She drove on autopilot, without a destination.

Bored by the motorway, she turned off towards the south coast. She wasn't in the mood to talk to anyone, so when she saw a signpost to a picnic site in a wood, she made her first conscious decision since leaving 'Littletrees'. Turning off the main road, to her delight she found the car park and picnic site deserted. With the handbrake firmly pulled on and the ignition key thrown into the glove compartment, she released the swivel seat and turned to face the table, looking around her compact little home as if seeing Goldilocks for the very first time.

"Home sweet home, Helen McGuire. This is it. Robert and James, my dear boys, you have no idea where I am, or for that matter, who I am. So fuck off."

She hadn't eaten all day, but what was needed right now was a drink. She limped to the fridge and took out a bottle of red wine. Twisting the top off, she filled a large glass and drank it straight off, and then limped to the bedroom and took Phil's photo from her bedside drawer. She took a second clean glass from the cupboard and set it down on the table next to Phil's photograph, sat down, wriggled herself into a comfortable position, and filled the two glasses.

"Cheers, Phil." She raised her glass to the photograph. "I don't suppose it's appropriate to say 'good health', you having being dead two years."

Swinging absentmindedly from side to side in the driver's seat, Helen took her phone from her bag, and with a giggle, switched it off. The cool liquid chilled her throat, relaxing her mind with a mellowing sensation as it slipped into her stomach.

"It's like this, Phil. Those boys of ours each need to get a nice girlfriend. They need to get away from Chester and my apron strings." Her glass emptied, she poured another, looking incredulously at the empty bottle. "Wasn't much in there, was there?" She grinned. "Did you sneak some when I wasn't looking, Phil, you old sod?" The smile left her face to be replaced by an overwhelming sadness. "I need to be free, Phil. Free from Robert, free from James and free from you…free to talk to myself if I fucking want to."

As the daylight faded, she could just make out the silhouette of a small town. The last embers of the sun played on the sea beyond. She took Phil's glass and raised it to his photograph, as her lips began to tingle, all the pain dissolved from her ankle.

* * * *

The next morning dawned bright, sunny and spring-like. The birds sang their dawn chorus, waking her far too early. The bedroom window faced due east, and brilliant spring sunshine poured in without any consideration for a tired and emotional Helen, who couldn't understand why she'd forgotten to draw the blinds. She turned over and buried her head under the pillow, but it was no use, she was awake and needed a wee, and those bloody birds weren't going to let her go back to sleep. No way.

She staggered to the bathroom with one hand clutching the door frame, the other supporting her head. A brief glance in the mirror made her groan. "Not a pretty sight this morning, are you?"

Maybe when she'd had a shower and washed her hair, her face would wake up a bit and return to normal. The combined forces of a headache and daylight were conspiring against her. She shut her eyes and felt as if she were spinning in a pirouette. The thought of putting her thumping head under a cool shower was tempting, but after careful consideration, she decided a black coffee and light breakfast should take priority.

Two empty bottles and two glasses sat on the table. She picked the bottles up, one in each hand, and read the labels. They were both hers, all right, and so, with a groan of self deprecation, Helen accepted the hangover for what it was. A sharp pain in her right foot made her wince.

"Shit." It was the wrong foot for the ankle pain. She looked down to see blood pouring from her big toe, cut by the shattered glass of Phil's photograph. "How the fuck did that happen?" Phil didn't reply. "Well, answer me, then!" she shouted, putting her hand to her temple as her voice echoed around inside her head. She grabbed a tea towel and wrapped it around her foot, and then picked up the photograph. Bending down was not good, her head wanted to burst. Even her teeth ached. She swept the broken glass under the table with a hand brush. It could be cleaned up properly later, when bending down was more of an option.

The kettle whistled louder than ever. Helen turned off the gas and the high-pitched scream descended slowly into silence. The first sip of coffee burned its way through her alcoholic dehydration. It helped a little, but the cornflakes were way too noisy. She pushed the bowl away and picked up the bloodstained photograph. With a huge sigh, she ripped it up into tiny pieces. "You're gone, Phil. Fact. It's just me and Goldilocks and the worst hangover

I've ever had."

She stood up, closed the windows and shut the blinds before staggering back to bed, lying on her back with one foot firmly on the floor, in an attempt to stop the spinning. There was bugger all to do about it, she was stuck out there in the woods, and didn't fancy adding drink-driving to her list of misdemeanours. The only option was to sleep it off. A driving ban really would fuck things up.

* * * *

Five hours and a deep sleep later, the warm shower soothed away the remnants of her hangover. She was grateful for the small size of the bathroom; it meant she could sit on the loo seat whilst enjoying the shower. She took a deep breath and tipped her head back, enjoying the scent of the shampoo. The clear water ran down her face, droplets of it massaging her skin. Bliss. Unadulterated heaven, until a whirring noise, as the water pump stuttered, brought her back to earth with a bump. There was a loud 'click' and the shower stopped. She watched the last of the water drain down the plug hole. Her eyes closed in disbelief. No water left. Stark naked, hair full of shampoo, the reality of life on the open road was definitely not living up to the dream.

"Bollocks!" she shouted, kicking the wall with her right foot. "Ouch!" Blood streamed from her big toe. She'd forgotten about that. "Fucking bollocks." As she leaned forward to stem the bleeding with a face cloth, shampoo ran into her eye. Pulling open the bathroom door, and with her stinging eye closed, she limped from one foot to the other, not knowing whether to laugh or cry. The sound she made was a peculiar mixture of the two, a keening wail interspersed with little giggles. Blood spurted all over the carpet and the bed. She rubbed her eye, and then bound her toe as tightly as she could with some tissues.

With her shampoo-laden hair wrapped in a towel, Helen dressed in the first clean clothes that came to hand. Next, and with great difficulty, she brushed as much shampoo out of her hair as she could, changed the bloody bedding, and wiped the worst of the blood from the carpet. She swept the floor, clearing the shards of glass from Phil's photo with a dustpan and brush. The photograph, frame and broken glass were thrown into a litter bin, along with the empty wine bottles. Soggy cornflakes were scattered for the birds. Her hair felt awful, the shampoo was drying to an itchy crust. Helen resigned herself to the fact there was nothing she could do about it.

About a cupful of water remained in the kettle. This presented a difficult decision. Should she use it to rinse her hair or make a strong black coffee? In the end, the coffee won because there wasn't enough water to make a significant difference to her hair. She found a bottle of lemonade next to the cafetiere in the cupboard, unscrewed the top, leaned over the sink and tipped the lot through her hair. Her scalp still itched, but not so badly, and with her hair rubbed dry with a towel and combed through, she thought it didn't look quite so bad. Next job was to put a proper dressing on her toe. The bleeding had stopped, and with a large plaster carefully applied courtesy of her first aid box, things were looking better. She put on some loose fitting socks and her slippers, and then looked at her watch. Half past two.

"Your priority now, Helen McGuire, is to get to a campsite and get some water." She turned the driver's seat to face the front and took the keys from the glove compartment.

* * * *

Five minutes later, she passed a sign requesting that

she drive carefully in Pennington-on-Sea. She parked Goldilocks in the town square, near the Tourist Information Centre. In the centre of the square was a seating area with benches and a few shrubs. A War Memorial pointed its pinnacle towards the sky.

Helen locked Goldilocks with the press of a button and an electronic 'peep-peep', and crossed the road. The glass door of the Tourist Information Centre made a 'bing bong' noise, announcing her arrival. The usual leaflets encouraging visits to castles, wildlife parks, art exhibitions, museums, etcetera, were arrayed in neat piles. All manner of souvenirs of Pennington-on-Sea from baseball hats to teaspoons were on display. A large mirror behind the counter gave the impression of a much larger room. There were no other customers.

Helen headed straight for an assistant who was engrossed in her computer screen. In the few seconds it took her to reach the desk she saw a very neat assistant in her mid forties. Her immaculate, well cut hair bobbed around her ears, her uniform suit French navy with a crisp white collared blouse. The plastic badge on her lapel identified her as Miss Sheila Forrester.

"Do you have a list of caravan sites?"

The assistant looked up, her eyes widening.

"Didn't you hear me come in?" Helen noted the perfectly applied make up and beautifully manicured nails.

"Yes, yes. I heard you. Sorry. What was it you said?" The assistant stared at her.

"Campsites. Do you have a list of campsites?" Helen heard her own voice rising.

"Yes, of course. They're all for holidays."

"That's what I expected. What else would I want?"

"Residential?" Her one word question puzzled Helen.

"What? I have a motorhome."

"It's just I thought maybe you...never mind." She opened a drawer and gave Helen an A4 sheet of paper with a list of caravan sites, and a map. Helen cast her eyes over it, acutely aware that the assistant was watching her.

"Do you need any help with it?" Miss Forrester asked.

Her attitude annoyed Helen. "No. I can read." As she spoke, Helen looked up and caught sight of herself in the mirror. Everything fell into place. She looked terrible. Individually, she liked her flowery print blouse and striped skirt, but together her random choice of clothes made her look like a jumble sale. Her hair had dried into matted clumps.

Obviously, the assistant thought she was homeless. An itinerant. Nomadic. A traveller. To make matters worse, dried blood from her toe was stuck under her fingernails. She wanted to scream a denial, but thought better of it.

With as much dignity as she could muster, Helen stood straight. She thanked the assistant and wobbled out, limping from one injured foot to the other, her awkward gait adding to her dubious appearance. No doubt the assistant had noticed by now that she wore slippers.

The door 'bing bonged' her out, and she hobbled back to Goldilocks as quickly as possible. She closed the door behind her with a deep sigh, grateful to be in her sanctuary. Sitting at the table, she studied the list of sites. One name jumped out at her. 'Ten Acres.' If it was as big as the name suggested, she could get lost in the crowds. She would be anonymous.

Helen punched the post code into the satnav and seconds later drove out of Pennington-on-Sea town square. 'Ten Acres' was half a mile or so outside the town, on the cliff tops of the Devon coast. Helen asked for a site for a week. The receptionist barely looked up, which, given her recent experience, suited Helen very well.

"Site three-two-six. Over there." The receptionist pointed to the left. "The toilets and other facilities are over there." She pointed to the right, working with the speed of a bored sloth. Helen eventually left the reception area with a bunch of paperwork and a burning desire to punch all receptionists.

* * * *

By five o'clock, Helen had returned to the land of the living. She'd filled up the fresh water tank, hooked up to mains electricity, and had a lovely shower. Her toe was suitably dressed in a plaster from her first aid box, and all traces of the night before erased from Goldilocks. She dried her hair and cooked a single portion of macaroni cheese. Site three-two-six was in a lovely spot, right alongside the top of the cliffs. She could hear the waves gently turning on the pebbles below, and the town and its little beach could be seen in the distance. Yachts danced by on the sparkling sea. Happy voices and the delicious smell of barbecued food filled the air.

Her first experience of binge drinking had somehow drawn a line in her life. Phil was dead. Helen didn't like the term 'closure', and until now hadn't understood it. With a sense of relief, she recognised that for the past two years, three months and eight days, she had been grieving. She no longer needed his smiling photograph, which was just as well considering it was a ripped-up blood-stained mess, destined for landfill. She smiled at the thought. At last she was living the dream. The dream she'd had when drinking hot chocolate and eating crumpets at the kitchen table in Jumbles Lane.

Was that really only four weeks ago?

Her emotions soared with the seagulls as they floated effortlessly on the thermals of the cliff top air. Helen took her laptop from the cupboard to check her emails. To her surprise, she no longer felt angry with James about the tracking device. He was wrong to have done that, very wrong, but she accepted he would have done it for the right reasons. She'd give it another week and then come clean, tell them she was staying away for at least the summer. Her laptop played its four note tune, informing her she was connected to the internet. Her home page was set to the weather forecast. It showed heavy rain in North Wales for the next few days, so travelling south had been a good move. She turned on her phone. There was a text message from James.

Pls check email.

"Okay, okay, I'm onto it." She logged on to her hotmail account. There were two, one from James and one from Robert. No surprise there. She opened Robert's first in the hope of hearing about his date in London.

Hi Mum, Where are you? We've just got back from Llandudno. We wanted to say Happy Mothers' Day to you. Can I phone sometime? The tracking device thing was James's idea. They told us at the campsite about your ankle. When are you coming home?

With love from Robert.

"Shit. The cat's out of the bag, then." She returned to her inbox and opened James's email.

Hi Mum, Sorry about the tracker. We went to see you in Llandudno to wish you 'Happy Mothers' Day'. Where have you gone? What about your ankle? How can you drive?

When are you coming home? I have something to tell you, and I'd rather say it face to face.

Love, James.

Helen sat back and read the emails again and again. A wave of guilt washed over her. Robert and James were good sons. She hadn't realised it was Mothers' Day. It was kind of them to travel to Llandudno. They barely spoke to each other as a rule. Maybe her absence was having an unexpected effect. She would have to word her reply carefully. There was the question of whether or not to tell them where she was. They knew where she wasn't, and they knew about her ankle. They weren't stupid and would have worked out she'd lied to them about her long walks on the beach. What they didn't realise was that she was doing this for them, to make them independent.

In the end, she decided to come clean. She would send the same reply to both of them.

Hi Robert and James,

Thanks for the emails. I apologise for being less than truthful regarding my plans. I was very cross about the tracking thing, but realise you did it for the right reasons. I'm on the south coast at a place called Pennington-on-Sea. I don't know how long I'm staying here but promise to let you know when I set off again. I sprained my left ankle, so driving isn't a problem. Whatever it is you want to talk about, James, it will have to wait. Please don't phone unless it's an emergency. I need a bit of time to myself, that's all.

I do miss you both, but I'll be away for most of the summer. I need to do this for all our sakes. With love, Mum.

Helen read it through several times before clicking 'Send'. She thought it sounded rather cold and formal, though perhaps brutally honest was a better description. It was honest anyway. She wasn't ready to speak to them yet. She feared they would try to persuade her to go back to Chester. She missed their voices, missed her home. At the same time she loved Goldilocks and her freedom. Lying to her sons had never been on her list of things to do. The bad tempered drama of leaving 'Littletrees' was gone, replaced by a roller coaster of mixed up feelings. She closed her laptop and put it away, turning to Miss Sloth's leaflets as a distraction.

* * * *

Robert was glad to be back at work, in a world he understood. The trouble was he couldn't concentrate. His measured day of twenty minute time slots unachievable, even worse than Friday, when the anticipation of meeting Jayne had occupied his mind. Thoughts leapt between Jayne, his mother, his brother, Maddie Ridgeway, Llandudno, and the south coast.

The office vending machine spat hot chocolate to the rim of the cup. He walked carefully to his desk on the first floor of a neo gothic building in Chester town centre. Normally he would never take a drink to his desk for fear of spilling it, but nothing felt normal that day. Maybe he would go to the golf club after work and fire off a few shots at the driving range. He drank the hot, sweet liquid and threw the empty cup into a waste bin, only to realise it wasn't quite empty and dark brown sludgy dregs splattered across the plain blue carpet.

"Bollocks!"

Several heads turned towards him. He blushed as a momentary silence spread across the room, followed by a Mexican wave of giggles. He returned to his desk and logged onto his private email account. There was one from Mum, and one from Jayne. Jayne would be telling him she was sorry, that she'd changed her mind and didn't want to see him again, so he opened hers first, wanting to get it over with.

Hi Robert,

I really enjoyed your company today, though as it's now after midnight, strictly speaking it was yesterday. I hope you manage to see your mum soon, I meant it when I said I would love to see you again, and hope you feel the same about me.

Jayne.

Robert was stunned. Jayne had emailed him as soon as he'd left London. She wanted to see him again. She'd said she'd go to Llandudno with him the following weekend if he wanted. A lot had happened since then. Maybe she'd come to Chester anyway, but that would mean introducing her to James.

He clicked 'Reply'.

Hi Jayne,

Thanks for the email. I'll phone tonight and we'll arrange something soon.

Robert.

He opened his mother's email. A sense of relief

washed over him as he read her news, but what on earth did she mean by '*I need to do this for all our sakes*'? The email was addressed to both himself and James. He'd have to speak with his brother about it before replying. His thoughts returned to Jayne, and he determined to get on with some work. A promotion to the London office suddenly seemed like the answer to everything.

* * * *

James was home first. He wanted to talk to Robert about Mum. Maddie was right. They needed to communicate better.

"Sweet and sour pork okay with you? It was the first thing I came to in the freezer." The shocked expression on Robert's face was priceless. James smiled.

"Yes, fine…did you get Mum's email?"

"Certainly did." James took a mobile phone from his shirt pocket and waved it at Robert. "What do you reckon? Mum's email came through as soon as I programmed everything in." He put two plates in the oven before handing the phone to his brother. Sweet and sour smells came from the microwave.

"How much did this cost you then?" Robert asked as he examined the phone.

"I got a good deal. You should get one."

Robert ignored the suggestion. "Did you reply to her?"

"Not yet, I thought we should talk about it first." James reached into the fridge for a beer. "You were right about her not coming back, though. Funny, isn't it? I'm supposed to be the copper, and I didn't see what was right under my nose. I thought you were wrong." He took a swig of beer from the bottle. "What I still don't get is this bit about 'doing it for all our sakes'. What do you reckon she means by that?"

"I've no idea. That's what I was going to ask you

about."

"The trouble is if we are both going to London, this house will be empty." James stabbed a bag of rice and put it in the microwave. "Food won't be long."

"I don't think we should tell her we might be leaving home." Robert looked serious. "She wouldn't like that." He took a lager from the fridge, pulled the ring and poured it into a glass.

"No. I know. But if we are, I mean, when we know for definite, we'll have to tell her."

"Sufficient unto the day," Robert muttered.

"What?"

"It's a quote. Don't know where from. It means we'll do something when we have to, and not before."

"Right." James tipped steaming rice onto the plates and poured on the sweet and sour pork. They ate in silence for a while.

Robert put his fork down. "Will you be seeing Maddie at the weekend?"

"Probably, depending on our shifts. What's it to you?"

"We could ask them what they think. Maddie and Jayne. Women seem to have this intuition thing."

"Jayne? Who the hell is Jayne?"

"My girlfriend."

"Tell me more, big brother." James leaned back in his chair. His sarcastic tone wasn't wasted on Robert. It was no more than he expected.

"She's from London. She might be coming up at the weekend, and I thought it might be a good idea if we put our heads together."

"Well, is she or isn't she? Might means might not, in my book."

"Look, James. I'm trying to be constructive here." Robert's face was getting redder by the moment. James didn't want to enjoy his brother's discomfort, but he was just so funny.

"I'm speaking to Jayne tonight to make arrangements for the weekend. I wanted to talk to you about that, and about Mum, before I did anything else. I thought maybe we could all go to this Pennington place."

"Okay, okay. Who's bitten your arse, then?"

"You have, you self righteous pillock. You're not the only one with a life, you know."

James was taken by surprise by the uncharacteristic outburst. In fact, a lot of things surprised him lately. He felt uneasy, but didn't know why. Maddie's news about London had been a nice surprise. Everything was going well between them. Work was no more stressful that usual, so that wasn't the reason.

"Sorry, mate, I was out of order there. What's she like?"

"Well, hopefully, you'll find out at the weekend. I think she's fantastic, and I'm going upstairs to call her now." Robert put down his fork and pushed his empty plate to the middle of the table. "I'll wash up later, seeing as you cooked."

The conversation hadn't gone according to plan. James was annoyed with himself for being annoyed with Robert, and they hadn't really discussed Mum's email at all. He kicked the kitchen bin, causing a dent in the side, and then started to wash the dishes.

CHAPTER TWELVE

'Ten Acres' had a shop, spa and swimming pool, bar, restaurant, games room, a gym, barbecue facilities and a laundry. Hundreds of identical static caravans lined the concrete avenues in regimental order. The only problem with Helen's sea view pitch was its distance from all these wonderful facilities. Plot three-two-six was a commute away from everything the place had to offer.

Her ankle improved by the day, and her toe had almost healed, but the walk to the little town, or even to the shop on site, became a drag. Helen browsed through the leaflets supplied by Miss Sloth. As she studied the local map with its picture of a happy family cycling along the seafront on the cover, the words 'King's Cycle Hire' jumped out at her. She hadn't ridden a bicycle for years, but it would be easier than walking everywhere. She could see herself with a basket on the front, for her groceries, and a rucksack on her back, for a packed lunch, or swimming things, or anything else, for that matter. Closer inspection of the advertisement informed her 'King's Cycle Hire' offered a delivery service. She dialled the number before any second thoughts had the chance to divert her.

"King's Bicycle shop. Jim King speaking."

"I'd like to hire a bicycle."

"Then you've dialled the right number, madam." His enthusiasm made Helen smile. "What size wheel?"

"I haven't a clue. I just want a lady's bike."

"Ah, madam. If only life were so simple. How tall are you?"

"Five foot four."

"And what do you want to do?" The question puzzled her. What on earth did he think she wanted to do?

"I want to ride a bike, of course." An exasperated sigh came from the cycle shop owner.

"Do you want a mountain bike, a racing bike, a—?"

"Mr King, I'm fifty years old. I haven't been on a bike for over thirty years. I don't want to go up a mountain, and I don't want to enter any races. I would like a bicycle with two wheels and a basket on the front. I would like you to deliver it to plot three-two-six of Ten Acres Caravan Park as soon as possible." She hung up. "Fucking twat."

* * * *

An hour later, and to Helen's great surprise, a large van pulled up outside Goldilocks. The sign writing left her in no doubt as to whom it could be. 'King's Cycles' and the happy family in the advertisement stared at her. She could hardly believe her eyes. It was seven o'clock in the evening, and there was Mr King with her bicycle. She stepped outside.

"Sorry, I couldn't get here any sooner. I've been on my own in the shop today." He held out his hand. "Jim King. Don't think I caught your name when you rang."

Helen felt thoroughly ashamed of herself. She had been a bad-tempered cow with this happy man, whose only crime was trying to be helpful. They shook hands. She guessed he was about forty-five. Tanned and toned, Jim King clearly loved his job. Every inch of him screamed 'serious cyclist'.

"Helen McGuire."

"I'll get the bike out. You can tell me if this is what you want." He opened the back doors of the van and climbed inside, still chatting. "If it's not right, I can bring another in the morning, no charge for delivery, of course." He lifted a shiny pink and black bicycle onto the grass. It had a brand new basket on the front, and was exactly what she wanted. Perhaps not her first colour choice, but that didn't matter.

Her face lit up like that of a child at Christmas. "I'm sorry I was rude on the phone, Mr King."

He looked puzzled. "Rude? You weren't rude, Mrs McGuire, and please call me Jim. Everyone calls me Jim. I might not answer to 'Mr King'," he laughed.

"If I call you Jim, you must call me Helen." Strangely shy, she found herself checking his left hand for a wedding ring. There wasn't one. Not that it meant anything. Lots of married men didn't wear rings. "The bicycle is perfect, thank you."

"The security chain's in the basket. Give me a ring when you've finished with it."

"What if I want to buy it, Jim?"

He looked at his watch. "Tell you what, Helen, call round at the shop sometime and we'll talk about it then. I have to be off. Mrs K will have dinner on the table, and I don't like to ruffle her feathers." He closed the back doors of his van with a bang.

She mounted the bicycle, tested the brakes and inspected the gear controls before setting off around 'Ten Acres', wobbling quite a lot as she set off, but soon getting the hang of it. Her ankle ached, but it was easier than walking. Fifteen minutes later, she was back at plot three-two-six. Her bum and thighs hurt more than her injured feet. She'd see Jim the following morning about buying the bike. The garage in the back of Goldilocks would be useful after all.

"Bobby Billington would be impressed if he could see me now," Helen said as she put the bicycle in Goldilocks's garage.

* * * *

Next morning found Helen in an unsettled mood, and she didn't know why, which made it all the more unsettling. She'd been like an awkward schoolgirl in front of Jim King.

"How ridiculous is that, you fat old bag? And another thing, it's time you stopped talking to yourself." She tucked into her cooked breakfast, and then leaned back, running her thumb under the tight waistband of her trousers.

"Better get out on that bicycle, old girl." She put her waterproof cagoule in her rucksack, along with some sandwiches and an apple, a small bottle of water, and a serviette. Wearing her smart blue trousers and a white top, she managed, with considerable difficulty, to get her trainers on. Once on, they didn't feel too bad. She hadn't worn a pair of shoes since Llandudno A&E, but all that was in the past. She combed her hair and put a splash of perfume on her wrists. There was to be no repetition of the débâcle at the Tourist Information Centre.

There wasn't a cloud in the sky as she locked up Goldilocks and peddled off towards Pennington-on-Sea. An off-shore breeze chilled her left cheek as she peddled towards town. Thankfully, there were no steep hills, and the gentle undulations gave her the opportunity to master the gears of the shiny new bicycle.

She made her way to 'King's Cycles' in the town square. The shop front was quite large, with rows of bicycles lined up outside. Why hadn't she noticed it the day before? Then she remembered her haste to leave the town square. It all seemed so long ago.

Her bicycle chained up, she went inside. A very attractive young blonde dressed in dayglo pink and black lycra stood behind the counter. Jim King knew how to choose his staff. She was young, beautiful, fit, and would, Helen was sure, know all about cycling. Her ready smile greeted Helen, but her appearance made her feel old and frumpy. A sparkling wedding ring, encrusted with diamonds, with a matching engagement ring, adorned her left hand. Someone loved her very much.

"Can I help at all?"

"Yes, I hope so. Jim delivered a bicycle to me yesterday, initially for hire, but I'd like to buy it."

"You must be Helen McGuire." She smiled.

Helen was struck by the kindness that shone from her face, and smiled back.

Just then, Jim King came through a door to the rear of the shop. "Ah, Helen. I see you've met Mrs K."

Helen paled.

"I told her you might be calling in this morning. She told me off, didn't you, Mrs K? She says I'm too trusting, but here you are to prove me right. There are lots of bad people, I know, but I reckon I'm a good judge of character. After all, I picked Mrs K here, didn't I?" He laughed at his own joke. His wife poked him in the ribs, and they laughed together.

"I'd like to buy the bicycle, Jim. It suits me well, and I may not be staying in Pennington-on-Sea very long."

"Right, I see. I'll throw in the basket and a matching helmet too, if you like. The bike's new, but old, if you know what I mean."

Helen looked puzzled.

"I think the colour scheme put people off."

"He means," his wife said, "it's old stock. It's been here years, longer than me, in fact."

"Pink and black suits you well enough, Mrs King," Helen said.

"But Mrs K here isn't a bicycle, is she?" There was a short silence, and then his wife laughed. This time Helen laughed too. Ten minutes later, she had paid with her debit card and was the proud owner of a pink and black bicycle, basket and helmet.

She cycled round the town, catching her bearings. A high street showed some interesting shops. Many were touristy, but Pennington-on-Sea appeared to be a prosperous little place with some posh dress shops and shoe shops, and several hairdressers. On impulse, she chained her bicycle up in the town square and limped over to Kirstie's Kutz.

"Do you have any appointments available today?"

The receptionist had the name "Jodie" embroidered on her black tunic. "What would you like to have done?" Jodie had the obligatory bizarre hairstyle, dyed in an unnatural shade of red. It reminded Helen of Bobby Billington. She thought they'd make a good couple.

"I don't know, Jodie. There's nothing interesting about brown with a touch of grey, so a bit of a make-over would be nice."

A glimmer of a smile crossed Jodie's face. She was looking at Helen's hair, summing up the possibilities. "Now with Annie, or four o'clock with Kirstie?"

"I'll take the four o'clock, please."

"Would you like that written on a card?"

"No, thanks. Memory not that bad yet." Helen smiled.

Jodie looked blank. She was pleasant enough, Helen thought, but not old enough to appreciate the joke.

* * * *

Helen sat alone in a shelter on the sea front, her lunch in a rucksack at her side. Even though her watch told her it was only a quarter to twelve, she was hungry. The breeze coming straight from the sea hit her full in the face. Why on earth she had packed a lunch she didn't know. It would have been far more pleasant to sit in a cafe. The shelter gave no shelter at all. Her mind returned to Jim King. What on earth had she been thinking there? She ate a sandwich and thought of Mrs K's trim body. "You're jealous, you stupid old cow."

"I beg your pardon?"

Helen turned quickly to see a woman of about her own age sitting at the far end of the bench. She hadn't heard or seen her arrive.

"Sorry. Bad habit of mine—talking to myself. No offence intended."

"None taken." A short silence followed. The two women stared out to sea.

"If you don't mind my asking, what are you jealous of?"

"I really don't know."

"My name's Gillian, by the way, Gillian Halstead."

"Helen, Helen McGuire."

"You on holiday here?"

"Yes, is it that obvious?"

"Locals don't come down here much, and definitely not with a packed lunch."

"Fair comment. These shelters could do with a clean and a coat of paint."

"That's what I told my husband." Her voice was flat, not exactly a monotone, but dull, lifeless. Helen admired the way she was dressed, so casual and yet so smart. She wore trainers and cropped trousers, a yellow T-shirt and body warmer. A yellow bum bag was wrapped around her middle. Her clothes were happy clothes, and yet she sounded sad.

"I take it you live here, then?"

"Yes, I live here. I've always lived here. That's part of the problem. Pennington-on-Sea. A little town full of little minds."

"So why are you here in this shabby shelter with the wind in your face?"

"How long have you got?"

"Me? All the time in the world, until my hair appointment at four o'clock."

"If I told you I was here to meet a junkie, would you believe me?"

Helen didn't answer.

"They hang out around here, come to buy drugs from the dealers. That's why you won't see many locals."

"Go on," Helen said. "I'm listening."

"My daughter's an addict. A junkie. I want her to come home."

"Does your husband know you're here? He'd be worried."

"He's dead. And he wouldn't be worried, he'd be furious."

"Sorry, it's just that you said you'd told him about the state of the shelters and I assumed…"

"Don't apologise. Please don't apologise. The day he died was the happiest day of my life. I couldn't stand the sanctimonious bastard."

Helen was lost for words. She reminded herself of her rule, 'don't ask the question unless you're sure you want the answer'. But she couldn't even think of a question right then, so her rule didn't matter. She finished her sandwiches and ate her apple. Her companion continued to stare out to sea. Helen considered asking how long she had been a widow, or she could make small talk by asking how old her daughter was. In the end, she broke the silence by talking about herself.

"My husband died two years ago. Heart attack." She threw her apple core in the litter bin.

"Same here."

"Your husband died two years ago?"

"No. He had a heart attack two weeks ago."

"Two weeks!"

Gillian nodded, her gaze fixed on the horizon.

"Fancy a coffee?" Helen had no idea why she said it. The words were out before she gave any thought as to whether she wanted to befriend this strangely sad woman. Still, it would do no harm to have a coffee and a chat. If Gillian wanted to talk about her daughter, Helen would listen.

"Why not?"

The two women walked side by side, Helen pushing her bicycle.

"There's a new coffee shop just around the corner,

towards the square. They have outside seating."

"I think I saw it. Do you mean the one called 'Fresh Ground'?" Helen asked.

"That's right."

"Well, let's hope it is, then. Fresh ground, I mean." They walked the short distance in silence. When they arrived, Gillian insisted on buying the coffee. Helen stayed outside with her bicycle propped against one of the aluminium chairs. Away from the sea front and out of the breeze, the day was pleasant enough.

Before long, Gillian emerged from the coffee shop with a tray bearing two large cups of coffee and two large portions of carrot cake. "Comfort cake, I call it," she said. "Hope you like it."

"I don't know anyone who doesn't like carrot cake." Helen laughed.

Gillian set out the plates of cake and cups, stirring her coffee pensively. Helen noticed the pale band of skin on the third finger of Gillian's left hand where her rings had been.

"You're the first person I've spoken to in years who doesn't know my husband." Gillian continued to stir her coffee. Helen was trying to remember if she'd seen her put any sugar in it. "Sorry, that should be past tense. Who *didn't* know my husband, the wonderful Councillor Keith Halstead."

"It takes a bit of getting used to and it *is* early days for you." Helen had seen through the sarcastic comment. She saw that this woman was still in shock. Raw grief could take the form of anger for a while. Helen knew all about that.

Gillian looked up and smiled a thin, sad smile. "Oh, I'll get used to it, all right." She bent down and rummaged through her handbag. "He left me everything." She pulled out an envelope and took a key from it. "Including this." She placed the key on the table between them.

"What is it?"

"A key."

"I can see that. What's it for?"

"Safety deposit box number two-five-six-nine at a bank in Camford."

"What's inside it?"

"I haven't a bloody clue, but you can bet the taxman doesn't know it's there."

"Why are you telling me this, Gillian? You've only just met me. I might be a tax inspector."

"Oh, Christ, you're not, are you?"

"No, I'm not." The two women laughed together nervously.

Gillian's face became serious. "I feel guilty when I laugh, not because of Keith, but because of Caroline, my daughter. How can I be happy when she's in such a bad way?"

Helen didn't attempt to answer the question. She waited for Gillian to carry on with her story. For the next half hour, Gillian Halstead poured out her troubles: how Caroline had left home, and how she felt guilty for not standing up to Keith. She told of the way she had allowed herself to be controlled by Keith, and how his position as councillor had meant more to him than their daughter, and how he'd taken bribes from builders. "He made sure their planning applications went smoothly."

Helen tried to understand, but she couldn't, not really. She felt ashamed and ungrateful, and desperately sorry for this woman whom she had met barely an hour before.

"Would you like me to go with you to the bank?" Helen looked at the key lying on the table.

Gillian gave her a thin smile. "I would, yes. I'd like that very much."

CHAPTER THIRTEEN

Helen and Gillian walked back to 'Ten Acres' and stowed the bicycle away in Goldilocks's garage before ordering a taxi to Camford.

For some reason, which she was unable to explain, Helen had always thought safety deposit boxes were small, like little money boxes, big enough for a few pieces of jewellery maybe, but no more. The box on the table between them was more the size of a small suitcase. The clerk left the room, closing the door quietly behind him.

Gillian pushed the key across the table to Helen. "You open it."

Helen did as she was asked. The key turned easily. She lifted the lid. Gillian showed no emotion as they stared at the bundles of used bank notes.

"Bloody hell, Gillian, how much d'you reckon's there?"

"No idea. But it's proof, if proof were needed, that he was taking back-handers. This will be the money he took as bribes."

"What are you going to do?"

"Spend it, of course. Let's call it compensation for the years of misery he put me through."

Helen felt faint. *What would Robert and James say? This was like robbing a bank.*

Gillian noticed Helen's pale face. "What else am I going to do with it? It's okay, Helen. He left me everything, remember?" She started stuffing the money in her handbag. "You'll have to put some in your rucksack, Helen. It won't all go in here."

She was rooted to the spot, staring wide-eyed.

Gillian grabbed the rucksack and then shook it upside down. Breadcrumbs rained down onto the carpet as Gillian methodically packed the remaining rolls of notes into it. She bounced it on the table to settle its contents, and crammed more money in, zipping it up with difficulty. As soon as it was securely fastened, Gillian pressed a button on the wall and the clerk returned. She signed the relevant papers and told him the box was no longer needed, thank you.

They were travelling back to Pennington-on-Sea before either of them spoke.

"The taxi can drop you off first, Gillian."

"Won't you come in for a cuppa?"

"Sorry. Hair appointment."

"Tomorrow?"

"Maybe." Helen had deep reservations about continuing her friendship with Gillian. She felt sorry for her, but she was as mad as a box of frogs.

* * * *

Helen flopped into the styling chair of Kirstie's Kutz, tired out by the day's events. Kirstie's energetic smile made her feel quite exhausted.

"Jodie said you wanted a make-over." Kirstie combed Helen's hair slowly back from her face, making a professional assessment of the possibilities. Stylist and client looked in the mirror. "Any ideas?"

"None." Helen thought how unflattering it was to have her hair scraped back. Anything would be an improvement on that. "But I need brightening up a bit, don't you think?"

"Come over to the sinks, and I'll shampoo you first."

Helen did as she was told, and Kirstie enveloped her in a bright green gown and tucked a towel around her neck. Helen leaned back, resting her neck on the edge of the back-wash sink, grateful for the opportunity to close her eyes and relax. The warm spray of water and the massaging rhythm of Kirstie's fingers made her feel sleepy. Kirstie rinsed, shampooed and rinsed again before putting a towel over Helen's wet hair and invited her back to the styling chair.

Helen's skin looked tired and wrinkly. Green had never suited her, and the gown made her look ill. She sighed deeply. "I'll leave it up to you, Kirstie, but I need a change."

Kirstie smiled. Helen didn't feel capable of making a decision. She tried to focus on her reflection in the mirror but her eyes grew irresistibly heavy; the snip, snip, snip of Kirstie's scissors hypnotic. Before long, she lost the battle with her eyelids and drifted into a deep sleep. The snip, snip, snip became the swish, swish, swish of Goldilocks's windscreen wipers, and she was driving through torrential rain. Suddenly, the rain stopped and the road before her was a desert track. In the distance she could see a long queue at a bus stop. She drove on. As she drew closer to the queue, a familiar voice shouted from somewhere behind her, 'Next stop, please.' Helen signalled and pulled up. She swivelled round in her seat. Phil was stepping out of the side door. She opened her mouth to speak but no words would come. He smiled at her and faded into the shimmering heat of the desert. The people in the queue started to push their way on board. Goldilocks had turned into a mini-bus. Bobby Billington was first, followed by Jeff and Miranda from Littletrees. John was there, but no Betty. John smiled and waved. Tashy was next, her headphones on, looking down at her feet. Gillian was about to get on when Helen pressed a button and said, 'Sorry, I'm full. There'll be another one along in a minute.' The door closed with an electrical buzz, squashing Gillian's handbag. It fell inside Goldilocks and rolls of fifty pound notes scattered all over the floor. None of her passengers noticed.

Helen felt hot, very hot. Sweat trickled down her temples. She set off again, pressing her foot to the floor. Goldilocks raced through her gears, her engine screaming in protest, gathering speed. A siren wailed behind her. In the wing mirror, she saw a police car approaching fast, blue lights flashing. It swooped in front of Goldilocks, forcing Helen to stamp on the brake pedal. James jumped out of the driver's side of the police car and ran to her door, pulling her from her seat. Robert stood beside him, shaking his head. He pursed his lips and screwed up his nose in a look of disgust. She was wearing a dayglo pink and black cycling outfit that was far too small, and she could feel herself getting fatter and fatter.

"I'm arresting you for selling heroin," James shouted at her as he snapped handcuffs around her wrists. "You are also guilty of robbing a bank, and of looking like a fucking idiot. Anything you say—"

She tried to pull away, and woke up with a start. Her wide eyes stared at the face in the mirror before her. For a few seconds, she didn't know where she was, what day it was, or even who she was, her head still in the desert. The face before her in the mirror was haloed by a roll of cotton wool, tucked under a variety of clips, tin foil, and strips of pink plastic.

"You all right, Mrs McGuire?"

Helen's head struggled back to reality.

Kirstie held her wrist. "Did the siren wake you?"

Helen didn't know what to say. How could Kirstie know James had arrested her?

"An ambulance just went by, sirens blaring. I think it woke you up."

Helen still didn't speak. The faces of her dream faded, and the jumble of memories fell back into place. She hadn't been arrested, and Gillian's cash was not her problem.

"Sorry, I nodded off, didn't I?" Helen said.

Kirstie nodded. "Everyone else has gone home. I usually stay a bit later to tidy up. Come back over to the sink. One more shampoo and some nice conditioner."

With clean, dry towels softly wrapped around her,

Helen leaned back and Kirstie removed the clips, foil, and plastic strips from her head. The shampoo smelled lovely. Kirstie's gentle massage helped Helen back to the land of the living.

"Did you put some highlights in, then?"

"We-ell...I brightened you up. Nice and colourful. Just like you asked. I didn't like to wake you up, see." She rubbed Helen's head with a towel, rather vigorously. "Back over here now, Mrs McGuire."

Helen remembered saying she needed brightening up, but the words 'nice and colourful' worried her.

"Please call me Hel—" She caught sight of herself in the mirror.

"Do you like it?" Kirstie's voice had lost some of its confidence. Not exactly a whisper, but much quieter. Helen's hair was jet black with a streak of shocking pink from her parting, over the top of her head and down the side.

"Christ almighty. I match my bicycle!"

"What?" Kirstie looked scared.

"Sorry...no...yes...oh dear, I'm not making any sense, am I? It's just that pink and black keep cropping up. I'm sure it will be fine when you've dried it." Helen had no idea why she was being so conciliatory. She looked bloody ridiculous.

Kirstie picked up a brush and a drier and set to work. The pink grew brighter and brighter as it dried, and her haircut took shape, a very odd shape. Bobby Billington came to mind as the asymmetric cut revealed itself. She made a conscious effort to stop glowering at the mirror, and tried to think of something to say.

"Do you know Gillian Halstead?"

"Oh, yes. She's a regular. Been coming here every week for years. Do you know she doesn't have one grey hair? Not one, lovely brown curls, all natural. Such a shame her husband dying like that, so sudden. They were devoted to each other, you know. He was a councillor."

"So I heard."

"Very well thought of, he was, and she was always there by his side. Don't know how she'll go on without him." Kirstie's brush twisted and turned in the hot air of the drier, her voice raised above the noise. "She's due in tomorrow. She's my ten o'clock. Lovely lady. How do you know her?"

"Oh, just a chance meeting. We chatted for a while. We have a few things in common." Helen smiled. Kirstie had known, and no doubt chatted to Gillian on a weekly basis for years, but didn't know her at all.

"Oh, that's nice."

"Well, it is if you count husbands dropping dead of heart attacks."

Kirstie stood like a statue, her mouth open. "Sorry. Bit of a conversation stopper that one, and yes, I'm sure you're right. She's a lovely lady."

Ten minutes later, after a bit more snipping and a lot of hairspray, Helen emerged from Kirstie's Kutz. She told Kirstie how she loved her new look and thanked her repeatedly, when, in fact, she thought she looked like a toilet brush from the pound shop. She paid and gave a generous tip, all the time annoyed with herself for lying, and being too scared to be honest. It was all her fault for falling asleep.

As she pedalled off across the car park, the woman from the Tourist Information Centre was locking up. Helen waved. The woman looked past her to see who the cyclist with a crazy hair style was waving at, and on seeing no one, returned her concentration to her keys. Helen pedalled on, unaware she was grinning all over her face. As she pedalled, she thought of her sons, and decided to send each of them a separate email.

CHAPTER FOURTEEN

Everything changed when Jono died. Naz was locked up, Jorge gone away, Dad was dead. Not that Dad being dead really changed anything, not for her, anyway.

Carrie sat on a bench in the town square, her chin tilted to face the warming afternoon sun, her hands curled inside the little pockets of her denim jacket. A police car cruised around the perimeter of the square. She turned her head to see if it was Pete Levens. *He was a funny guy. Funny peculiar, not funny ha-ha. He actually seems to care.* Part of her thought he was only being nice because she'd given a statement, but then he had always been okay, for a pig. The two wraps from Jorge would be her last. She was determined to get clean this time. With Naz locked up, quitting would be easy. She had been to the police station and given her statement. Pete had told her there would be new dealers moving in to take up Naz's business, and as she'd left the police station, even before she'd reached the next street, she'd been approached.

Carrie knew deep down that if it hadn't been for Pete's warning, and the fear of being dragged into prostitution, she would've bought. Pete had asked her several times if she knew where Jorge was.

"Jorge," he had said, "is the key to getting Naz convicted, and Jorge has disappeared. If we can't persuade him to give evidence, Naz will walk free." He had told her Jorge's statement wasn't enough, that Naz had pleaded 'not guilty', and there was to be a trial. Jorge would be needed to give evidence.

Carrie had told Pete he'd be too scared. "Let's face it," she'd said, "Naz will be out one day and Jorge has already grassed him up. You won't find Jorge if he doesn't want to be found."

Pete had argued that if Jorge was in fear of Naz, then it was in his own interests to get Naz put away. She understood the logic in that, but as she didn't know where Jorge was, there was nothing she could do about it. Jorge and a lot of other people were afraid of Naz. She was one of them.

Carrie had been clean for over a week now, and the mist was beginning to lift.

The rent and the gas and electric bills had been paid with the money from the pawn shops in Camford. The jewellers in Pennington-on-Sea would've bought the stuff, possibly given her more cash, but even her heroin-soaked mind knew most of the jewellery had been bought there, and might be recognised. For all she knew, her mum had been to the police.

There were three pawnbrokers in Camford, and she had sold a few pieces in each, not wanting to attract attention. The money was getting her life back on track, and now she was over the worst of the cold turkey.

Carrie still regarded herself as being an honest person. She was no good at shoplifting. She reasoned that her mother would rather she stole from her than steal from a shop.

The police car cruised on. It wasn't Pete.

She closed her eyes to the bright sunshine. Her mind drifted dreamily, her thoughts cosseted by the warm sun.

"Where is he, Carrie?" Her eyes opened wide in a terrified flash. At the opposite end of the bench, sitting sideways, staring with cold hatred, was Naz.

"W-w-what you doing here?" She tried to shrink away, instinctively making herself a smaller target for her enemy.

Naz slid along the bench; she could feel his breath on her face. "What I'm doing here, Miss Princess Carrie, is I'm asking you where my shitbag grassing brother Jorge is." His expression echoed the threat in his voice.

"I don't know, Naz. Honest, I don't. How…how

come—?"

"How come they let me out? That what you're trying to say?"

Carrie nodded, tears of fear welling up in her eyes.

Naz put his arm around her. "Think about it, Princess Carrie. What have they got on me? Nothing. That's what. They got nothing on me but the word of a jealous kid brother who's run away to some rat hole. When it comes to my trial the pigs will lose, you see if they don't. No evidence, see? Innocent 'til proved guilty and all that, and they ain't got evidence, so I got bail. Now, let me tell you what's gonna happen. We gonna hold hands like the good friends we are, and we're going to walk over to my car. Right?" With his free hand, he pulled something from his pocket. His eyes lowered, telling Carrie to look down. He held a syringe. "You see, Carrie, if you don't do like I say, you're gonna get this little present right in your princess body. This is real special stuff."

Carrie stood up and took his hand, and they walked to his car. Naz opened the passenger door and she got in. The car sped away with a squeal of tyres.

* * * *

The sea was flat, calm. The breeze had dropped and crystal-clear visibility gave a sharp edge to the horizon. Helen gazed at the scene. Tiny wavelets flopped lazily at the shore line. In the far distance, huge container ships dotted the Atlantic Sea, looking like toy boats on a village pond.

'Ping!' Two warm croissants, strawberry jam, fresh orange juice and cafetiere of fresh coffee. Bliss. Today was going to be a good day. She already felt better for being honest with James and Robert. The email she'd sent the night before had been more chatty. It would reassure them she was just fine, enjoying the break. She had promised to let them know if she moved, but for now was staying in Pennington-on-Sea. She wrote politely about how she was confident they could cope, and that she looked forward to hearing their news. She hadn't told them about her hair, of course, that had been a bit of a shock when she had gone into the bathroom. In her not-quite-awake state, she had forgotten about Kirstie's creation. For a split second she hadn't recognised herself.

She hadn't mentioned the matching bicycle either, or her new bonkers friend Gillian, or the other stuff like getting drunk, running out of water, and smoking dope. In fact, she hadn't told them very much at all, but she had told them the truth; all that other stuff was best forgotten. On a need-to-know basis, they didn't need to know, and while she may not have told them everything, she hadn't told any lies either. So why, oh why, did she still have this nagging elf sitting on her shoulder? Was it her conscience, like Pinnochio's Jiminy Cricket? Why should she feel guilty when she was doing all this for them? Something felt all wrong. On this beautiful morning, she sensed an elephant in the room, or rather an elephant in Goldilocks.

Helen thought about that for a while. 'Goldilocks and the Three Bears meet an Elephant.' Or, 'The Nagging Elf and the Elephant.' She smiled at the idiotic train of thought, and then frowned. *What's wrong? Why do I feel happy and sad at the same time?* She sighed and ate the croissants. The jam oozed out of the sides because she had put too much on them.

"Greedy cow," she said, wiping the jam from her fingers with a piece of kitchen roll.

The coffee was good. It washed down the sticky breakfast with its hotness and flavour. She stared out of the window for several minutes. Then, unbidden and unexpectedly, the reason for her mood became as clear as the Atlantic air before her. She hadn't thought about Phil for over twelve hours. Not since she'd made that stupid comment in Kirstie's Kutz about her and Gillian Halstead having husbands dropping dead of a heart attack. Then her dream came back to her, the part where Phil had said, 'Next stop, please,' and she had seen him getting out of Goldilocks.

She sat back, throwing herself into the curve of her chair, not knowing whether the feeling was good or bad.

"Does this mean I'm moving on? And do I really want to?"

Helen thought she'd done with grieving, but the impact of the elf and the elephant was frightening. The sun still shone, the wavelets insisted on lapping the shore, and the container ships continued on their chartered course. Nothing had changed, and yet the day was no longer a good one. It stretched before her like an infinite chore. She poured the last drops of coffee into her cup and sipped the not-quite-so-hot liquid. She thought of Gillian, and how she had been quick to decide Gillian's raw grief had manifested itself in hatred.

"Who am I to even have an opinion on anyone else when I have failed so miserably to recognise my own grief?" She looked at her watch. Ten o'clock. Gillian would be at Kirstie's Kutz. She suddenly felt lonely, very lonely. She was treading water. Passing the time from cradle to grave. Neither moving on nor going back. There *was* no going back, so what was happening to her? She'd tried to make things happen by setting off on her travels. *Am I really trying to make James and Robert independent? Or am I running away from something? I have two wonderful sons who need me, and I've walked out on them. What sort of a mother am I?*

The kettle on again, she refilled the cafetiere, recalling the day she had thought to travel in Valerie Drobshaw so she could be with Phil. Freddie Dixon's voice echoed in her head, 'G'mornin', Mrs McGuire.' She saw Valerie Drobshaw being taken away by that nice Leonard Bulmer. Then there was Bobby Billington, Tashy, Littletrees and the M5. Red wine and a hangover.

She had thought when she had thrown away Phil's photo that there had been 'closure', but it hadn't been the end of it. Throwing away the photo had been no more than a milestone, and not the end of the journey. This was the end of the journey. She felt sure, this time. The thing that really mattered, the deciding factor, was the image of Phil leaving Goldilocks and fading into the desert. *He* was saying good-bye to *her*. He had said 'next stop, please,' and had got off the bus.

* * * *

James and Robert sat opposite each other outside the Lock-Keepers. They'd come to discuss the emails, but neither of them spoke. They watched the swirling debris in the black water of the lock. Plastic bottles, carrier bags, driftwood and a twisted umbrella jostled together as the water rose. They watched the old wooden gates open and two narrow boats glide into the lock, skilfully positioned by their masters. The gates closed, great handles were turned at the lock side by willing volunteers and the water level dropped, rapidly and noisily. The boats descended into the stone abyss of Victorian engineering that was the lock.

"They're called paddles." Robert broke the silence as he put his glass down.

"What are?" James's tone hinted that Robert was ever so slightly mad.

"There are ground paddles and gate paddles, and when the handles are turned, the paddles open and let the water through. Brilliant. Simple and brilliant."

"Ri-ight." James nodded slowly.

"The ground paddles run from the upper level into the lock. The gate paddles are in the gates."

"How d'you know all that, then?" James had never given a thought as to how canal locks worked.

"An old guy told me once when I came down here as

a kid…but that's not why we came here, is it? And I'm sure you're not remotely interested."

"Right again." James took a long drink from his pint. He wanted to stand up and have a look at the lock, to see what Robert was rambling on about, but pride kept him in his seat. He'd agreed with Robert that he wasn't interested, so had to stay put. "What do you think of this email, then?"

"Not a lot, really, she's on the south coast and will let us know when she moves. She was cross about the tracker, and her ankle is getting better."

"I don't mean all that crap. I'm talking about the fact there was no mention of coming home, and this *'doing it for all our sakes'.* I still can't understand what she means by that."

Robert leaned back in his chair as James went to the bar, returning a few minutes later with two pints and two bags of crisps. He threw a bag at Robert. They sat in silence once again, the air filled with the general hum of conversation around them and the crunching of crisps. The narrow boats made their slow progress down the canal.

"Americans call them chips." James broke the silence this time.

"What?"

"Crisps."

"What do they call chips, then?" Robert actually sounded interested, much to James's amusement.

"Fries."

"Right. I never thought about it before." Robert sounded disappointed. "They sell fries at McDonalds."

"Yeah. I…well, I never thought about how the water gets from up there to down there." James pointed at the lock, his finger sweeping from the upper to lower level. "They don't just open the gates slowly, then?" He paused.

Robert didn't reply. He was probably too surprised by his brother's ignorance.

"But they're chips, thin chips, and anyway, they call them shoestring French fries, and McDonalds is American." James stuffed the empty crisp packet into his empty glass and drank from his second pint.

"So," Robert said, "when are we going to tell Mum we're both leaving home?"

"Dunno. I tried to tell her by email last night but it sounded all wrong, so I deleted it."

"You tried to tell her we were both going?"

"No. Just me," James said. "That was part of the problem. I might come across to you as a callous bastard, Robert, but even I realised this was a tricky one. When I read it through, it sounded like a 'Dear John' letter."

"So you haven't told her anything?"

"No. Maddie said I should speak to you first and that we ought to tell her face to face."

"Mmmm. That's what Jayne said."

"You've seen her again, then?"

"No. Just email."

"You say she works for Carleton's Bank?"

"Yes. I don't know exactly what she does. She sort of avoided the question. I reckon she must be quite high up. She's got a beautiful apartment by the river."

"Lucky you. I suppose that's your accommodation problem solved then." James grinned.

"Don't be daft. I've only met her once."

Robert's indignant tone amused him. "How many times a day does she email you?" He was teasing his brother now, and Robert blushed. "Lots, I bet. She's keen on you, Robert, isn't she? And you're blushing, so that means you like her more than a little bit."

"Shut up."

"I dare you to phone her."

"What, now?"

"Yes. Right now."

"She'll still be at work. They work all hours at head office."

"So?"

"I don't have her extension number."

"Just phone head office and ask for her. If she's so important, they'll know how to find her…go on."

"They won't put me through. Security. Someone can't just phone up and be put through, just like that."

"Give your name and say it's personal. Switchboard will ask her if she'll take the call, she'll say yes, and bingo! You're talking to Jayne."

"Who says I want to talk to her right now?"

"Course you do. You can tell her we've decided to go to Pennington-on-Sea. Tell her I'm going with Maddie, and you want her to come along as well, to meet everyone."

"Have we?"

"Have we what?"

"Have we decided to go to Pennington-on-Sea?"

"Well, I'm sure Maddie will be up for it. It was Jayne and Maddie's idea, wasn't it? Telling Mum face to face about leaving home and all that."

"When will we go?"

"Why don't you call the lovely Jayne and ask her when she's free?"

"Okay, I will. I'll do just that." Robert took out his phone and dialled. He waited. The tone rang twice. A female voice answered. "Carleton's Bank. Do you know which extension you require?"

"Jayne Manners, please. Sorry, I don't know her extension number."

"Robert? Is that you?" Jayne's voice asked.

"Y-yes. I didn't expect you to answer the phone."

"I can't take personal calls, Robert. I'll phone you tonight." She hung up. Robert pressed the red button on his phone, and then put it on the table before him, staring at it.

"What was all that, then?" James asked.

"I don't know…I mean, I don't get it."

"What's to get?" James took a large gulp of beer.

"Jayne answered the phone." Robert sounded incredulous, his face blank.

James spluttered beer down his shirt as he attempted to stifle a laugh. "Ah-ha!" He grinned. "Perhaps not so high up as you thought, brother dear."

"I just don't get it. It's weird. How does she afford that apartment? She was well known at the restaurant…and the hotel."

"So what did she say?"

"She's phoning me tonight."

"Well, not too long to wait, then. C'mon, let's go. We can microwave one of Mum's frozen dinners, if you like."

The brothers stood up and walked together along the tow path.

"I could check up on her on the police computer, if you like."

"Whatever for? What makes you think Jayne would be on the police computer?"

"She's not what you thought. That makes me suspicious. I can't help it. It goes with the job."

"Well, I'm not in the least suspicious. I'll speak with her tonight and ask about her coming to Pennington-on-Sea."

"And?"

"And nothing. I'm not going to say, 'I'd like you to meet my mum and, by the way, how do you pay for that apartment?'"

"Okay, okay, I take your point." They walked on in silence.

Robert looked at his watch, trying to work out how long it would be before Jayne phoned.

* * * *

Jayne stood before the window watching the River Thames flow by. The timeless river with its variety of boats and cargoes had fascinated her when she had first moved in. Inevitably, the novelty had quickly faded, like a new picture on the wall, carefully chosen, but disappearing into the background in a matter of days. Her eyes focused on the rectangular sections of river, segregated by the famous London bridges. They saw it all, but her mind was elsewhere. She'd told Robert she'd phone him that evening, and it was nine o'clock already. She wanted to talk to him, oh yes, she'd love to hear his voice, and yet she was apprehensive. He'd be disappointed that she was just a telephonist, and their relationship would be finished before it really started.

What was wrong with her? Why hadn't she told him straight away? It had seemed such a good idea to have a bit of fun. Internet dating with no strings attached, no personal details, and no long-term plans or talk of the future. The trouble was she liked Robert, and didn't want to lose him. She'd pretended to be independent, both emotionally and financially, whereas in fact she was neither of those things. Robert had thought her unattainable, probably still did. How wrong was that?

She turned away from the window and sat on the sofa, her phone on the coffee table before her. She couldn't be in love with Robert, not yet. It was mad, she'd only met him once, but even in the hotel, when he'd fallen into that plant, she'd felt drawn to him. More than anything, she wanted to see him again. She argued with herself that she hadn't lied to him. But what she had done was create a false impression. She wanted him to like her for what she was, but he didn't know what she was, though even that wasn't strictly true, not now. He knew now that she was a telephonist. Daddy had been right when he had said, *'People judge by what they see, for they can do no other.'*

Jayne wished she hadn't shown Robert her apartment, and she wished they'd gone to a restaurant where she wasn't known. She wished she hadn't recommended 'The White Dolphin Hotel', but rather some anonymous place where no one knew her. She put herself in Robert's shoes and knew he would have concluded, with good reason, that she was really clever and had a brilliant job at Carleton's.

She picked up her phone and dialled his number.

He answered immediately. "Jayne. I was afraid you weren't going to call."

"I'm sorry, Robert. I would've called earlier, but I only just got home."

"Is something wrong?"

"N-no." She paused, not knowing what to say. "I thought maybe you were disappointed."

"In what? Why might I be disappointed to hear your voice?"

"I'm just a telephonist, Robert." There was another pause. Jayne was afraid he would accuse her of being a liar, or at least of deceiving him, somehow.

"Jayne, I phoned to ask if you would like to join me and my brother and his girlfriend on a trip to the south coast this weekend. You know you said we should talk to Mum face to face about leaving home, and Maddie—she's James's girlfriend—she said the same." His words came tumbling out, as if they were in a race. "Will you come, Jayne? Will you? Please say 'yes'."

Jayne felt rising bubbles of excitement inside her. Robert still wanted to see her again, even though he knew about her lowly position at the bank. He didn't seem to care. "I'd love to. Are you sure? I mean…"

"There's nothing I'd like better…" His voice trailed off.

"If you remember, I was willing to go with you to Llandudno before your Mum moved on."

"Yes, I know. I'll never forget going to that caravan site. Hopefully, she'll still be at Pennington-on-Sea when we get there."

"I was wondering where she was. I've been to

Pennington-on-Sea loads of times. It's lovely down there."

"You can show us around, then." His high-pitched laugh was somewhere between nervous and happy. "What about this weekend? I'll have to check it with James and Maddie."

"That's fine by me, and if James and Maddie can't make it, there's nothing to stop you and me going, Robert." Jayne paused for a moment, afraid she had been too pushy. "I'll check out some B&Bs, if you like."

"Y-yes. Yes, please. I'll speak with James and get back to you."

"Speak soon, then."

"Bye, Jayne." He hung up.

Jayne laughed out loud with happiness.

* * * *

Robert leapt down the stairs, two at a time, and gave James the good news.

"So you arranged it all, just like that. You know me and Maddie have to work shifts. We can't just take a weekend at short notice. We're not all nine-to-fivers, you know, Robert."

"I'm fully aware of that, James, and as a matter of fact, no, I didn't. I said I would have to check it out with you and Maddie, though I have to say, if it had been the other way around, you would have assumed the right to make decisions for *me.*"

"Sorr-eee!"

"Just for once, James, it would be nice if you could be happy for me, you smart-arsed pillock." Robert grabbed his jacket from the hooks by the back door.

"I said I'm sorry."

"I heard you." Robert wasn't exactly shouting, but his voice was raised and quivering with anger. A few moments ago he'd been so happy, chatting with Jayne, now, after a brief conversation with James, he was in a foul temper. "You think you can say whatever you want to me. Then you just have to say 'sorry' and everything's all right again. Well, it isn't. You're not a little boy hiding behind Mum anymore. It's time you learned some social skills. In particular, it's time you stopped thinking the world revolves around you. You're a sanctimonious bastard, James. You should listen to yourself sometimes. When Mum was here, you just took her for granted." He pointed his finger, jabbing the air between them. "You never let her know when you would be home, just breezing in and out. I suppose you'll do some laundry when you run out of clothes, or will you just go and buy some more?" Robert's face turned from pink to red. A vein pulsed in his left temple. He put his jacket on, throwing his arms into the sleeves. "I'm sick of it. I'm sick of you, and I'm sick with worry about Mum."

"Wow."

"Is that it? Is that all you can say? Wow."

"Well, you told me not to say sorry."

"So they're your only options, are they? 'Wow', or 'sorry'?"

"No, 'course not."

"Fuck off, James." Robert slammed the door behind him as he went out.

James slumped down in a chair. He'd never heard Robert say 'fuck'. He picked up his phone and sent a text to Maddie: *'wot yr shifts wkend?'* She replied almost immediately. *'none not due back til tues wot yrs?'* James hadn't expected her to be free all weekend. He was to work Friday night through until ten on Saturday morning. If Maddie drove, he could sleep in the car down to Pennington-on-Sea.

His argument with Robert had been completely unnecessary. He had no idea why his brother had gone off on one like that. This Jayne was having a weird effect on him.

He replied to Maddie: *U up 4 Pen-on-c sat/sun?*

Again, she replied almost immediately. *Yes. gd.*

There was no way he wanted to stay in a B&B with Robert and the mysterious Jayne. He googled hotels in Pennington-on-Sea, and booked a double room at 'The Turning House Hotel' for Saturday night, then dialled Maddie's number. He wanted to talk to her.

* * * *

Robert walked quickly down Jumbles Lane, past Freddie Dixon's garage and onto the tow path. His pace slackened, his bad mood dissipating with each footstep. He walked on past the 'Lock-Keepers'. The path was lit by streetlights from the adjacent road, and by the lamps of narrow boats moored up for the night.

His thoughts were with Jayne. He cursed himself for telling James he thought she had a well-paid job, and for telling him about her apartment. There had to be a perfectly logical explanation. Why had he jumped to conclusions? Maybe he had even been showing off a bit. It didn't matter to him whether she was rich or poor. No doubt she'd tell him more about herself at the weekend. He grinned. He'd enjoyed telling James what he thought of him. That had been a long time coming, and James deserved every word of it. No regrets there.

"Pillock," Robert said aloud, then realised he was within earshot of a couple sitting at the back of their narrow boat. "Sorry," he called, "not you." He walked on a few paces, and then remembered the canal took a curve into woodland, away from the road and the lights. He turned back. The couple had shut the door at the back of their boat and had drawn the curtains. No doubt, Robert thought, to protect themselves from weird guys swearing to themselves.

He felt unsettled. His life was spiralling out of

control. Everything had gone wrong since Mum had left. No, he corrected himself. That wasn't true. Everything had changed. He had Jayne in his life now, and already he couldn't contemplate life without her.

His pace quickened as he passed the Lock-Keepers, deciding against any more beer. Tomorrow, he'd call at the golf club and fire off a few practice shots before going home. If he was going to Pennington-on-Sea at the weekend, there would be no chance of a game. As he headed up Jumbles Lane, he wondered if Jayne played golf.

As the driveway of number fourteen came into view, he was pleased to see James's car was not there.

* * * *

James could have sent Maddie a text about the hotel, but he was bursting to tell her about his big brother's tantrum. He giggled as he told her about it, and about Jayne answering the phone at Carleton's.

"You should've seen him, Maddie, all red in the face. I've never seen him in such a temper. I guess he's missing his mummy."

"And all this because he was trying to fix up some accommodation at the weekend?"

James didn't reply. He'd expected Maddie to share the joke.

"There was no need for it, no need at all. Don't you see?"

"Yeah, you're right." He stopped laughing. "You don't think it's funny, then?"

"No."

"Well, you don't know Robert like I do. Him and his mysterious girlfriend. I bet she's ugly, or fat, or both."

"James, have you any idea how childish you sound?"

Ten minutes later, James set the running machine in the gym two paces faster than his usual speed. After twenty minutes, he slowed the pace, sweat soaking his T-shirt. The effort had done nothing to improve his temper.

He switched off his iPod. Even his favourite tracks annoyed him, and he hadn't a clue why Maddie had been so mad with him. He knew he had been teasing Robert, but she had gone on like it was some major thing. He'd make it up to her at the weekend. She'd like 'The Turning House Hotel'. It would be worth the cost.

The thought of sharing a table with Robert and Jayne in some silent little dining room in a B&B overlooking the sea front made him wince. The sort of place where people say 'good morning' to the strangers at the next table, then sit in silence, the uncomfortable air filled with the sound of rattling cutlery and crockery, and of not enough butter being scraped across cold toast.

CHAPTER FIFTEEN

Helen cleared away her breakfast and washed up. She swept the carpet, made her bed and cleaned the little bathroom. When she was near the mirror her bright pink hair caught her eye. It would take time to get used to it. She peered forward in the mirror to check if her eyebrows needed plucking. She could always go back to Kirstie and say she'd changed her mind about the pink bit, or she could go to a chemist and buy a bottle of something.

Goldilocks was spick and span in no time, so she put her duster and polish away.

"That's better. Better than cleaning a whole bloody house. I think a long bike ride would do you good today, Helen, but first of all, check your emails to see if either of those two sons of yours has replied."

Lifting her laptop out of the cupboard, she jumped when a knock came on the door, and she bumped her head on the cupboard.

"Shit!" Helen rubbed her head as she opened the door.

Gillian Halstead stood in the doorway.

"Oh, it's you." She was aware her tone was less than welcoming. "I thought you were at Kirstie's Kutz this morning."

"Can I come in?" Gillian's voice was no more than a whisper.

Alarm bells rang in Helen's head. Something about Gillian's demeanour told her something was wrong, badly wrong. Helen had a gut feeling she didn't want to be involved in whatever it was that had made Gillian miss her hair appointment. She inhaled and exhaled loudly, and then stood to one side to allow her unwelcome visitor to step inside.

She closed the cupboard door, making a mental note to check her emails as soon as she could get rid of Gillian.

"What happened to your hair?" Gillian's voice was still quiet.

Helen found it impossible to look her in the eye. "Great, don't you think?" She patted the top of her head. "I asked Kirstie to brighten me up a bit, and she certainly did that." Helen's voice trailed off as Gillian put her head in her hands and burst into tears. Helen was bemused. Only then did she notice Gillian was still wearing the yellow T-shirt she had worn the previous day, and still had the yellow bum bag around her waist.

"What is it, Gillian? Whatever's happened?" She put her arm on the other woman's shoulder. "Would you like a cup of tea…or a coffee?"

Gillian cried and cried for what seemed like an eternity. As the kettle started its rumbling noise, Gillian took a tissue from the box Helen had put on the table and wiped her eyes.

"I'm sorry, Helen. I shouldn't have come, but I didn't know who else to turn to."

Helen didn't know what to say. Surely, Gillian must have loads of friends, people she could talk to. They'd only met yesterday for the first time, and Gillian had lived here all her life.

The kettle boiled and she made two coffees. Gillian stared out of the window, dabbing the now silent tears from her blotchy, swollen face.

Fear struck Helen. "Is this to do with all that cash in the safety deposit box? We'll be on the CCTV at the bank. I don't know what my sons will say if I'm an accessory to a fraud." She sipped the coffee she didn't really want.

Gillian sipped hers. "It's Caroline, my daughter," Gillian whispered.

Helen sighed. Gillian probably thought it was an

expression of sympathy, when in reality it was a sigh of relief that the tears were nothing to do with all that cash.

"What about her?"

"She's in hospital." Gillian took another sip of her coffee. "Thank you."

"For what?"

"For letting me in…and for the coffee."

"What's the matter with Caroline?"

Gillian continued to stare out of the window.

Helen lowered her voice to a whisper. "Was it an overdose?"

Gillian shook her head. "Not exactly. The police aren't sure. The doctors are running lots of tests."

"Have you spoken to her? What does Caroline say?"

"She's unconscious." Gillian's words hung in the air. "In intensive care. The police rang me yesterday, soon after you left. I've been at the hospital all night. They told me to go home and get some rest."

Helen leaned back. She looked down at her thumbs as they turned in circles around each other, with her fingers linked together. All selfish thoughts disappeared as she tried, without success, to imagine what this woman must be going through. The police must have called when she was dozing in the chair at Kirstie's Kutz.

"What time did they call you?"

"About quarter to five."

"Where was she?"

"Down on the front, in the shelter, you know, where I met you yesterday…why?"

"Oh, it's nothing. Just that I heard an ambulance go by. I'd nodded off as Kirstie was doing my hair, and a siren woke me up."

They sat in silence for a while, each deep in thought. Eventually, Gillian spoke. "I didn't want to leave the hospital. I wanted to stay with her, just looking at her, you know? Talking to her. I'll go back now. Thanks for the coffee."

"No, please. Stay a while. You've got your mobile with you, haven't you?"

Gillian nodded.

"And the hospital have your number?"

"Yes, of course."

"I think you'd better have a bite to eat and tell me all about it. Right from the beginning." Helen meant it. Deep inside, she truly meant it. Only a short while ago she had resented Gillian's presence, and now she wanted her to stay, to feel welcome.

"You're very kind, but I couldn't eat a thing."

"Well, I'll get some ginger biscuits out and you can nibble if you want." She made fresh coffee.

Gillian took a tiny bite from a biscuit and began to tell Helen all about Caroline, about her being an only child, the apple of her eye. She spoke with pride of her GCSE successes, smiling at the memory, and then her face clouded as she told how Keith had put pressure on her to take "A" levels. "She wanted to leave school, you see, and they argued about it all the time. Caroline rebelled, and started staying out late. The police brought her home once, unable to stand up, she was so drunk. Her father went mad. Said she would ruin his reputation. Soon after that, she met Jono and left home. I think— that's to say I'm sure—it was Jono who introduced her to the drugs."

"And where is this Jono now?"

"Dead. I hoped she'd come home after he died. Then I hoped she'd come home when Keith died."

"But she didn't?"

"No. Well, yes, actually, she did. She came home on the day of Keith's funeral, when she knew I'd be out. I'd left a note at the house where she and Jono were living together, telling her where I had left a key, and that she was welcome to come home any time she wanted." Gillian looked up, and the two women looked each other in the eye. "That was when she took my jewellery."

Helen's jaw dropped with an involuntary intake of breath. She thought of the sentimental value of the jewellery Phil had bought for her, and she thought of Robert and James.

"She did what? Did you tell the police?"

"No. No, of course not. I don't care about the jewellery. I would never have worn it again. Keith bought it all, you see. It's knowing she sold it to buy heroin that worries me so."

"Did you not think, Gillian, that if you'd involved the police, it might have brought her to her senses? How many times do you want to be kicked?"

"I know, I know. Maybe you're right. It's all water under the bridge now, anyway. I just had to keep the door open in every way. She's my daughter."

"I'm sorry, Gillian, I didn't mean to criticise. Who knows what any of us would do under the same circumstances?" Helen thought of Robert and James, and how lucky she was. She thought how she had wanted them to leave home. The unavoidable comparisons flooded in. Gillian wanted her daughter back and was glad her husband was dead, whereas she had only just accepted the finality of Phil's death, and wanted her boys to leave home. It was all very sobering. "What do you mean when you say it's all water under the bridge?"

"Her condition is critical. She's been badly beaten up. I could hardly recognise her. Her face is all bruised and swollen." Gillian's voice returned to a whisper. "If she survives this, and it is an 'if', she may be brain damaged."

Helen couldn't speak for several moments, but when she did, she whispered, too. "When will you know?"

Gillian shrugged. "They can't tell me. But at least Keith's dead, so it could be worse."

"Would he have been upset?"

"I don't know, and I don't care, but he would have tried to stop me seeing her. You see, the difference between you and me is that your husband's death was a nasty shock, and mine was a pleasant surprise. Keith was a little fish in a little pond who thought he was a big fish in a big pond, him and his precious, all-important reputation. He would have failed to keep me away, of course, and wild horses won't keep me from seeing her now. They know me at the hospital. I used to be a volunteer there. They're all very kind."

"Would you like me to go with you? To see Caroline?"

"I have to go home and get changed." Gillian stood up quickly, as if she had just remembered something. "Thanks for listening. See you later." She opened the door and was gone, waving from her car window as she drove off.

Helen stood on Goldilocks's step and watched until the car disappeared from view down the 'Ten Acres' concrete avenue. She washed and dried the two coffee mugs slowly, thinking of all Gillian had said. She tried to put herself in her situation, to walk around in her shoes, but found it impossible. Pennington-on-Sea was not what it seemed, but was it any different to anywhere else?

"Probably not, bad stuff happens everywhere." She wasn't in the mood to check her emails any more. Robert and James could wait. Nothing either of them could say would compare to Gillian's story. They would phone her in an emergency, and they hadn't phoned. She needed some fresh air. A rush of guilt swept over her again. Why did she feel guilty whenever she thought of her boys? They were good sons. They hadn't stolen from her as Caroline had stolen from Gillian. They both had good jobs. She had no reason not to love her sons, and she did love them dearly. "Of course I do. So why am I here in Pennington-on-Sea?"

Unable to answer her own question, Helen went outside and pulled her bicycle out of the garage. Ten minutes later, she was pedalling along a country lane. She twisted the grips on the handlebars, taking her through the gears as she cycled up and down the hills. With no pavements, just grassy banks and high hedges, any potential view was blocked from sight. She dismounted and walked up a particularly steep hill.

A seat at the top bore a small plaque that read: *In memory of Sidney Banderby, 1920 to 2008. He loved this place.*

Helen propped her bicycle against the hedge and sat down by a gap in the hedgerow, opposite the seat.

"Well, Sidney Banderby, you had a point."

Sitting back, she admired the view, her mind wandering over the rolling Devonshire countryside spread out before her, the epitome of England. She screwed up her eyes to focus on the distant hills of Dartmoor. The dark hills frowned on the farmland at their feet. The hills had their freedom, they would not allow change, and they would not be manipulated to do the bidding of the farmer. They said, *'here I am, and here I stay. I'll let you walk on me, but you will never change me'.* The hills were, she thought, just as Sidney Banderby had seen them, and if legend were based in any fact, as King Arthur had seen them. In all probability, she mused, even the dinosaurs had seen them.

Her eyes moved away from the hills. About half a mile away, a herd of Friesian cattle stood noisily near a gate. Mature trees dotted the fields, providing the cattle with shade from the sun and shelter from the rain.

Helen twirled her right ankle in circles. The exercise had become a habit. She looked down at her foot. It hardly hurt at all.

A farmer opened the gate, and the cows filed lazily along the road towards the farm at the bottom of the hill. A collie dog tried to hurry them, but the cows had their own pace. When the last of the herd were in the farmyard and the farmer closed the gate, Helen set off again, freewheeling down the hill, gathering speed. The wind in her face felt good, the fresh air was just what she needed to blow away her deep thoughts, and maybe blow away a bit of reality, too.

Helen congratulated herself on buying a bicycle. This was fun...and then she came to the gate which had, until recently, held back the cows. From there onwards, the lane was covered in cow pats of varying size and wetness. The air was no longer fresh, and she hit the shit at speed. Applying the brakes, the bicycle skidded to a stop. Her trainers were in it, too, and her wheels. She cursed the cows, the countryside and everything that went with it. As far as she was concerned, right now, milk came out of plastic bottles.

Helen turned her bicycle round and pushed it back up the hill. She would have to go back to 'Ten Acres' and clean herself up. As she passed the seat, she thought how Sidney Banderby would have laughed at her, and she laughed with him.

The bicycle and trainers were cleaned first, and then she took a shower. Even a generous dose of perfume could not disguise the smell of the countryside that still hung around. In the end, Helen concluded that the smell was up her nose and in her imagination. There was no one to ask, "Do I smell of cow shit?"

Her thoughts returned to Gillian and her daughter. Now, that was a different sort of shit altogether. Gillian was in the metaphorical stuff.

With a deep sigh, she set off for the hospital. It was no good, she had to go.

She followed the signs to 'Intensive Care', taking the lift to the third floor. She smiled at a policeman sitting on an uncomfortable looking plastic chair beside a door marked 'I.C.U.' and pressed the buzzer. He smiled back. A cheerful, female voice crackled through a small speaker.

"Who do you want to see?"

Helen put her face close to the speaker. "Caroline Halstead. I'm a friend of her mother." The policeman stood up and stepped towards her. "And who are you?" he demanded.

She found his manner intimidating. "My name is Helen McGuire," her voiced trailed to a whisper.

The policeman spoke into his radio. "She has a visitor." The door opened, and Gillian stood there, beckoning Helen to follow her into the Intensive Care Unit. She didn't look as if she'd had any sleep.

"What's it all about, Gillian? Why is there a policeman at the door? Is it to do with Caroline? What's she done?"

Helen became aware that her voice sounded far too loud in the hushed atmosphere of the ward. Life hung in the balance there. Everyday noises were replaced by the bleeping of machines.

Gillian tipped her head to one side, indicating to Helen to follow her. They went into a small sitting room where low chairs in a soothing shade of lilac surrounded a small table. A vase of artificial flowers fought for space with worn magazines on the windowsill. Gillian went to the hot drinks machine in one corner of the room, made two coffees, put one down in front of Helen and sat down before she spoke.

"She hasn't done anything."

"Then why—?"

"Why the policeman?" Gillian interrupted.

Helen nodded.

"They think whoever did this thought they had killed her, and might try again." Gillian stirred her coffee as she spoke.

Helen's hand flew involuntarily to her mouth, and her eyes widened at the shock of Gillian's words.

"They want to speak with her as soon as possible, but the doctor says that won't be for a few days. She's heavily sedated."

"Why would anyone want to kill her?"

"They haven't said much about that. Only that they

have a suspect and are looking for him."

Helen stood up and went to the window. The hospital car park spread out three floors below. She could see her bicycle, all pink and black and conspicuous, chained to the bars near the main entrance. A large sign with the words 'Welcome to Pennington-on-Sea General Hospital' stood next to it. The words struck her as odd. No one wanted to be here, welcome or not. If you were here, either you were ill or you knew someone who was.

"Can I see her?"

"Yes, of course you can." They left the coffees on the table, and Helen followed Gillian out of the dull little room. "We're lucky to have this ward, or this hospital, even. They talk about closing it and everyone having to go to Camford."

There were three beds, all occupied. Helen had never been in an intensive care unit before, and wasn't prepared for what she saw: patients wired up to banks of complicated equipment, machines bleeping and monitors flickering as nurses checked and rechecked their patients.

Gillian stood to the side of Caroline's bed and spoke to her softly. "This is my good friend Helen, Caroline. You'll like Helen, she's very kind and understanding and a good listener. I should know because I've told her all about us, and she listened to it all." She held her daughter's hand, gently stroking it with her thumb as she spoke.

Helen was quite shaken by the extent of Caroline's injuries. Her face and arms were indeed badly bruised and swollen. Her head had been shaved at one side, and a long gash stitched. Congealed blood stuck to the threads in her distended scalp. Her swollen eyelids remained closed. Her hair had been bleached blonde a long time ago. Straw-like rats' tails lay on the other side of her pillow. She looked so vulnerable, her life dependent on the equipment surrounding her.

"Can she hear you?" Helen whispered.

"I don't know, but the nurses say it's a good idea to talk to her because she might be able to."

Helen looked around the room.

Gillian inclined her head towards the man in the next bed. "He came off his motorbike, and the man over there had a brain haemorrhage."

Helen nodded. The machines bleeped. "What does all this equipment actually do?"

"Monitors, mostly. This one measures the pressure in her veins. C.V.P., central venous pressure. Deep vein thrombosis is a concern because of her drug use. This one is E.C.G., electrocardiogram. Look." Gillian pointed to the scars on Caroline's arms. Helen was taken aback by the ugly, irrefutable evidence of the girl's heroin addiction.

"What's that little clip on her finger for?"

"Oh, that. Yes. I think it measures the oxygen in her blood. I've no idea how it works, or any of it for that matter. She has broken ribs and there's damage to her spleen. Then there's the question of brain damage. All they say is that time will tell." Gillian smiled at her daughter. "Come on, Caroline. You can make it, my lovely girl. Your face will be all pretty again soon, and I'll see your gorgeous blue eyes. I'll be right here when you open them, yes I will."

They returned to the sitting room and the cold coffee.

"Can I bring anything in for you?" Helen asked.

"No, but thank you. Maybe tomorrow they'll reduce the sedatives. I must be here when she comes round. I simply must. It's very kind of you to come. I meant every word I said to Caroline, you know."

Helen looked down at her trainers, embarrassed by the compliment. She noticed a brown mark on one of the laces.

"Do I smell of cow shit?"

Gillian smiled for the first time in two days. "Oh,

Helen, you are a tonic, and no, you smell of perfume, not shit of any sort. Whatever are you talking about?"

"Good. I mean I'm glad I'm a tonic to you, because if anyone needs one right now, it's you. And I'm glad about the other, as I had an unfortunate encounter this morning after you left. I'll tell you about it sometime. Right now, I think you want to get back to Caroline. Give her my love. I'll come again tomorrow, if that's okay with you."

"Of course." Gillian nodded. "I'll be here. I expect they'll tell me to go home at night, and I suppose they're right, but I find it hard to leave her."

Helen rummaged about in her bag and found a scrap of paper and a pen. She scribbled her phone number down and gave it to Gillian.

"Here. Call me any time."

Gillian smiled and shook her head.

Helen looked up and waved as she set off, her pink and black hair with matching bicycle making an unmistakable sight.

CHAPTER SIXTEEN

The emails were mostly to do with the house in Jumbles Lane. Gas and electricity accounts, council tax and so on. She dealt with them first, so she could relax and read the ones from Robert and James. There was another address in her inbox. 'tashyd@hotmail.com'. "Now, what is it you have to say, Tashy, dear?" She opened it. Robert and James could wait a bit longer.

Hi Helen.

I hope you are enjoying your travels. Are you anywhere near Scarborough? I'd like to see you if you are. My Mum is very ill. She has cancer and is in hospital and it's really not fair. I can't talk to my mates about it, they don't understand, they just say stupid things like, 'Oh my God', and my dad doesn't know what to say. He's hopeless. Fiona and baby Alex are fine, and I'm trying to be OK, and they think I'm OK but I'm not. Mum's having treatment and all her hair will fall out soon. They say she won't die but if you saw her you wouldn't believe them. I'm scared she will die and they're just saying that she won't, to try to keep it from me. I'm sorry to go on like this. Just typing it has helped a bit. I hope you don't mind.

Your friend,

Tashy.

Helen rested her elbows on the table, her chin in her hands, reading it again. Her reply would have to be worded carefully. She opened the next email.

Hi Mum,

I expect you're having a wonderful time. I checked the weather in Devon, it looks good, if a bit windy. What are your neighbours like? You can tell me in person at the weekend, I'm coming down Friday evening and bringing my girlfriend with me. We'll be staying at the 'Blue Seas' bed and breakfast. Jayne has booked it.

See you soon,

With love, Robert.

Helen grinned. *Robert was coming and bringing his girlfriend.*

The next was from James.

Hi Mum,

Hope everything is OK with you and your travels. Will you still be in Pennington-on-Sea at the weekend? Maddie and I can come down Saturday morning if you're around. I've booked 'The Turning House Hotel'. We have some news for you.

Looking forward to hearing what you've been up to.

James.

So James had a girlfriend too. Helen's grin got wider. James had some news. Was he getting married? That would mean he was leaving home. Was Maddie having a baby? That would be even better news.

She wondered what these girlfriends were like. Robert had told her about the cyber girlfriend, and Helen was pretty sure he had said she was called Jayne, so this must be her. The date in London must've gone well. The boys and their girlfriends were staying in separate places, which could mean that each didn't know the other was coming, or maybe they had fallen out over it. Or maybe decided they wanted their own space with their own girlfriends. Maybe the girls had met and didn't get on. Today was Wednesday. Robert would be here the day after tomorrow, and James the morning after.

She typed her replies quickly.

Hello Robert,

I'm looking forward to seeing you and meeting Jayne. I'm on plot three-two-six, Ten Acres caravan site. I haven't met any of the neighbours here yet.

Love, Mum.

Hello James,

I'm looking forward to seeing you and meeting Maddie, and hearing your news. I'll still be here at the weekend, plot three-two-six, Ten Acres caravan site. See you Saturday,

Love, Mum.

She made herself a sandwich and a cup of tea before attempting to reply to Tashy. The *'Hello Tashy'* bit was easy. She leaned back in her chair and considered how to allay the girl's fears when, for all she knew, Tashy was right, and her Mum was going to die. She brushed breadcrumbs from her blouse. Some of them landed in the laptop's keyboard, and she blew on it to dislodge them. Tashy hadn't told her where the cancer was, and Helen didn't want to ask. Tashy would tell her in her own time, if she wanted to.

It took over half an hour for Helen to write, delete, and cut and paste her email, before she was satisfied it was as good as it was going to get.

Hello Tashy,

It's good to hear from you, but I'm sorry to hear your mum is in hospital. I'm in Devon at the moment, so nowhere near Scarborough, I'm afraid. You should listen to what the doctors say. I'm sure they won't lie, and cancer is very treatable these days, even though the treatment can have horrid side effects. Perhaps you could make a list of questions for the doctors and take it with you when you go to see your mum.

People always find it difficult to know what to say. I'm sure your friends are good friends. Sometimes you will want to talk about it, and sometimes you won't. That's how it usually works, and I'm sure your friends will listen. I'm happy for you to email or text me as much as you want.

My sons and their girlfriends are coming to visit me at the weekend, so I'm looking forward to that.

Lovely to hear from you. If I decide to travel up your way, I will let you know.

Your friend, Helen.

It all sounded rather wishy washy, but she sent it anyway, and hoped for a reply.

* * * *

Helen lay awake for hours that night. At two o'clock,

she got up and made herself a drink of hot milk, and ate the remaining ginger biscuits. The image of Caroline's bruised and battered face wouldn't go away. She marvelled at Gillian, a woman whom she had originally thought was bonkers, and whom she now respected for her calm devotion to her daughter. What if Robert or James had rebelled as Caroline had? She couldn't imagine that she would have been able to cope.

From Gillian and Caroline, her tortured thoughts switched to Tashy. Poor girl. She was clearly worried sick about her mum. Perhaps she should go to see her after the weekend. Perhaps not. In the end, Helen decided to wait and see if Tashy replied to her email. She went to the bathroom and looked in the mirror, running her fingers through her hair. The shocking pink wasn't quite such a shock any more, and she wondered whether or not to forewarn Robert and James.

"Whatever will their girlfriends make of me?" She smiled, and decided to keep it as a surprise. It would give them something to talk about.

At four o'clock, she went back to bed and fell into a deep sleep.

* * * *

Pete Levens was in the driver's seat when the call came through. Dan switched on the blue flashing lights, and Pete put his foot to the floor. At seven-fifteen in the morning, the roads of Pennington-on-Sea were quiet. There was no need for a siren. Pete parked on a slipway, and the two policemen ran towards a small group of people gathered near the high water mark.

"Okay, everyone," Dan said, "please stand back." His arms outstretched to herd the little crowd away. "Who discovered the body?" A man in a T-shirt and jogging shorts stepped forward, a little brown and white terrier at his feet. Pete crouched next to the body. It was face down with seaweed draped over the legs and torso. More police cars and an ambulance arrived on the slipway and, within moments, a young female police officer was pushing poles into the sand and tying police tape around them to section off the immediate area.

"Did anyone else see anything?" A negative murmur and shaking of heads rippled through the crowd. "Okay, we'll need all your names and addresses, and may need to speak with you." Dan beckoned to the jogger. "We'll definitely need a statement from you, sir."

The crowd moved off towards the slipway. Pete turned the body over. Jorge Sadler's bloated face couldn't stare at him because his eyes had been eaten by some sea creature after an easy meal. Pete felt bile rise in his gut and briefly tasted the cornflakes he had eaten an hour earlier.

A tent was erected over the body, and a doctor declared him dead. Forensic officers did their work, and Jorge was taken to the hospital for a post mortem. Pete knew the investigation would take time, and that everything had to be done according to procedure, but he and all the other officers on the beach were convinced this was Naz's work. Naz thought he'd killed Carrie, and now he'd killed Jorge. Naz had to be found.

His hands formed into clenched fists. This was sleepy little Pennington-on-Sea, for God's sake. Jorge's statement had effectively closed Naz's businesses down. Warrants had been issued to search addresses in Camford, Plymouth and Exeter. Jorge's information had been good. Three brothels had been raided and closed. Some of the girls were in a bad way, and little more than slaves, working for the heroin supplied by Naz. The whole thing was mushrooming into a major investigation. A good score. The man should never have been released, but there was no going back, no point thinking about that.

"P.C. Levens."

Pete looked up to see his sergeant beckoning him towards the slipway. He walked over and sat beside him in the car.

"I know you took an interest in Caroline Halstead."

"Any news?" Pete feared the worst. The sergeant shook his head.

"No change, but just before we got the call to come here, the hospital sent over the test results."

"And?"

"Medic speak says there is 'evidence of sexual activity'. But put that with the beating she got, I'm thinking rape. The toxicology report backs it up."

"How?" Pete asked. He wanted to know the exact details.

"There was Rohypnol in her blood, but no opiates or benzodiazepines."

"She was raped, then." Pete let out a quiet, long, slow whistle. "Rohypnol. That's the date rape drug, isn't it?"

"Yes. They have a good DNA sample. Whoever did this wasn't careful."

"We know who did it. We've just got to find the bastard. How's her mother taking it?"

"She's upset. What else could she be? Her daughter's been beaten within an inch of her life, which she may lose, brain damage can't be ruled out, and she could be pregnant. Then there's the question of HIV. The only good news is that Carrie, or Caroline, seemed to have been getting herself off the heroin."

* * * *

Helen opened her laptop. No emails. She shut it down again. *Maybe the boys wouldn't reply, just turn up at the weekend.* With her elbows on the table, she cupped her chin in her hands, and her mind started to wander.

If Tashy was fifteen, her mum was probably in her

late thirties. Something like that. Unless there's been a personal experience, you assume only people older than yourself will die before you. Young people, say under twenty, like Tashy, think that only really old people die. Tashy wanted answers, but there probably were none, not absolute, definitive answers, and for Tashy no other sort was an answer at all.

Helen started to make a shopping list.

Coffee, sugar, tea, milk, bread.

There was no way they could all comfortably be seated in Goldilocks, and anyway she couldn't be bothered cooking. They would eat out. There were plenty of cafes and restaurants in Pennington-on-Sea to choose from.

Helen ran her fingers under the waistband of her trousers. She had to admit they were a bit tight, even when she sat up straight. Sighing in resignation, she looked out at the endless seas. Her attention was taken by flashing blue lights near the beach. Several police cars and an ambulance were on the slipway, and a small tent had been erected on the sand. The pavement was packed with people near the shelter where she had met Gillian.

She went outside and stood on tiptoe for a better view, but it was impossible to make out what was going on from that distance.

"Looks like bad news for someone," she said to herself as she went back inside.

"What did you say?"

She turned quickly to see Gillian.

"Oh, hello. Sorry. I was talking to myself again. I keep telling myself I must stop it." Helen giggled at her own joke. Gillian looked back at her with a blank expression. "Never mind. Come in. I was just saying it looks like bad news down on the beach."

"I just walked past that way. They say there's a body been washed up."

"You not in your car?"

"No. I fancied a walk. I feel so stiff with all the sitting."

"Fancy a cuppa? What news of Caroline?"

"The doctors say they will reduce the sedatives soon, not today, though. Maybe tomorrow." Gillian paused and took a deep breath, but said no more.

"That's good news, isn't it?"

"Yes." Gillian took a breath as if to say more. She clasped her hands together tightly in front of her, then spread her fingers out on the table.

"Do you want to tell me more, Gillian? I'll listen if you want, but if you'd rather not talk, that's okay by me."

"They say she wasn't taking heroin. The results were negative."

"That's good news, too." Helen smiled. Gillian didn't. "There's something else, isn't there, Gillian?"

"She was drugged and raped."

"Good God!" Helen tried to take in Gillian's words. Undeniable, irrefutable, overwhelming words.

"And they still can't tell me whether there is any brain damage or not." Gillian looked up, her eyes brimming with tears. "I want to know, and at the same time I'm scared to find out. She could have HIV, she could be pregnant, I suppose, but no one has actually said so."

"My sons and their girlfriends are coming to see me at the weekend." The words sounded flippant. Helen wished she could take them back.

"I didn't know you had any sons. How many do you have?"

"I'm sure I mentioned it, but never mind. I have two. Robert and James. Twenty-eight and twenty-six."

"Do you have any daughters?"

"No. Just the boys. I've never met their girlfriends before…" Helen's voice trailed off as she saw Gillian's expression. "You can cry if you want, Gillian. I hope I didn't hurt you by talking about my family. I didn't mean to upset you, honestly, I didn't."

"No. Of course not." She sniffed, and forced a little smile. "I know that." She took a tissue from her bag to wipe her eyes and blow her nose.

"Tell you what, Gillian," Helen said, "let's go into town. We could buy a handbag each. That'll cheer us up."

"You don't need cheering up, do you?"

"No. But I've put on a bit of weight, and I'm not buying clothes any bigger than a size fourteen."

"I'm not following this, Helen. What are you talking about?" Gillian frowned.

"What I'm saying is you can buy handbags on a fat day. Come on. We'll walk. I need some exercise, too." Helen saw Gillian's expression and read her thoughts. "You can go from the shops straight to the hospital to see Caroline." She put on her jacket.

Gillian smiled at her friend. "Oh, Helen, what would I have done without you these last days?"

They set off on foot towards the town. Helen's ankle ached a bit, but not much. She didn't mention it, it was nothing.

* * * *

On the command of the officer in charge, D.I. Andy Greatorex, an empty office at the back of Pennington-on-Sea police station had been cleared as an incident room. The building teemed with officers from Camford and the recently-formed National Crime Agency.

It wasn't rocket science to link Jorge's death with his brother. If Pete Levens had been a betting man, he'd have put money on there being a link between Naz and Jono Lister's death as well. They'd know soon enough. Jono's body was to be exhumed in Leicester and further tests carried out. Luckily for them Jono hadn't been cremated. If there was a link, the forensic evidence would be there. Pete studied the boards around the room, lists of names linked by arrows, addresses and photos of known associates. Anything and anybody with a connection to Nathan Sadler was on the board. Naz: every force in the country was on the lookout for him and his four-wheel drive. It was only a matter of time. His brothels had been closed and his house had been thoroughly searched. All his known contacts had been interviewed, or would be by the end of the day. Either they didn't know or were too scared to say where he was. Pete suspected it was the former. Naz was smart enough to know the only way to keep a secret was to tell no one. He wouldn't want to be found. No doubt he knew by now that Carrie Halstead was alive. What Naz didn't know, what none of them knew, was whether or not she would be able to give evidence against him. Naz would assume she could, and would. He was hiding somewhere, but the world wasn't going to be big enough, not in the long term. Pete wanted him found quickly, if only so Carrie and her mother knew he wouldn't be turning up on their doorstep. He was a dangerous man. No one who knew him could fail to know that.

Dan Greenway came into the room and headed straight for Pete. "They found his car."

Pete turned quickly. "Where?"

"That's the not-so-good bit. It's at Gatwick Airport."

"Shit."

CHAPTER SEVENTEEN

Robert headed out of London a happy man. Jayne sat at his side as he drove along the M3 past Farnborough and on towards Basingstoke. 'Radio Two' played its uncontroversial music, punctuated by the disc jockey's banter. After a while he began to feel silence between them and wondered if this was a companionable silence or an awkward one. Maybe Jayne didn't want to meet his mother after all. Maybe she was regretting the whole thing. He didn't dare ask in case he didn't like her answer.

"Penny for them?" she asked.

He laughed nervously.

"What's so funny?"

"Nothing, only I was wondering what you were thinking about. I was worried that you might think it a bit bizarre that I'm taking you to meet my mother on our second date."

"It can't be a *bit* bizarre, Robert. That's a contradiction. Like someone being a *bit* terrified. Either it's bizarre or it isn't. You can't do bizarre in bits."

He thought she sounded cross. "Well…yes. Strictly speaking, you're right, I suppose. It's just a turn of phrase. I didn't mean—"

"I know, I know. I'm sorry. It's just me being grouchy."

"We can turn back if you like. You don't have to come. I mean, I feel I have to go, but I can take you back home if you like."

"Of course not. I want to come with you and meet your mum, and your brother and his girlfriend. Did you say they are called James and Madeleine?"

"Yes. Maddie. He calls her Maddie."

"And when am I going to meet your dad?"

"Dad? You can't meet him, he's dead."

"Oh, Robert, I'm so sorry. I assumed your parents were divorced, like mine."

"Then I'm sorry. Sorry I didn't explain properly. I should've told you, and I'm sorry about your folks."

The silence returned. The M3 rumbled beneath them.

"Dad died two years ago. Heart attack. No warning, he just dropped dead at work." Robert was surprised to feel tears pricking his eyes. Whatever was wrong with him? He took a deep breath through his nose and willed the tears away. He felt Jayne's eyes upon him.

"Your poor mother."

"Yes. She coped well, but I…never mind."

"Go on."

"It's nothing. Just that everything changed, then. I can see it now, better than at the time, but I don't think Mum has ever gotten over it. Closure and all that stuff. Whatever you like to call it."

"Is that why she's taken herself off?"

"Maybe. I don't know." He felt the prickling tears again. "Can we change the subject?"

"Okay. What do you want to talk about?"

"Let's talk about you." Robert smiled.

"I knew you'd say that," Jayne groaned.

"And is it so bad?"

"I feel I've misled you, Robert."

"Oh, yes. And how have you done that? I mean, in what way?"

They had driven off the motorway and were heading down the A303 towards Yeovil.

Jayne turned her head to the window and closed her eyes to the passing countryside. She spoke clearly. "I'll tell you, Robert, but please don't interrupt or I won't be able to carry on."

Gripped with a strange fear, he didn't reply. What could be so bad? What could she have done? James's offer to do a criminal records check on her flashed through his mind. He dismissed it, refusing to think anything bad of her. It was not possible.

"As you know, Robert, I work at Carleton's Bank as a telephonist. You also know, because you have seen it, that my lifestyle in London could not possibly be paid for with my salary."

Robert felt his heart beating as if it were about to burst through his chest. Jayne had asked him not to speak, so he didn't.

"No doubt, when we first emailed each other, you thought I had some high flying job at head office. Then, when we met, you saw how I was well known in London, at the hotel and all that. You saw my apartment. You must have been impressed. I was showing off like a stupid girl. Well, that's what I am, Robert. I'm a stupid girl. I'm not clever like you. The truth is my father pays for the apartment, and the truth is that my name is really Jayne Green. My father is Martin Green."

He couldn't prevent an intake of breath.

"I know what you're thinking and, yes, he is *the* Martin Green, chief executive of Carleton's Bank." Jayne opened her eyes and stared at the road ahead. "I'm sure you've had other girlfriends, as I've had other boyfriends. The trouble was they always knew my family background. I felt they were all interested in me because of my father, or more to the point because of his money. I did the internet thing under the name Jayne Manners to avoid all that. I wanted a friendship that was based on me as a person, even if that meant it had to be based on a lie. I don't know if any of this makes sense, like I said, I'm not very clever, but I know I want to be honest with you before we get any more involved. Now I've been totally honest with you, and what I've said can't be unsaid, so if you want to end it now, I fully understand. When we get to Pennington-on-Sea, or if you'd rather drop me off in Yeovil or somewhere, I can get the train back to London, and you won't have to introduce a lying little rich girl to your mum. That's it, Robert, I've finished."

Robert still didn't speak. He drove on and pulled into the next lay-by. The traffic roared past in the Friday afternoon race out of London. He put his hand over hers, and they dared to look each other in the eye. Two tearful faces stared at each other, and then, in a split second, they were hugging each other tightly, as if fearing they would be parted for life should they let go. Robert laughed through his tears, and Jayne started to laugh with him.

"I love you, Jayne Manners. I love you, Jayne Green. I love you whoever you are, and for what you are, I love everything about you, and I'm the luckiest man in the world." He released his grip on her and wiped his tears away with the back of his hand. "This is all crazy. We should be on the top of a mountain, or on a silver beach, not in a lay-by on the A303." They laughed again. The rest of the journey was going to be so happy. Robert knew the rest of his life was going to be so happy. He adored her, he admired her, and Jayne looked as if she was bursting with happiness.

She wiped her eyes, laughter and tears mingling together.

"This is about you and me, Jayne. I don't care if you're rich or poor, or who your father is, or isn't. I'm glad I didn't know. I'm glad you lied to me. This way, no one can ever say I was after your money. Don't you see?"

Jayne nodded. "Now I really am looking forward to this weekend." Her whole face smiled. "I'm looking forward to being with you, and to meeting your family. I feel I can do that now everything is out in the open."

His eyes sparkled. Her hand covered his on the gear stick as he pulled out of the lay-by. His head was full of happily ever after, of engagement rings and a self confidence he had never known before, not ever.

* * * *

Robert parked at the rear of 'Blue Seas Bed and Breakfast'. The white pebble-dashed walls and blue window frames of the large Victorian house were typical of an English seaside B&B. The garden was immaculately tidy; not a blade of grass dared to stray out of place. He carried their bags around to the front of the house. As they crossed the threshold, a bell automatically rang in the far regions of the house, and as if by magic, a young receptionist—her pale foundation and heavy black eyeliner making her look ill—popped up behind the little desk in the hallway. She looked both frightened and frightening.

"Is it Ms Manners?" she asked anxiously.

"Yes, that's right," Jayne replied. "Is there a problem?"

"I've made a mistake with your booking. I haven't dared tell Mrs Hughes, she's the boss, and she'll sack me for sure. It's the third one I've made, and I've only been here two weeks."

"Do you not have rooms for us?" Jayne asked.

"No. Well, I mean, yes. There is a room, a double room, not the singles you asked for. Sorry."

"It's okay," Jayne said with a smile.

Robert could only stand there, bags in hand, barely believing his eyes and ears.

"We'll take the double, thanks. No need to tell Mrs Hughes."

The girl's face relaxed and even the make-up couldn't disguise her relief. Jayne and Robert followed her up the stairs and were shown into the room, complete with en-suite bathroom and sea view. It wasn't until they were alone that they burst into hysterical laughter and fell together on the bed. The giggles subsided and they kissed, each savouring the moment. Robert's phone rang, breaking the spell.

"Robert, it's me, Mum."

"Why are you ringing me? You never ring. Is something wrong? Where are you?"

"I thought I'd surprise you. I'm here, outside your B&B. I've seen your car around the back. Come on, I'll buy you an ice cream. He'll be shutting up shop and going home soon, and I want to meet Jayne."

"Okay, we'll be right down." He hung up.

"Was that your mum?" Jayne asked.

"It certainly was. She's here, and wants to buy me an ice cream." Robert was incredulous.

Jayne went to the window and smiled mischievously. "Has your mum got pink and black hair?" In two quick strides he was at Jayne's side, looking down on his mother, her hair, and her matching bicycle.

* * * *

Helen shook Jayne's hand. "Delighted to meet you. Just delighted." She turned and hugged Robert, embarrassing him. His mum never used to be a huggy sort of person, but then she was never a pink hair sort of person either. He began to wonder if she'd gone completely mad.

Jayne stood behind Helen and, rolling his eyes skywards, Robert gave her a 'don't-ask-me-what's-going-on' look over his mother's shoulder.

Jayne stifled a laugh, pretending to sneeze.

Helen released her grip. "You don't have a cold, do you, Jayne?"

"No, I'm fine, thanks, just a tickle."

"Good. This way. There's an ice cream van just a bit farther down the road towards the town centre." Helen led the way, pushing her bicycle.

"Three ninety-nines, please." Helen gave the order without asking what they would like, and the bored young vendor of Mr Freezy Creams went about his work, skilfully holding three cornets in one hand. She handed them the cones with their little chocolate flakes. "I never knew anyone who didn't like a ninety-nine."

Robert and Jayne exchanged amused glances. They walked along the seafront, Jayne and Robert hand in hand, while Helen pushed her bicycle with one hand, holding her ice cream in the other.

"You like my hair then, Robert?" she said between licks.

Jayne squeezed his hand, and out of the corner of his eye, he saw her give an almost imperceptible nod. "I think it's terrific, Mum. Just great."

"No, you don't. You think I'm bonkers. But thanks, anyway."

They walked on, concentrating on their ice creams. They walked round Pennington-on-Sea window shopping and making small talk. Helen pointed out the Tourist Information Centre, and the 'Fresh Ground' coffee shop. Robert and Jayne held hands the whole time.

A clock struck eight, as the light began to fade.

"Well, I must be off, back to Goldilocks. I'll meet you tomorrow at 'Fresh Ground', about eleven. James and Madeleine should be here by then. I'll send him a text, or I might even phone him."

"But, Mum—" He glanced at Jayne "—we thought we'd go for a meal together tonight."

Helen's face softened into a smile. "You two can barely keep your hands off each other. Whatever you want to do this evening, I'm sure you'd rather do it without me, and anyway, I have a friend to visit in hospital. She's expecting me. In fact, I'm late." Before Robert or Jayne could say anything, she had switched on her bicycle lights and pedalled off, waving as she wobbled along the road.

Jayne turned to Robert. "Who's Goldilocks?"

"It's a long story."

"I'm sure it is, so you'd better start now, so I'm ready

for your mum and your brother tomorrow. By the way, I think she's great."

* * * *

Helen kicked off her shoes and placed them neatly under her bed. She had no intention of going to see Gillian, not tonight. Visiting time was over, and she didn't want to go to her house. Perhaps she would see her in the morning before she met up with the boys, perhaps not. She pulled down the blinds and sent a text to James.

C U Fresh ground coffee shop, near c front. Elevenish 2moz. OK. Met Jayne and Robert. V nice. Mum X

Her phone buzzed back almost immediately.

OK Mum, lookng 4wd 2 c u. J n M

She switched off her phone and cracked open a bottle of red wine. Robert seemed happy, and she had no reason to think James was not. She sighed deeply. So why was she so fed up again? What was the problem? The closure thing had been done, thanks to the weird desert dream. If Goldilocks had been bigger, she would have paced up and down; instead she made circles with her ankles simply because she could, without pain.

The warmth of the wine spread through her. She twirled her glass and watched the red liquid cling to the sides. Phil had once told her it was the sign of a good wine, and that the little rivulets were called 'legs'. Her own legs were feeling the effects of the wine in a relaxed sort of way, but she wasn't going anywhere, so it didn't matter.

She switched on the television. An episode of 'Poirot' was just starting. She'd seen it before, of course, but she could never remember the endings, the whodunnit, so she settled back to watch it again. Poirot and his sidekick, Captain Hastings, were guests at a wedding. Helen visualised herself at Robert and Jayne's wedding, wearing a big hat and high heels. Gillian and

Caroline would be there. Robert would look so smart in a morning suit and Jayne the picture of beauty in her wedding dress.

She refilled her glass. The groom had just been shot on 'Poirot', and Captain Hastings said 'I say, what rotten luck.' She liked Captain Hastings. He was so delightfully useless. Robert wouldn't be shot, of course; he and Jayne would provide grandchildren. A baby girl would be nice. Or maybe James and Maddie would get married first.

James and his work no longer worried her. She was no longer a witness to his unsociable hours, the coming and going in the night, the snatched meals. She'd seen James's world from the other side, of course, with poor Caroline, and before that with Tashy and her dope.

Had she, Helen McGuire, widow of Jumbles Lane, really been under the influence of cannabis at a hospital?

She took another sip of wine and giggled at the memory of Llandudno A&E. Time and wine made it amusing.

"It's far more likely they will just live together." Helen heard her words slurring, but didn't care. "You'll never get to wear a big hat and high heels, you silly woman. Couples just live together these days, and think about getting married when babies come along. And anyway, what if Jayne and Maddie become fed up with my boys?"

She had no idea how long James had known Maddie, but she did know that Robert hadn't known the lovely Jayne very long at all. It was as plain as the nose on her face that they were madly in love, or her hair wasn't pink. Giggling again, she drained the bottle into her glass, telling herself she'd find something to eat and go to bed when 'Poirot' finished.

* * * *

Robert and Jayne, James and Maddie, all arrived at

'Fresh Ground' before eleven o'clock. With four cups of coffee before them on a table near the window, they waited for Helen. Jayne put her handbag on a vacant chair between herself and Maddie. Constant rain—the fine drizzly 'set-for-the-day' type of rain—had been falling since dawn. Customers dripped in from the gloomy weather. The window was covered in condensation from the wet clothes and the steaming espresso machine. After ten minutes, there was still no sign of Helen. Introductions had been made, and Jayne and Maddie were chatting as if they had known each other all their lives.

Robert and Jayne held hands under the table. He cleared a patch of condensation from the window with the sleeve of his free arm. "Still no sign of her."

"She's probably waiting for the rain to ease up a bit," James said. "You say she's got a bike?"

"Yes. You can't miss it—pink and black with a basket on the front. What I didn't tell you is that it matches her hair. She's had it dyed."

"Black?"

"Pink and black." Robert's face was serious.

James threw his head back and laughed loudly. Customers turned their heads and smiled, wondering what the man with untidy fair hair found so funny.

"It's not funny, James. She looks ridiculous." He squeezed Jayne's hand, and she turned to him. "Doesn't she, Jayne?" Jayne frowned, giving him a quizzical look. "Mum—" He thought she hadn't heard him "—her hair, it's ridiculous?"

Jayne's face softened into a smile, and Robert was certain she'd confirm his opinion until she replied, "I think it's rather fun. And why not? It's her hair, Robert, and it's not like she had a tattoo. It will grow out."

"I bet your mum wouldn't have her hair dyed shocking pink."

James smiled as Jayne said, "Probably not. But then,

from what I've seen of her, your mum isn't anything like mine. Maybe you should ask her why she did it, you know, just come out with it and say, 'Why pink, Mum?'"

"I think I'll leave that to you and Maddie here. She's more likely to tell you."

* * * *

Helen was woken by the sound of people arguing and, with her eyes still shut, she recognised the unmistakable sound of 'The Jeremy Kyle Show'. It puzzled her. Jeremy Kyle was on in the morning, and she was watching 'Poirot'. She opened her eyes slowly and raised the blind next to her. The grey wet day matched her mood. Two empty bottles stood in front of her. She was seeing double. To confirm her suspicions, she reached forward, only to realise there was nothing wrong with her eyes, and she'd drunk two bottles of red wine on an empty stomach. Groaning, she put her hands to her temples.

"Not again. Please, not again."

The time check in the corner of the TV screen showed 11.10 am. Feeling stiff and cold, her little grey cells—as Poirot would have put it—started to function, and reality set in. She'd got drunk, slept an alcoholic sleep in the chair, and was hung over, big time and…Christ Almighty…she was late for meeting Robert and James.

Helen leapt out of her chair, dashed to the bedroom, dragged a brush through her hair, and put on her shoes. In the bathroom she splashed cold water on her face and, two minutes later, was pedalling through 'Ten Acres' on her way to the coffee shop.

Rain trickled down her neck as she chained her bicycle to the railings. She rubbed her hands over her face and her fingers through her hair in a vain attempt to improve her appearance.

James stood up and waved. "Over here, Mum."

She made her way between the tables and was rewarded with a hug from James.

"You look marvellous, Mum." He did not look as if he meant it. "Mum, this is Maddie." Maddie stood up and shook Helen's hand. Greetings were exchanged, and Robert introduced Jayne, who moved her handbag.

Helen sat down. "Sorry I'm late, everyone. Get me a large black coffee, will you James? I've got a bloody awful hangover." James did as he was told and went to the counter. "Why are you staring at me like that, Robert?" Reaching across the table, she patted her elder son's hand as she turned to Jayne and Maddie. "Poor boy has never seen his mother with a hangover before."

Jayne and Maddie clearly tried not to laugh, but somehow when they looked at each other they burst into fits of giggles.

"I've never seen you with pink hair before, Mum."

"Yes, you have, you saw me yesterday."

"You know what I mean. What's gotten into you? You've changed."

James returned to the table and put a large mug of black coffee in front of Helen.

She leaned forward to inhale the steam before taking a sip. "Don't know." She stared into the coffee. "But you're right. I have changed."

"What's all this?" James asked. "Confession time?"

Helen looked up. "Maaaay-beeee," she replied thoughtfully.

James, Robert, Maddie and Jayne all waited for her to continue.

"It's difficult to know where to start, because nothing has turned out quite the way I expected." She supported her head with one hand, her elbow on the table.

"What did you expect?" James asked.

"I don't know, but not this. I didn't expect you two to come after me like I was a naughty teenager, running away from home."

"But we wanted to see you," Robert said.

"I know, I know, and it's nice to see you, especially nice to meet Jayne and Maddie." She smiled towards them. "I suppose I needed to get away from home for a while."

"Well, you have," James said. "I don't see any problem with that."

"What I don't understand," Robert said, "is why you felt the need to lie about it. To pretend you were just going away for a couple of weeks, when it's obvious you planned to stay away for much longer."

Helen paused, summoning the courage to disclose her original intentions, and to explain her reasoning, still not knowing if it was the right thing to do. She took a deep breath. "I thought, that is to say, I still think, it's high time you two left home and stopped hanging on to my apron strings. I thought if I went away for a while you'd become more independent."

The noise of the coffee machines and the chatter of the customers filled the air. It was a full ten seconds before James once again threw his head back and laughed.

Robert stared open mouthed at his mother.

Jayne and Maddie stared into their empty cups.

Maddie stood up slowly, scraping her chair on the tiled floor. "How about you and I take a walk, Jayne? The rain has let up a bit. I think it best if Robert and James discuss this with their mum on their own."

Jayne nodded with relief and followed her out of the café.

As they left, Helen turned to her smiling son. "What's so funny, James?"

"Oh, Mum, it's you. Why didn't you just tell us? Robert and I both want to leave home. As it happens, we both have job offers in London. We have been worried about leaving *you* on your own."

Helen turned to her elder son. "Is this true, Robert?"

He nodded in agreement.

"And how long have you known this?"

"A while," Robert said. "James and I discussed it that night we went for a drink at the 'Lock-Keepers'."

"Now, that is a surprise, you two discussing something." Robert and James glared at each other, and Helen sensed she had touched a sore point. "Have you two been arguing?"

"No!" They answered together, too quickly.

"Let me get this straight. You both knew, or knew it was a possibility, that you would be leaving Chester, before I bought Goldilocks?"

"Oh, yes." Robert said. "I'd known before then, and I expect James had known about his promotion for a while, too."

James nodded. "Well, I knew it was a possibility, not confirmed. It was the same with you, wasn't it, Robert?" He turned to his brother.

"That's right. We sort of decided to tell you when it was confirmed. It's still not a hundred percent. We didn't want you worrying about being left on your own when it was all still up in the air, so to speak."

Helen sat back in her chair, cup in hand, sipping her coffee as she mulled over the chain of events, from her selling Valerie Drobshaw and buying Goldilocks, to buying her bicycle, and meeting Gillian. She didn't know whether she was relieved or cross. She wanted to shout at them for not discussing it with her, while at the same time knowing she was equally guilty. Her head hurt like it was going to burst, which didn't help.

"Whatever must Maddie and Jayne think of me?" She looked from one son to the other and back again. "I bet they're laughing at me for being so stupid."

"I don't think so, Mum," Robert said. "Jayne likes you. She told me so last night."

"That was when she thought the daftest thing I'd ever done was have my hair dyed pink and black. That was a mistake, by the way. While I'm confessing, I might as well tell you I fell asleep at the hairdressers and when I woke up I was pink and black."

James roared with laughter again and, this time, Robert joined in, and then Helen. Heads turned once again to the happy table in the corner.

The laughter subsided and Helen wiped her eyes.

"I thought you said you were visiting a friend in hospital last night," Robert said. "So how come you have a hangover?"

"Ah. Yes. Well, that wasn't true. I suppose this is another confession."

"Do you have a friend in hospital here? You've only been here a few days."

"I met a lady called Gillian the second day I was here." The smile left Helen's face. "Her daughter has been attacked. She's the one who's in hospital, so it wasn't a total lie. I didn't go to see her, though. I rather got the impression you and Jayne wanted to be alone, so I thought I'd clear off."

Robert blushed.

James smiled at his brother's discomfort. "Anything else to confess, Mother?" he asked mockingly. "Must I interrogate you, or will you tell all?"

"Oh, lots, James. You wouldn't believe what wicked things I've done since I left home."

"I knew you weren't coming back in two weeks," Robert said. "You left enough food in the freezer to last six months."

"Yes, I know. But my conscience was giving me trouble. I had to keep telling myself I was doing it for you, but in truth I'm not so sure now."

"I thought," James said, "that you were going off for a couple of weeks at a time, doing a 'find myself' thing."

"Don't be daft, James. I know perfectly well who I am. You may think I've changed, but I haven't, not really. I'm just being more honest with myself." Helen heard her words echoing in her head, knowing nothing could be further from the truth. She had changed. It was the biggest load of rubbish she'd ever come up with.

"So what's all this 'don't phone or text me' stuff, then? Only email, blah blah blah?" Robert asked. "And what exactly do you mean when you say you've done lots of wicked things?"

"It doesn't matter."

"Yes it does, Mum. We got in this situation by not communicating with each other."

"Well, okay then, but you might not like it. I need more coffee, your turn, Robert, and I think I'll have some carrot cake. I need something sweet if I'm going to shift this hangover."

Robert joined the queue at the counter.

James took the opportunity to talk to his mum about Robert and Jayne. "What do you think of Robert finding such a beauty, Mum? I didn't think he had it in him."

"It's early days, but they make a nice couple."

"Is that all you can say, 'they make a nice couple'?" James had clearly hoped for more, but Helen had no intention of gossiping about Robert and Jayne.

"How long have you been seeing Maddie?"

"Quite a while. You'd have to ask Maddie to know exactly. Women seem to remember these things better than men. Better than I do, anyway."

"Where did you meet her?"

"Work."

"And what happens when you go to London?"

"Maddie's moving to London as well. She has a two year secondment. It's all worked out very well. We'll be looking for an apartment." James looked relieved when Robert returned to the table. "Thank goodness you're back, Robert."

Helen heard the sarcasm.

"Mother here was giving me the third degree."

"Really? I thought you'd be talking about me and

Jayne."

"Don't flatter yourself, big brother."

"Will you two stop it?" Helen had raised her voice, and the sound of it bounced around inside her skull. "Ow!" She put her head in her hands. Heads turned again to the not-so-happy table. She lowered her voice, hissing her words. "You're behaving like two little boys. What's the problem? You both have lovely girlfriends, you have good jobs with exciting futures, and still you behave like jealous children, trying to get one over on each other."

They were about to object, to defend themselves, but she continued.

"When I think of the people who have real troubles I begin to wonder where I went wrong. Didn't your dad and I bring you up to consider the other person's point of view? Well, that includes each other. You two have very different personalities, but that doesn't mean you have to constantly compete."

Robert and James stared at their mother.

"Well? What do you have to say for yourselves?"

They shuffled uncomfortably in their seats. "Sorry, Mum," they chorused.

Helen took a breath, about to launch into another lecture. They still sounded like little boys with their shallow apology. Helen wasn't convinced they meant it, but they were saved from further humiliation by the return of Maddie and Jayne.

"There you are, girls. I was about to tell them all about my adventures and confess all my wrong doings, but I've thought better of it."

James and Robert looked at each other. James shrugged his 'I don't know' shrug, and Robert pursed his lips.

"Don't tell them anything, Helen." Maddie laughed. "Jayne and I have worked out why they're so grumpy with each other."

CHAPTER EIGHTEEN

Gillian's thumb gently rubbed the back of Caroline's hand, her eyes fixed on her daughter. Helen sat at the opposite side of the bed. Neither of the women spoke for some time.

"Did your sons come down, then?"

"Yes, and their girlfriends. We're having a meal tonight at 'The Turning House'. James and Maddie are staying there. Is it any good?"

"Oh, yes, I've had a few meals there. It's one of the few hotels that stay open all year round."

"Will I have to dress up?"

"Depends what you call 'dress up'. Smart, I suppose."

"I didn't really pack anything suitable for dining out. It wasn't on my list of things to do. To tell you the truth, I don't really want to go."

"Oh, Helen, you must." Gillian turned to face her. "They've come all this way."

"I know I must, and I will. It's just the way Robert and James were bickering at each other this morning. They were just the same when they were little boys, and I thought they'd have grown out of it by now."

"What are their girlfriends like?"

"Very nice from what I've seen of them. I suppose it's not surprising that James's girlfriend is in the police, and Robert's girlfriend works for a bank."

"That's what they do, is it? Your sons, I mean."

"Yes...I know this sounds awful, but I wish they hadn't come. It's my own fault for not keeping in touch or telling them what I was doing."

"Where are they now?"

"Dunno. I left them in 'Fresh Ground'. I told them I

had to visit a friend in hospital."

"You didn't have to." Gillian turned her gaze back to Caroline.

"I know that, but I was finding it all a bit claustrophobic in there, so I'm afraid I used you and Caroline as an excuse. Hopefully, they'll do something together before we meet up tonight."

"And what would you be doing if you weren't going out for a meal tonight?"

Helen thought for a while. "What I'd really like to do is set off to see a friend of mine in Scarborough. Her mum's ill."

Gillian turned to look at her. "Scarborough? That's quite a drive."

"Mmnnn." Helen looked at Caroline, so pretty despite the bruises, and so vulnerable. With a sudden pang of guilt, she realised she hadn't asked Gillian how she was. Part of her wanted to ask, and yet she'd avoided it, in case Gillian didn't want to talk. There was no apparent change. Helen decided she must say something. If Gillian didn't want to tell her, that was okay. The only thing she'd noticed was that there was no longer a policeman outside the ward.

"How is she? Any change?"

"No, but the doctors have reduced the dose of sedatives a little, so they must be pleased with her." Gillian lowered her eyes, focussing on Caroline's hand. "A policewoman came to see me this morning, at home."

"And?"

"They're linking Caroline's attack to the death of her boyfriend, and to the body found on the beach. They are waiting for the pathologist's reports, but it looks as if Jono—he was Caroline's boyfriend—and Jorge Sadler— he was the one found on the beach—were both killed by an overdose of heroin."

"But you said Caroline's blood tests showed no heroin. Am I missing something here?"

"There are still more questions than answers from what I can gather, but the police seem to think the person who supplied the heroin to Jono and Jorge was the one who drugged and raped Caroline. You see, they found Rohypnol in her blood. They're doing more tests. If she's pregnant, she will have the option of an abortion. To be honest with you, all I want to hear is that she isn't brain damaged. They still don't know. Anything else seems trivial."

Helen made no reply. She had no words for this courageous woman who bore her terrible burden as if it were no weight at all. Her estimation of Gillian Halstead was the complete opposite to her first impression that morning, not so long ago, when they had met by chance. As she watched Gillian's tears fall onto the thin white bedspread, she stood up and walked slowly round to the other side of the bed. This woman, this wonderful woman had listened to her moaning on about her sons while bearing this terrible burden.

She put her hand on Gillian's shoulders. "I'm so, so sorry, Gillian. I'm so lucky, and you are so brave." She took a tissue from the box at the side of Caroline's bed and handed it to her.

"Thank you." Gillian wiped her eyes. "Are you going to Scarborough, then? I'll miss you if you do."

"I don't know yet. I'm waiting for my friend to email me. She's only a young girl, younger than Caroline, and her mother is ill." The comfortable silence of friendship fell between them.

After a while, she said, "Can I ask you something, Gillian? If you don't want to answer, you can just say so."

"Of course you can. Anything at all."

"Why did Caroline start taking drugs?"

Gillian thought for a while before replying.

"When she first left home, and I realised what was going on, I went to a meeting in Camford. It was one of these support groups. I never told Keith about it. He had already forbidden me to mention her name. I only went once. I would have liked to go again, but I knew Keith would find out and create an argument about it. Looking back, I should've stood up to him, but that's hindsight. There were counsellors there, specially trained people, and one of the things I remember them saying is that you should never ask 'why?' They don't know, you see, the addicts, nobody knows, not really. They can talk about peer pressure and all that, but it doesn't entirely answer the question, does it?"

"I suppose not." Helen thought of Tashy and her dope, and shuddered at the thought of her getting involved in the hard stuff. She looked around the ward slowly before her eyes rested on the white bedcover. It showed every contour of Caroline's thin body; even her hip bones showed through. She felt ashamed. She was a selfish, ungrateful bitch with two healthy, intelligent, successful sons who deserved a better mother. In the strange encapsulated environment of intensive care, Helen suddenly didn't like herself, not one little bit.

"I'd better be getting off. I need to wash my hair and dig out some clothes for tonight. I—" She never finished her sentence.

"Nurse! Nurse!" Gillian was on her feet. A nurse appeared in a split second. "She squeezed my hand...she did, she did."

The nurse checked the monitors. Caroline's hand moved slightly, and her eyelids gave the faintest flicker.

* * * *

The two couples walked along the beach, hand in hand, their backs to the wind and the rain.

"Come on then, girls," James shouted above the roar of the waves and the wind. "What can you tell me about Robert that I didn't already know?"

"It isn't all about you, James, or Robert," Maddie

shouted back.

"What, then?"

"It's about your mum. In your own very different ways, you are both—perhaps to some extent subconsciously and definitely understandably—worried sick about her."

Neither of the brothers had an answer, so they walked on for a while.

Robert and Jayne linked arms closely as they were all blown along the beach. "You're right, of course," Robert shouted. "But where does that take us? I mean, what are we supposed to do about it?"

"Nothing, nothing at all," Jayne shouted back, indicating they should leave the shore via a slipway and go into a shelter on the sea front, out of the wind and rain. They sat in the shelter with the litter and broken glass, looking out to sea. Robert and James sat on opposite ends of the bench, their partners next to them, in the middle.

"Your mum's doing just fine. Let her get on with her life." Jayne was grateful to be out of the wind, and able to speak in a more normal voice. "It's the way you two are in competition with each other. That's the problem."

"What do you mean, 'in competition'?" James asked.

"Respect."

"You sound like a teenager." James laughed. "'Respect, man…I want respect.'"

"Don't speak to Jayne like that." Robert was on his feet, challenging his brother, fists clenched at his sides.

"Sit down, Robert." Jayne pulled him back to his seat. "This is exactly what we mean. You two need to accept your differences, stop being so childish, and think of your mother."

The brothers fumed.

"You do realise," Maddie said, "that your mum actually left home so you two could sort yourselves out. You really have got to stop this. One minute you seem to be getting along just fine, and then you're off again. Maybe you never will be best of friends, but you have to admit we're right. You both think the world of her, and she of you. You can't argue with that, can you?"

Neither of them answered.

"I take it you agree, then?"

There was still no reply. They had been forced to face the truth about their stupid stubbornness and the futility of their bickering. Feeling awkward, they were embarrassed to have their faults highlighted by their girlfriends. Maddie and Jayne were spot on, and the brothers knew they couldn't deny it.

Robert stood up, walked over to James and held out his hand. James had no choice but to take it and shake it.

* * * *

A black mini dress showed off Maddie's long slim legs while Jayne's red chiffon blouse complemented her white mini skirt. Robert and James's open-necked shirts looked smart and relaxed with casual trousers. 'The Turning House' was not a place for jeans. They each had a gin and tonic before them on the bar.

James's seat gave him a view of the entrance to the lounge of 'The Turning House'. His jaw dropped when he saw his mother at the door.

"Oh, my God. She hasn't even changed. She's still in the same clothes she had on this morning, and looks like a drowned rat."

Maddie looked up. Robert and Jayne had to turn to see Helen. Robert waved and beckoned her to them.

"Don't say anything. There'll be a reason for it," Jayne whispered, just loud enough for the other three to hear.

"Sorry, everyone. I've come straight from the hospital. Marvellous news. My friend's daughter, Caroline, is coming round."

"Can I get you a drink?" James asked.

"I'll have a large G and T please," she said, her hangover forgotten, a thing of the past. "I have a lot to tell you. I've made my plans." Her phone buzzed. She took it out of her pocket and read the text message. It was from Tashy.

Hi Helen, I did like u said. Mum home today, things OK. I stopped smoking. Tashy.

Helen tapped in her reply while everyone waited.

All excellent news. I'll come to see you very soon, would love to meet your mum, Helen.

Robert and James exchanged smiles; the girls struggled to stifle their giggles. Helen put her phone in her pocket.

"Can I take your coat, Mum?"

"Thank you, Robert." Helen peeled off her wet anorak.

James handed her a tall glass packed with ice and lemon. She raised her glass.

"Cheers!" They followed suit. A waiter handed each of them a large menu. Helen put hers on the bar without opening it.

"That was a text from my friend in Scarborough. I think I'll be going there tomorrow, after all."

Four blank faces stared at her.

"I don't think you told any of us you were thinking of going to Scarborough, Mum," James said.

"Sorry, I thought I had. I have a friend there whose mum is ill. She had asked if I was anywhere near, which of course I'm not. Anyway, her mum is out of hospital, and the doctors say she's doing well. It has been a tricky decision, because I felt I should stay here."

"What do you mean, 'you felt you should stay here'?" Robert asked.

"Well, it's all to do with why I haven't had a chance to change since this morning. Like I said, my friend's daughter is coming round. I want to be here to help them.

219

It's a long story."

"Do you want to tell us about it?" Jayne asked.

"Yes, I do, but not here. I feel uncomfortable in more ways than one. You all look so lovely, and I look like something the cat dragged in." There was a short pause. No one disagreed with her. "I could go back to Goldilocks and change, but I'd be at least an hour."

"Tell you what, Mum," James said. "I'll cancel the table. You go back to Goldilocks. We'll get a take-away and meet you back there in half an hour."

"That's fine by me, if the girls agree," said Robert.

"It'll be a squash," Helen said, unsure if Jayne and Maddie would be happy with James's suggestion.

"I don't know about you, Jayne," Maddie said, "but I've heard so much about Goldilocks I'd love to see her, and I'm starving."

* * * *

Helen was right, it was a squash. They ate their pizzas straight from their boxes. Helen supplied paper serviettes.

"So," she said, "my plan has worked. You're both leaving home. Now I'll tell you what's happened these last few weeks, and what I propose to do." Wiping her fingers on her serviette, she spoke briefly of Llandudno and the people she had met there, of her twisted ankle, and Tashy from Scarborough. Her story moved swiftly on to Pennington-on-Sea, omitting the matter of smoking dope, the tracking device and her first hangover. She told them how she had met Gillian in the shelter, feeling no need to mention the safety deposit box. Caroline's problems, the body on the beach and Gillian's friendship were relayed in detail. "Sometimes events and people make these decisions easier."

"Oh, do get on with it, Mother," James said. "You're making an awful drama of it. Are you emigrating or something?"

"Not quite, James. I've decided to settle here in Pennington-on-Sea."

"What, and live in here?" Robert sounded horrified at the thought of his mother permanently living in a motorhome.

"Why not?" Jayne said. "I think Goldilocks is great."

Maddie nodded in agreement as she ate her pizza.

"No, Robert, I do not intend to live permanently in Goldilocks, and please stop interrupting."

Robert frowned.

"I intend to sell the house in Chester and buy a house here, or maybe a bungalow."

He opened his mouth to speak, but Helen put up her hand to silence him. "Number fourteen Jumbles Lane has served its purpose. It is a family house, and I don't want to be left there on my own. I suppose that means you were right in a way, you know, about leaving home. You can visit me here just as well, if anything it will be easier than travelling up north. Pennington-on-Sea is, in my opinion, a very lovely little town. People here have their troubles like anywhere else. I'm not expecting utopia."

"You're not thinking of getting married, are you, Mum?" James paled at his own suggestion. "It's all a bit quick."

"And if I were…?"

"Er…nothing, Mum." James's voice was almost a whisper. "It's your life."

"Exactly, and it's not a rehearsal, not for any of us. But the answer to your question is no. I have no intention of getting married, either now or in the future. No one will ever replace your dad, but I have many years ahead of me, I hope, and I intend to enjoy them. As far as it being 'a bit quick', as you put it, time, or lack of it, doesn't matter when you know something is right." She turned to Robert and Jayne. "Isn't that right, Robert?"

He squeezed Jayne's hand and nodded.

"When you get back home, I want one of you to get in touch with an estate agent and start the ball rolling. I'll be back to pack up, of course. Meanwhile, I'm going to Scarborough for a few days. I can be back here before Caroline is out of hospital. There'll be plenty of time for you two to move to London. You won't be homeless. Any questions?"

"Have you told your friend about your plans?" Robert asked.

"No. I thought I'd tell her when I come back from Scarborough. She has quite enough to think about at the moment without me nattering on."

"When exactly did you decide all this?" James asked. "It all seems rather sudden. There was no hint of it this morning."

"To be perfectly frank with you, I had a bit of a lightbulb moment when I was cycling back here. It all fell into place. I like this little town, and the winters will be much milder than in Chester. I can help Gillian when Caroline is out of hospital. We get on like a house on fire."

Neither James nor Robert dared contradict her. Both probably had misgivings, but knew better than to say anything.

"I think a celebratory drink is in order. There are some glasses in the cupboard behind you, Maddie, and a bottle of champagne in the fridge."

James popped the cork carefully and filled five glasses. They toasted 'the future'.

Helen thought back to her kitchen in Jumbles Lane as they sipped the fizzing champagne, recalling a similar toast.

CHAPTER NINETEEN

Sheila Forrester had never been in a police station before. She'd lived in Pennington-on-Sea all her life, and was happy to say she had never had cause to darken those particular doors. After closing the Tourist Information Centre, as the good citizen she aspired to be, she walked straight up to the desk, where a sergeant pored over some papers, a mug of steaming tea in his hand.

"My name is Sheila Forrester, and I think I may have some information regarding the attack on the young girl, Caroline Halstead."

The desk sergeant looked up.

"I believe I saw her, you see, with a young man. I read about it in the Pennington-on-Sea Gazette, and saw you were asking for witnesses to come forward."

She was quickly ushered into an office.

P.C. Pete Levens handed the witness a cup of tea. "It's very good of you to come in, Miss Forrester."

"Would I be right in thinking this girl is the daughter of the late Councillor Halstead?"

"That's right."

"Strange. I'd forgotten he had a daughter. His poor wife—losing her husband—and now this. I tell you what, constable, I'm glad I never married, never had children, and that's the truth."

"You say you may be able to help us, Miss Forrester?" Pete Levens was beginning to wonder if this very neat and tidy woman had just come in to gossip. The story of Caroline Halstead being assaulted, and Jorge Sadler's death, were hot news. The team working in the incident room had quickly linked in Jono's death. Preliminary post mortem reports on Jorge Sadler and the exhumed body of Jonathan Lister showed similarities, but as yet that wasn't public knowledge. In a way, the reports gave more questions than answers. Jono Lister had been a known heroin user, had known what he was doing with the stuff, and suicide seemed unlikely. Jorge Sadler, on the other hand, was not a known user. The pathologist had confirmed there were no needle marks on his arms. The general consensus of opinion was that Naz had murdered them both. They believed he had knowingly supplied Jono with uncut heroin, and forcibly injected Jorge. Naz was the only suspect, the link, and right now a missing link.

"On Wednesday afternoon, I saw a young girl sitting in the square, wearing a denim jacket and jeans. Her hair was a mousy brown sort of colour, straggly on her shoulders and blonde at the ends. She wore scruffy old trainers."

Sheila Forrester had Pete's undivided attention. She had described Caroline and her clothing precisely.

"It was a sunny afternoon and the girl was enjoying the sunshine, she had her eyes closed and her face in the sun. I thought she looked rather pale, like she could do with a bit of fresh air and sunshine. A large black four-wheel drive entered the square and parked nearby."

Miss Forrester took a notepad and a pair of glasses from her handbag. With her glasses perched on the end of her nose, she continued, "Registration number B-sixteen-N-A-Z." She took her glasses off and carefully returned them to their case. "A young man with dark hair and dark clothing got out and sat next to her, next to Caroline Halstead. It was her I saw, wasn't it, Constable?"

Pete didn't answer.

She continued, "He wore shiny black and red shoes. I always take a note of shoes. I think they say a lot about a person. In this case, it told me he was rich, and she was poor. What I don't understand is why Caroline Halstead, whose parents have pots of money, was wearing a poor person's shoes." She looked at Pete, seeking his agreement, his approval of her observations.

He said nothing.

"Well, like I say, shoes say a lot about people. They looked friendly enough, like any young couple, I thought. He held her hand when they went to his car, and he opened the passenger door for her. I thought that was rather nice, chivalrous, if you know what I mean. I thought they looked like boyfriend and girlfriend, but with hindsight I may have been wrong about that. That bit was just an assumption. Do you think he did it? The man I saw her with. Do you?"

Pete was impressed by the detail. Her account was as precise as her appearance. If every witness was like Miss Forrester, his job would be much easier. There was no doubt in his mind that she had seen Caroline Halstead being abducted by Nathan Sadler.

"Well, Miss Forrester, you have given some very interesting information. Very interesting. I'd like you to give a statement, get it all down on paper, just as you told me, and I'll be speaking with the officers in charge of this case immediately. That's not me, you understand, I'm not in charge. It's my guess they'll want you to look at a VIPER identity parade. I'll get you another cup of tea."

"Have you caught him, then?"

"No. No, we haven't, I'm sorry to say, but there are lines of enquiry." Pete thought of Gatwick airport, Naz's car, and the fact that so far Nathan Sadler had not appeared on any passenger lists.

"So, how can there be an identity parade, then? And what is VIPER?"

"It's a video identity parade. You'll see clips of several men of similar appearance. Our suspect will be one of them."

"So you don't line them up for me to peer into their faces?" She smiled as she spoke.

"No. Even if we did do a line up, you would be

behind one-way glass."

"I was pulling your leg, P.C. Levens. Even I know that much."

* * * *

It took over an hour to give her statement. The young policewoman told her she must stick to the facts as she remembered them, not her thoughts or suppositions. Sheila found it all very interesting. The detail and precision of the process fascinated her. When it was finished, each sheet of paper had to be signed and dated individually.

The policewoman stood up and straightened the papers by tapping them together on the table. "Thank you, Miss Forrester. I'll go and see if the VIPER is ready. Would you like a cup of tea?"

"Yes, please." She found the paper cups disappointing, but the tea was drinkable. Sheila waited alone in the interview room, feeling important and valued. Her conscience made it a guilty pleasure, because her presence was occasioned by Caroline Halstead's adversity. She drummed her perfect nails on the table and waited. A third cup of tea was provided, this time with biscuits. Eventually, when she was beginning to think she'd been forgotten, she was taken to another room. The young man who accompanied her didn't wear a uniform. He introduced himself as Andy Greatorex from the National Crime Agency.

Sheila had no difficulty in picking out the man she'd seen in the square. "That's definitely him." She pointed to one of the photographs. "He looks younger, though."

"He's been on the books for a while."

Andy Greatorex escorted her to the front door of the police station. "Thank you very much for your time and assistance, Miss Forrester. You've been a great help. We'll be in touch, I'm sure."

The desk sergeant looked up from his papers and nodded towards her. Sheila thought he may have heard she was an important witness. She walked home as quickly as she could. She was dying for a pee.

* * * *

No one took any notice of the young man sitting in Dubai airport lounge, and that was just the way he wanted it. Alone in the crowds, even his clothing—a plain black tracksuit and baseball cap without any logos—helped him melt into the background. Every detail was exactly as he had planned, including buying his ticket with the credit card. Paying with cash would have attracted attention.

By the time the company realised the account belonged to a dead man, he would be settled in his new life, with another identity, and completely untraceable.

The two hour refuelling stop ticked away nicely, and in twenty minutes he would be in the air again, on his way to Bangkok, and then non-stop to Hanoi. Everything he needed was in his hand luggage. He could buy everything else when he arrived, and be through Noi Bai airport without the delay of baggage reclaim. He'd be in the rented penthouse in Golden Westlake, Hanoi, in eighteen hours. That part had been easier than he had expected. The agent in Hanoi hadn't asked many questions and was to meet him at the airport. He would look out for a man holding up a card with his new name. Mr Finch from England would then be taken to an apartment with a view of the lake.

England was his past. The businesses had given him money enough to live in luxury. Jorge, Jono, Carrie and all the slags in the houses had got what they deserved. Sooner or later stupid people had to pay for their stupidity, and dead people can't give evidence. He refused to allow Carrie into his head. She had to be discarded with everything else that had gone before.

He checked the flight departure board. The flight to Bangkok was delayed by four hours. The pretty girl at the airline desk assured him everything would be taken care of, and he would receive more information when he boarded to Bangkok. It wasn't what he wanted to hear, but there was nothing he could do about it. Jet lag was kicking in. He'd been awake for twenty hours.

He stretched his legs out in front of him and pulled his cap over his eyes.

* * * *

Andy Greatorex returned to the empty incident room. He put on his coat and was about to leave when Pete Levens came in. Andy knew the officer had an interest in the case, and he presumed he was going to give him an update on the girl.

Pete handed him a fax from Border Control.

Gatwick CCTV shows Nathan Sadler boarding plane to Hanoi, Vietnam, under false name but with a genuine passport in that name.

With the sort of money Sadler had, Andy expected him to disappear into the mist in Vietnam, a country where there was no likelihood of co-operation and no extradition treaty. Reliable witnesses were hard to come by, and Sheila Forrester's statement had been the breakthrough they needed to link him to Caroline Halstead. The forensics would confirm it, and the dead could give a lot of evidence these days. He was still waiting to interview Caroline, but it wasn't looking good for getting Sadler behind bars.

"Thanks, Pete. It looks like we missed him. See you tomorrow."

* * * *

Pete was back at the station at nine o'clock next

morning. He hadn't slept much. His shift didn't start until ten, but he wanted to know if there was any more news before he went out on patrol. As he walked through to the locker room, he heard shouting coming from the incident room. Not angry shouting, more of a cheering. He dashed through to be met by Andy Greatorex.

"Come in, Pete." Andy grinned, waving a fax in the air. The team were all smiling and shaking hands, giving the room a party atmosphere. Andy thrust the fax in Pete's hand.

Flight delayed while refuelling in Dubai. Sadler arrested and being held. Will be returned to UK on flight BA3452 to Gatwick, landing 2300hrs U.K. time.

"Our clever Mr Sadler wasn't as clever as he thought he was."

"How did they get on to him?" Pete asked.

"He made two mistakes, Pete."

Pete raised his eyebrows.

"Number one, he bought a one way ticket, and number two, he didn't check in any suitcases. Put those together and airport security, with the help of their computers, will pick him out as suspicious. We got lucky with the flight delay."

"Is it okay if I tell Carrie's mother?" Pete wanted to be the one to give Gillian Halstead the good news.

"I don't see why not. I'll be at Gatwick with the welcome party."

They shook hands. This was the sort of thing that made the job worthwhile. The sort of thing that gave the adrenaline rush of achievement, of success, of a job well done.

But it didn't compare to the moment when Pete saw Caroline sitting up in bed, her mother at her side.

Caroline's pale face, with its yellowing bruises, turned to him. She spoke very slowly. "Hello...Pete...Mum's... been...telling...me...what...happened."

CHAPTER TWENTY

Helen checked out of 'Ten Acres' at ten o'clock on Monday morning, bidding good-bye to a sleepy Miss Sloth. She sent Tashy a text saying she would be in Scarborough the next day. Tashy immediately texted back a simple '*gr8*'.

She drove away from Pennington-on-Sea with a sense of relief. The weekend had been a success insomuch as everyone had put their cards on the table, but it had been a bit claustrophobic, especially on Saturday night. They had all met up again for a coffee on Sunday morning before James, Maddie, Robert and Jayne had left for London, James and Maddie to do some house hunting, and Robert to stay with Jayne for a few days. He'd said he might be meeting her father, and seemed apprehensive about it. Helen hadn't wanted to appear nosey, but had then worried Robert might think she wasn't interested. In a way, she wished there had been more time, and felt guilty for talking so much about herself. *It was that bloody elf again.*

The A303 stretched before her, Rod Stewart once again her travelling companion. According to her satnav, Scarborough was three hundred and seventy-five miles and six hours and thirty-two minutes away. The journey time seemed optimistic, but there was no hurry. She would park up when she had had enough of driving, and would stick to soft drinks.

She stopped just past Oxford and made a smoked salmon and cucumber sandwich and a cup of tea. On the A1, she filled up with diesel, and by late afternoon she had bypassed York on the A64. The roads had been kind to her, traffic running smoothly all the way.

A road sign on the A170 informed her it was five

miles to Scarborough, and she was on the lookout for a caravan park when her phone rang. Cursing herself for not switching it to voicemail before setting off, she pulled into a lay-by. The phone stopped. By the time she'd retrieved it from her handbag, it was beeping a text message alert. She didn't recognise the number. It obviously wasn't anyone in her phone book.

Please ring asap. Susan

It took a moment to sink in that it had to be Susan Townsend, her neighbour in Jumbles Lane. Alarm bells rang. Robert and James were both in London, so the house was empty. She pressed the green 'call' button.

"Is that you, Helen?" The rising panic in Susan's voice was unmistakeable.

"Whatever's wrong, Susan? What's happened?"

"Oh, I'm so sorry to call, but you see, Robert and James must be away. I haven't seen their cars for at least two days."

"Yes, I know. They're in London. What is it?" Helen's stomach was a knot of impatience, not knowing if Susan was in panic mode without good reason. Images of a fire or a burglary at number fourteen flashed through her mind.

"I thought I should call a plumber, but I don't have a key. Oh, Helen, I wish you had left me a key."

"A plumber?" Helen relaxed a little. The house hadn't been burgled or razed to the ground.

"Yes. I looked out of my window and saw the water coming from under your kitchen door. I peeped through the lounge window and the ceiling's down. It's a terrible mess. Are you far away?"

"Not too far," Helen said, surprised at the calmness in her own voice. She thought of Tashy's disappointment, and of her own. "I'll be a couple of hours or so. Thanks for letting me know." She hung up. "Shit!"

Sorry Tashy. Can't make it tomorrow, will come asap. Helen.

Making a 'U' turn back towards Pickering and York,

the M62 and Chester, she drove in silence. This time Rod Stewart could piss off.

The motorways around Leeds, Bradford and Manchester their usual traffic-clogged selves, Helen had driven five hundred and twenty-seven miles by the time she arrived in Jumbles Lane, exhausted.

Susan came running out as the campervan turned into the drive. Light shone from her kitchen, reflecting in the water that sprang from beneath Helen's front door. It ran down the drive, underneath Goldilocks and onto Jumbles Lane. She turned the key and pushed. The water behind the door created a resistance. Leaning her shoulder against the door, she pushed harder. Water gushed from a tiny gap, soaking her feet. She stepped back to avoid the torrent that ran down the steps in a waterfall.

With the door wide open, Helen stepped inside. She flicked the light switch. Nothing. No power. She ran upstairs, feeling her way in the dark, to turn off the tap that must have been left on by Robert or James. There could be no other explanation.

The sound of running water came from her bedroom. To her horror, even in the dark, she could see that the ceiling was, for the most part, on her bed. She hurried downstairs and into the kitchen, flinging open the cupboard under the sink. Bottles of bleach and washing up liquid, along with all the other clutter, were thrown out in one sweep. Feeling her way to the back of the cupboard, she turned off the stop tap.

"Shit. Fuck. Bollocks," she shouted, her head still in the cupboard. "This is not part of the plan!"

"I've made a cup of tea."

The tap turned off, she stood up to see her neighbour silhouetted in the doorway.

"Milk, no sugar, right?"

Helen took the drink with both hands, wishing it were something stronger. Susan stared at her hair.

"Thanks. Sorry about the language."

"Understandable, I'd say. Would you like to stay in my house tonight?"

"Thanks again, but no."

"Is upstairs okay, then?"

"No, it isn't, it's a mess. Something's burst in the loft, I think. The ceiling is on my bed. I'll sleep in my motorhome."

"Of course. I wasn't thinking. Have you told Robert and James?"

"No, I don't want to spoil their weekend. It can wait."

"I don't suppose there's anything we can do tonight?"

"No…with no electricity. See you in the morning, Susan, and thanks for letting me know."

* * * *

The cold light of day dawned in Jumbles Lane, and Helen dragged her reluctant body out of bed. Exhausted by the long drive, and in spite of being parked on the sloping drive, she had slept for eight hours.

She squelched around the house in wellington boots. There was so much to do she didn't know where to start. Robert and James's bedrooms seemed to be unaffected, but everywhere else was a disaster. Her bedroom and the lounge directly below were worst. A tell-tale mark all around the downstairs walls showed the water had been about four inches deep.

She turned off the electricity at the meter and phoned her insurance broker. He assured her someone would be round in the afternoon to get the ball rolling, whatever that meant.

She sent a text to Tashy.

Sorry Tashy, I had to come home to sort something out. Will let you know when I can come over. Helen

And one to Robert and James.

Please phone asap. Mum.

It seemed too brief, but there was no point trying to go into details. Miserably, she realised her idea of selling up and moving would have to be put on hold for months. No one would buy a house in that state.

She wandered about, picking up familiar items and putting them down again: an ornament, a house plant, a sodden copy of the 'Radio Times'.

James rang first. "What's up?"

"I'm at home, James and—"

"Home? Home as in Jumbles Lane?"

"Yes. There's been a—"

"What you doing there? I thought you were going to Scarborough."

"Will you shut up for a minute and let me explain? There's been a pipe burst or something in the loft. Susan Townsend rang me yesterday. The whole bloody house is flooded. I'm waiting for someone from the insurance."

"The whole house? Seriously?"

"Yes, James. I'm not joking, and I'm not exaggerating."

"Do you want me to come home?"

"There's no point, really. You carry on with your house hunting. There's nothing you can do. I just thought I should tell you."

"I'll be home tomorrow. Does Robert know?"

"No. But I expect he'll call me soon."

"See you tomorrow, then."

"Bye, James." She hung up.

Robert rang five minutes later. James had already told him the news.

"You know what's happened then?"

"Yes. Is my golf bag okay?"

"As far as I know. Your room and James's escaped. The lounge and my bedroom are in a mess."

"It isn't in my room. It's in the hall near the

telephone."

"In that case, it's wet."

"I'll set off now."

"Up to you…"

Robert hung up before she could finish. Helen found his golf bag, carried it upstairs and put it in the bath. It was a waste of time and effort. Anything she tried to do would be a waste of time. It was all so depressing.

She rang Gillian.

"Oh, no! Helen, you poor thing. And you didn't even make it to Scarborough."

"No, and at best it will delay my plans about Pennington-on-Sea."

"What plans?"

"I didn't tell you, did I? But never mind about that. How's Caroline?"

"Doing well, thanks. She's out of intensive care and in a normal ward. She's being assessed today. It's looking good."

"Oh, I'm so pleased."

"What are these plans, then? What did you mean about Pennington-on-Sea?"

"Well, like I say, it's all going to have to go on hold for a while, but I've decided to move there."

There was no response.

"You still there, Gillian?"

"Yes, I'm still here. But before you go any further, I mean, I don't know if this will make any difference, but as soon as Caroline is better, we're leaving this place."

"Leaving? What do you mean?"

"I mean I'm leaving, selling up and leaving. I hate this town."

"But it's—"

"As long as I stay here, I will always be Counsellor Halstead's widow, and Caroline will be Councillor Halstead's daughter. You know how I feel about that. If she's to have a new start, we have to leave."

"I hadn't thought of that."

"Well, I'm not saying that you should change your plans, but—"

"It's fine, Gillian. I have a lot to think about. I'll ring in a day or two. Give Caroline my love. Bye for now."

"Bye."

Helen took her car keys out of a drawer, grabbed her handbag and stormed out of the sodding, sodden house, slamming the door behind her. She didn't bother to lock it. Susan would keep her eagle eye on everything, and if anyone wanted to steal anything, they were welcome to it. She reversed Goldilocks out of the drive, parking her on the roadside, before driving off down Jumbles Lane in her car. She had no destination in mind. It seemed strange after driving Goldilocks for so many miles, like being in a supercharged tin can. As she drove north, a billboard with the words 'Billington's Motorhomes, Next Left,' took her eye. She turned left.

Bobby, with his unmistakable hair, waved to her from the showroom as she got out of the car.

"Good to see you, Mrs McGuire. You had a nice holiday? I like your hair. How's your Goldilocks?"

"Fine, thanks, Bobby, no problems at all, you'll be pleased to hear. Your dad's not in, then?"

"No. Did you want to see him?"

"No, I came to see you, Bobby. I need cheering up."

"Black, no sugar, right?" He made her a coffee from the vending machine as she told him about the flood, and of her plan to move to the south coast.

"Oh, no, Mrs McGuire, you mustn't do that. You wouldn't like it, not one little bit."

"Why ever not, Bobby?"

"Because you live here in Chester. If you go to live at the seaside, whether it's this Pennington place or anywhere else, you're just another old duffer at the seaside, waiting for God, like. I've seen them. Sitting about on the seafront in St Anne's, looking dead miserable. My Auntie Margaret and Uncle Ron went there. Had only been there six months when he dropped dead. Dad reckons it was a mixture of boredom and naggin' what did it. Anyway, it left Auntie Margaret all on her own with no one to nag, so the next thing we know she's up sticks and back. Dad says the only one to make anything out of that palaver was the estate agents and the solicitors with all their fancy fees. There was the removal man as well, shiftin' everything there and back again. Anyway, you're a Northerner. You wouldn't settle down there. Think about it, Mrs McGuire, I'm right, aren't I?"

"I…"

"But here, you see, here you're somebody. Only the other day I was talking to some of me old school mates, and I said I'd sold you a motorhome, and they all remembered you. They liked you, see, not like that bossy old teacher we had. He was rubbish. And then there's your neighbours. I bet you got nice neighbours you've known for years and years. What I say is there's nothing wrong with making new friends—I'm all for it—but they're not old mates that really know you, like you don't feel you have to explain yourself all the time. Oh, no. Your old friends are the best. Don't go, Mrs McGuire."

"Thanks for making the coffee, Bobby, but I have to be getting back. The insurance man is coming." She left the untouched polystyrene cup on the desk. "And thank you for the advice. I can always count on you to say it like it is."

"You're welcome. Any time. I mean it, Mrs McGuire."

"I know you do, Bobby. That's what I like about you."

Helen drove home slowly with Bobby's words ringing in her head. She parked her car in front of Goldilocks and walked to the top of the drive. Four indentations in the tarmac showed where Valerie Drobshaw had been parked, as indelible as the memory of the old V-Dub herself. The house looked perfectly normal from there, apart from the condensation on the windows. A car door slammed and she made her way back to the house.

"Mrs McGuire?" A man in his late fifties stood before her, clipboard in hand.

She nodded.

"William Short, insurance. I believe you are expecting me."

"Please, come in."

He followed her into the kitchen. "Dear, oh dear, oh dear, what a mess." He started making notes. "Have you turned the electricity off at the mains?"

Helen nodded. She felt curiously detached from the scene before her.

"There are some stepladders in the cupboard under the stairs. You'll need them if you want to look in the loft." Even the sound of her own voice sounded strange.

"Thanks. I'll have a quick look, but I'll get a plumber here later today, then you can get the water back on. Was the house empty for long?"

"About three days."

"Water does a lot of damage."

"I'll leave you to it, then. I'll be in my motorhome if you want me."

"Right-oh. I won't be long."

Five minutes later, William Short knocked on Goldilocks' door.

"Come in, please. This is my home, there's plenty of room. I live here. Please take a seat."

"I'll turn down your kind offer, Mrs McGuire, if you don't mind, I have another appointment. I just wanted to tell you I've arranged for four dehumidifiers and three blowers to be delivered tomorrow. They will work on a generator until we get the electrics tested. We have to start drying you out. A skip will be here first thing as well."

Helen stared at him.

"You all right, Mrs McGuire? I can arrange for you to stay in a hotel if you like."

"No, that won't be necessary. I have Goldilocks."

William Short stepped back towards the door. "Yes, well…the skip is for the carpets, initially, but the kitchen base units will all have to come out. Chipboard doesn't like water."

"No, I don't either, not now."

"Good-bye for now, then." He handed her a business card. "Call me if you have any questions. I'll make sure things start moving quickly."

"Yes. Goodbye."

* * * *

Helen sat in her usual place at the kitchen table, rocking back on the chair legs. If William Short was right, the house was going to look a lot worse before it was back to normal.

"And what is normal? Tell me that, Helen McGuire."

A high pitched cry came from behind her tightly closed lips, catching her by surprise. Her head in her hands, the tears flowed, silently at first, then with great racking sobs. The tears weren't for Phil, and they weren't for the house. She'd seen real heartbreak in the intensive care ward. She cried because the truth, in all its harsh reality, had smacked her in the face. She'd got it all wrong, and it had taken Bobby Billington to make her see it. She rubbed her reddening eyes.

"This is your home, you stupid woman. Here. Jumbles Lane."

"Mum?" Helen turned to see Robert standing in the doorway. The next moment he was at her side, hugging her.

"Oh, I'm so glad you're here. Where's Jayne?" She stifled her tears, sniffing them away.

"She stayed in London, Mum, she has work tomorrow. Who were you talking to?"

"Oh, yes. Me. I talk to myself a lot, it helps sometimes." She managed a thin smile.

Neither of them heard James arrive. The first indication of his arrival was his hand tightly holding hers.

"James! I wasn't expecting you 'til tomorrow."

"I changed my mind. Well, Maddie did, really."

Helen stood up, and James kissed her on the cheek.

"She said I should come straight away. Poor old you, Mum, this has clipped your wings a bit, hasn't it?"

"You could put it that way. I'll go out to Goldilocks and make us all a cup of tea, shall I?" Not waiting for a reply, she left her sons and went outside.

* * * *

Robert waited until the door of the motorhome closed behind her. "I suppose it's all covered by insurance," he said.

"I suppose so. Dad will have always seen to that, and I'm sure Mum will have carried on with it."

"And I suppose she'll be off again as soon as it's sorted out?"

"I wish she would settle back at home. All this dashing here and there like a caped crusader, pretending she left home to make us more independent, it's crazy. Absolutely bloody crazy." James walked through the hallway to the lounge. "Christ Almighty! Have you been in here, Robert?"

"Bloody hell." Robert's eyes were like saucers as he took in the devastation. "It'll take months to get this lot right. Upstairs must be as bad, or worse." They went upstairs and into Helen's room. Neither of them spoke. James shook his head in disbelief. They made their way downstairs and back into the kitchen.

"It's like she's running away from herself all the time,

picking up other people's misery to mask her own," James said.

"I don't see anything wrong with going on holiday and making new friends, but moving to the south coast? No. She's in a fantasy world. She should stay in Jumbles Lane where she's got her roots."

"I couldn't agree more," James said, "but it's a braver man than me who would tell her."

The brothers laughed.

"Tea's ready. Come on," Helen shouted, and they all sat down in Goldilocks.

"I have something to tell you." Her tears had dried and she smiled. Robert and James exchanged suspicious glances. "It's all right. Nothing to be scared of. I've decided to come back here for good, that's all. I can stay in Goldilocks while all the work is done in the house."

"Wh-what about Pennington-on-Sea?" Robert asked.

"Oh, I'll go there again one day…you know, just for a holiday. I can chat to Gillian on the phone, keep up to date with Caroline's progress. I'll visit my friend Tashy in Scarborough as soon as I can, but this is where I belong. I'm already thinking of colour schemes for the house. I'm going to have new curtains and everything."

"Why the sudden change, Mum? What happened?" James sounded puzzled. "Apart from the flood, I mean?"

"Not *what*, James. *Who*. It was Bobby Billington. He told me I should stay where I belong."

"Bobby? Is he George Billington's lad?"

"That's right."

"Was he the one who told you about my tracking dev—" James never finished the question.

"Anyone home? Plumber here…"

Helen shouted back, "I certainly am. I'm home all right."

About The Author

Barbara Phipps was born in Liverpool in 1950. Her earliest memory is of moving to the West Riding of Yorkshire in 1953. The family travelled by train, few people had cars in those days. She attended Sandal Endowed Junior School and Wakefield Girls' High School, leaving in 1967 with a handful of 'O' levels, perhaps notably including English Language and Literature. Apart from a disastrous eight year marriage, when she lived in Norfolk, Barbara has lived in Yorkshire ever since. She re-married in 1982 and has a son and a daughter.

She describes her career as that of a serial assistant to the medical profession, having assisted doctors, pathologists, vets, dentists and pharmacists, all of which have been very interesting and very badly paid. Now retired, she has been a Magistrate in West Yorkshire since 2000.

Her hobbies include reading, cooking, walking and gardening. She shares an allotment, growing vegetables with limited success.

She has written several short stories. *Never Ask Why* is her second novel.

Lightning Source UK Ltd.
Milton Keynes UK
UKOW05f0719281113

222005UK00001B/3/P